The Original's Retribution

DAVID WATKINS

ISBN: 1534700889
ISBN-13: 978-1534700888

For Josh and Ethan

Chapter 1

1

Fuck me, it's dark. Corporal Jamie Bryant looked at the hole in the ground and couldn't help but shudder. Trees stood tall in a circle around him, dark branches merging in the twilight. Bryant could see some detail in the leaves, but that was about it. He turned back to the hole and leant over it. Loose earth fell to the floor of the cavern far below. He knew from the notes that it was only thirty feet, but right then, looking into the darkness, it felt a lot deeper.

"Let's get this done," he said. He looked at his team. All were in full camouflage and carrying large packs on their backs. The biggest man, Collins, was also carrying a flamethrower. They had tied ropes around the trees, secured with figure of eight knots.

Parker and Wills clipped themselves onto the ropes and abseiled quickly into the hole. "Clear," Wills whispered over the comms. Bryant and Collins nodded at each other and trusted the ropes to hold them.

Bryant's mood did not improve when he hit the cave floor. The cavern was roughly circular, with a black hole in one wall. He didn't want to go near that. Not yet. He'd read the file: they all had.

"Look at that," Wills said. He pointed at the only thing in the room: a large stone slab. Carvings littered the base of it and Bryant nodded. *Definitely the right place then.*

"Get some photos then, don't just stand there." Bryant scanned the rest of the cavern. *Exactly as Knowles' bunch of*

1

idiots described it. The slab was clear, rain had washed off any remaining dust or earth and the items it had on top of it were long gone. *Bones, massive bones.* Bryant shuddered at the thought.

The file had been very detailed. A man had died in here, bitten by a poisonous spider that shouldn't exist. Another man had landed on the bones and when he'd come out some very bad things had happened. *Not going there. I'm not sure I believe that part of this tale.*

He heard the whine of Wills' camera, the IR flash preserving their night vision. The carvings were exactly as described. Bryant knew that the brass believed it was The Green Man on the carvings, but it looked an awful lot like the Devil to him. Bryant was not a religious man, but he felt a chill all the same. He was more concerned by the complete lack of cobwebs in the cavern. *More ridiculous things in a report full of them.*

"Done," came Wills' reedy voice.

"Get ready Collins." Bryant took a deep breath and walked to the dark opening in the wall.

2

His thermal imaging gear didn't do much to alleviate the dark. Bryant stopped in the mouth of the passageway, willing the gear to make sense of the blackness. *Nothing there. It's just dark.* He grinned to himself. Scary stories in government files had successfully unnerved him. *Just take a step forward, nothing to worry about.*

Something moved in his peripheral vision. He turned his head, studying the rock walls of the passage. *Nothing. Jumping at shadows now.* Another movement in the corner of his eye made him turn again. This time he saw a thick black strand sticking out of the wall. Bryant watched as the strand unfurled, defying gravity until it was almost perpendicular to the wall. Another strand followed, then another. Each one was at least a centimetre thick.

Not a strand.

No.

A leg.

Lots of legs.

Bryant watched agape as the wall seemed to sprout the black strands. Large black bodies squeezed out of tiny cracks, more and more pouring out of the walls until the spiders were in full view and the passage covered in their grim bodies. They varied in size, but each was much larger than any spider he had ever seen; certainly they were far bigger than anything ever discovered in Britain before.

Not quite. This has been seen before.

And someone died.

Bryant did not want to think about Harry Meyers at that point, but pictures flooded his mind anyway. Meyers had been part of Knowles' team and had paid the price for the other man's incompetence. Knowles had ordered them into this cave with no idea what he was letting his men in for – unforgivable. Meyers had been attacked by the spiders and the photographs had made for grim viewing: his face so swollen that each orifice was shut; red welts covering his face and each one an area the size of a fifty pence coin. The report had not been specific about how many bites Meyers had received. It was clear that he had died due to the massive amount of venom in his system. *Meyers, the first - but not last - of the fuckwits to die.*

"Holy crap," Collins said, appearing next to him.

"Christ," Bryant said, "I nearly shat myself."

"That's a lot of spiders."

"Yeah," Bryant said, "Not showing up on thermal imaging either. Switch to white light." He blinked as the cavern suddenly lit up. Collins had pulled a head torch on whilst the others flicked on the torches attached to their Picatinny rails under their weapons.

"So it's true then."

"Yeah, looks like."

They paused, mesmerised by the mass of spiders in front of them. Wills and Parker peered past their shoulders and swore in unison.

"Makes you wonder what else is true in that report then," Wills said.

"Men who can turn into wolves? Seriously?" Parker said.

"Shut up you two," Bryant said. "We're here to investigate this cave, so let's get to it. Brass wants to know what's down this hole and we're going to tell them."

"What about them?" Wills pointed at the spiders. "I ain't walking through that."

"Me neither," Bryant said. He patted Collins on the back. "Light it up big man. Burn them all."

3

The flames licked the walls. Spiders burned, but didn't move. *It's like they want this.* Bryant refused to let that thought grow. He watched through shielded eyes as Collins moved the flamethrower methodically around the passageway. The heat was immense.

Spiders began to drop from the ceiling, flaming shooting stars falling to the stone floor. The air was filled with a smell like burning hair and the crackle and pop of superheated chitin. Eventually, the flames started to die down and Bryant could survey the damage without squinting. The entire floor was covered with the charcoaled remains of dead spiders. Embers glowed in the corridor casting long shadows on the walls.

The passage ran about twenty feet in length before the fires lit it no more. Bryant took a deep breath and started to walk down it. Residual heat made him sweat, and he could feel the warmth of the corpses under his feet. A loud crunching noise accompanied every step. It was a noise that would stay with Bryant for the rest of his life.

Moving forward, Bryant found himself in another circular cave. Once more, in the centre stood a stone slab but this was smaller than the one in the main cavern. Bryant's torch was doing a pathetic job of ridding the room of dark places and he could feel his heart hammering in his chest.

A rustle behind him made him turn quickly, rifle unslung.

"Easy," Collins said. The barrel of the flamethrower was still smoking. His torchlight joined with Bryant's, forcing shadows to the boundary of the room. Collins let out a low whistle, "Just think nobody's been down here for years."

"Centuries."

4

"What about that Stadler fella?"

"He didn't come in here, did he? The report said he stayed in that big cave," Bryant said. "Those spiders, I'm not surprised."

"How come we've never seen anything like those before?"

"No idea. We're not paid to think, remember?"

Collins nodded at that. He crossed to the slab and brushed a hand across the top of it. Thick dust blew into the air, and the trace of his hand could be clearly seen in what remained.

Bryant walked the perimeter of the room. Piles of rubble sat at several points in the room. He kicked at the bottom of a pile and some loose earth fell through the gaps in the rubble.

"I reckon there are more passages through here," he said.

Collins nodded. "Probably, but we're not going there now are we?"

"Nope."

"What do you want to do?" Collins leant on the slab but jumped up quickly. "It moved!"

Bryant crossed to him. The top of the slab had moved less than an inch. Together they pushed the top of it and were rewarded with a screech of stone on stone. The slab stopped moving after another inch. He swore to himself then turned to the long corridor of dead spiders. "Parker, get in here. You too, Wills."

The crack and crunch of dead spiders briefly got louder, then Wills and Parker arrived. Bryant pointed at the slab. "Push," he said.

The four of them heaved at the slab and with another loud screech it slid off the top of the dais and fell to the stone floor. A cracking noise echoed around the chamber and the slab smashed into four pieces.

"Oops," Collins said.

Bryant scowled at him, before coughing loudly for several moments. He spat phlegm onto the floor, looking for signs of blood. There weren't any, but he kicked loose soil over it anyway.

"Well?"

5

Collins was leaning over the dais, looking into the cavity they had just uncovered. "It's a skull."

Bryant peered in, letting his light illuminate the opening. It was a few feet deep and ran the length of the whole slab. *A giant stone box, like a coffin.* In the centre sat a large skull. It had the long mouth and nose of a dog, but he knew that's not what it was.

"Bingo," he muttered.

"So it really is true then," Wills said. "The spiders, now this." He looked at the other three, eyes wide. "That's a wolf's skull isn't it? It's the head."

"How the hell should I know?" Collins muttered.

"Shut up, Wills," Bryant said. "This is what we came for. Let's bag it up and get out of here."

Parker reached into the stone dais and picked the skull up with a grunt. Wills held open a large rucksack, and Parker lowered the bone into it. He zipped it shut and then hefted it onto his back.

"It's heavy," he said.

"Well, yeah, duh," Wills said.

"Just shut it, and let's get out of here," Bryant said, more sharply than he intended. "This place gives me the creeps."

4

Parker got to the passageway first, walking easily despite the weight of the skull. Bryant watched him then looked around the room again. Wills was taking pictures of the stone carvings, which were similar to the ones in the main chamber. Collins was tapping the barrel of the flamethrower and humming some god-awful dance tune. He turned and grinned at Bryant.

"Piece of piss, eh?"

Behind him, something large and black crawled out from behind a pile of rubble. As Bryant watched, more shapes started to move. He looked at the other piles and saw the same thing: masses of black legs and thick hairy bodies squeezing out of tiny gaps. The spiders were back.

"Don't turn around," he said. "We need to go."

"What-"

"Wills, stow the camera. Get after Parker. Do not stop until you get to the ropes. Wait there for us. Got it?"

Wills could see what Bryant was looking at and ran without another word. Collins started to turn to look over his shoulder.

"We run, then you light up this whole fucking place – got it?"

Collins nodded. The cavern was too small for the flamethrower. He had to get some distance or he would risk setting himself alight. He could see the spiders now. They were coming out of the holes in the walls and the gaps in the rubble piles.

They are slow at the moment. Waking up? Waiting for numbers? Bryant shuddered. The pictures of Meyers flashed through his mind again. Rumour was when they cut him open, all of his internal organs had liquefied.

All of them.

Just a rumour right?

"Let's go, big man. RUN!"

5

Bryant sprinted into the corridor, which now seemed twice as long as it had just minutes earlier. The crunch underfoot barely registered as the terror at what was coming out of the walls took over all his senses.

Bryant had seen combat many times. In Afghanistan, he'd been in some hairy situations. Some of his black ops had been worse, but he'd fed off that. It had given him a buzz.

This was different.

This was affecting him on an almost primal level. He heard Collins behind him, struggling to run and carry the weight of the flamethrower.

Spiders were coming out of the walls. Hundreds of them, pouring out of every hole or crack, regardless of size. The spiders also varied. Some were as big as his hand; some were larger still. *Impossible.*

He emerged into the main cavern, sprinting for the ropes. Collins stumbled out after him, tripped and fell. He pushed Bryant in the back and sent the smaller man crashing to the

7

floor. Collins rolled onto his back, lifting the barrel of the flamethrower and squeezing the trigger with a roar. The cavern lit up as suddenly as switching a light on. Flames roared into the tunnel, incinerating everything in their path.

Bryant leapt up, but could feel a million legs on him, could feel the spiders in his hair, on his arms. He brushed at himself, rubbing himself all over. Two spiders fell to the floor and he stamped on them quickly. The crunch of their bodies breaking was overpowered by Collins' roar and the sheer noise of the flamethrower. Bryant looked at his friend, who was now kneeling. His back was covered in spiders, their legs running over his back in some bizarre parody of the wind.

The thick clothing and tank of fuel had saved his life. The spiders could not find a way to bare skin. Bryant brushed them off with his gun and stamped on them as soon as they hit the ground.

"Come on!" Wills shouted from behind them as soon as the roar of flames died down. "Let's get the hell out of here."

Bryant couldn't agree more. "You bit?"

"No," Collins said. "Don't think so."

"I think you'd know."

"Yeah."

They ran to the others and clipped onto the lines.

"You last," Bryant said to Parker.

"You're kidding me?"

"No, you're carrying the skull," Bryant said. "Nothing happened till you left that other cave. You stay, until we're out." *Knowles report had said the same thing. His man hadn't been attacked until the bones left the cave. What is this?*

Parker did not look pleased, but Bryant pointed to his own stripes. "You stay."

"Just hurry up then."

The motors above started whining and the three men rose into the air. Bryant took one last look over to the corridor and saw more spiders gathering there. He shuddered. *I hope I'm right.* As soon as he cleared the top, he unclipped and shouted down, "Clear!"

He had never seen Parker move so fast.

8

6

They ran through the woods as quickly as they could with the equipment they were carrying. Bryant jogged at an even pace, trying to keep them moving fast without leaving Collins behind. Never the fastest man, the weight of the flamethrower was slowing him down. A wide path led all around the perimeter of the woods and they made better time when they reached it, leaving the undergrowth behind. By day this was a popular dog walking spot, but in the dead of night, they saw no-one. *Just as well. How would we explain this?* A bird exploded from the trees near them and they all started, before nervously laughing. They were out, had survived the cave and accomplished their mission. Nevertheless, Bryant had never been so pleased to see a gate in his life.

The Landrover sat with lights out the other side of the gate. Evans was leaning on the door, smoking. *He wants to stop that.* Bryant said nothing as he ran up to the car.

"Alright boys," Evans said.

"Get the engine started. We're leaving this shithole," Bryant said.

"What's-"

"Now, Evans, now."

Evans took in the men's expressions, tossed his cigarette and climbed into the driver's seat. Wills threw the motors and ropes in the boot of the Landrover, then helped Collins take the flamethrower off. It was considerably lighter than earlier.

Bryant helped Parker take the rucksack off. Parker tried to shrug it off himself, but Bryant patted him on the back and slid the heavy pack off. Parker clambered into the back of the car, asking Collins to move over.

"Just sit in the middle."

"For fuck's sake, if he's in the middle, I can't see out the back"

Bryant listened to them argue. The tension and fear were easing now and there was no sign of the spiders. He opened the rucksack and looked at the skull. *This better be worth it.* He slipped his glove off, reached into the bag and drew his hand across the teeth. They were still razor sharp and a thin red line appeared on his hand. *Not enough. Stadler was impaled.* One of the canine teeth stood proud of the others and Bryant knew what he had to do. He masked a coughing fit, to hide the noise of him driving his hand down onto the teeth.

Searing hot pain lanced up his arm and it took him two attempts to yank his hand free of the teeth. Sweat broke out on his brow, and he fought the temptation to scream. He looked at his hand. A perfect 'O' sat in the middle of his palm, filling with blood. Later he would be proud that he didn't make a sound. He quickly wiped his blood off the tooth then resealed the pack.

Bryant pulled his glove back on and got in the car.

Chapter 2

1

We have all read about the tragic events at the military base in deepest, darkest Kent last week. The explosion that killed ten serving military personnel, including Major David Smith, a twice decorated officer with considerable experience in combat. Major Smith had been re-assigned to the unit in Kent only a few months before his death.

Nobody will tell me what he was doing.

Nobody will say what his unit, which appeared to have many experienced soldiers in it, were actually doing in Kent. Why?

Why is there this secrecy about that particular base? This was British soil, do not forget that when you read the rest of this report. An army camp, seemingly staffed with experienced and competent men and women, all of whom had experienced the conflict in Afghanistan when it was at its height. This camp, which we are supposed to believe blew up in a tragic accident.

Reports from people near the base at the time of the explosion reported hearing helicopters before the explosion. Before. I'll write that again. What had happened? What were they doing? Incidentally, those people who reported hearing this can no longer be traced. Not one of them. People in the nearby villages don't say anything. Most of them say they were at work when the incident happened and so cannot help. One man, a Mr Fisher from Fosten Green, said these accounts were 'a load of crap'.

11

I don't believe him.

The same day, there were reports of a helicopter landing in a field in Huntleigh, Devon. An army helicopter. Coincidence? Irrelevant? If so, why won't anyone tell me why there was a helicopter in Huntleigh? Let us not forget that a couple of months before this incident, Huntleigh had been devastated by a pack of wolves attacking some of its residents. A policeman and a teacher, Jack Stadler, were amongst two of the casualties.

Why do I bring this up? Is it because Mrs Stadler still believes her husband is alive? She claims he was kidnapped by the army. Would that be the same army that landed a helicopter behind her house? Would that be the same army that has a mystery base in Kent?

There are many unexplained incidents from that day last week and I intend to find answers.

2

Simon Foster took a sip from his beer and scanned the room again. It had been four hours since he had uploaded his blog and three hours and fifty minutes since he had had the phone call. *Meet me, your local, if you want the truth.* All very Deep Throat. The Watergate one, not the famous porno.

Still, it had got him to the Dog and Duck in Wandsworth at 8 pm on a Tuesday night. The bar was quiet. Two guys sat on stools at the bar. They were drinking lager and their eyes were fixed on the screen at the far end of the bar. *Why do English guys watch any football match going? Who cares about Real Madrid and Barcelona or whoever the hell is playing?*

Behind him, at his usual table, not far from the pool table, sat literally one man and his dog. Simon struggled to remember the man's name. Derek or Clive or something old school like that. A man of few words, even when sober, Derek or Clive would not be capable of speech now. His dog had its head on its paws and it looked as fed up as it was possible for a dog to look. Simon grinned to himself and turned back to face the door. He took another sip of beer.

The door opened and a man roughly the same height as Simon walked in. There all similarity ended. This man was lean, muscles clear under his t-shirt. Clean shaven with short hair, almost cropped to the skull. Blue eyes regarded Simon with nothing short of contempt.

Oh crap.

The man slid into the chair opposite Simon. "Foster?"

Simon nodded.

"You the one writing that shit on the internet?" The man didn't wait for Simon to reply. "I lost friends in that accident, mate, so why are you stirring?"

"I'm sorry your friends died-"

"I'm not interested. What I do want to know is who has been filling your head with the lies you've been putting on the net."

"Who are you?"

"Wrong question, Foster."

"I have my sources, and I will not discuss them with some thug like you. Good night." Simon started to get up but realised the two men at the bar were no longer watching the football. They were standing right behind him. One of them put a hand on his shoulder. Simon suddenly felt sick to his stomach.

"Who are you?" he repeated.

"Nobody important, and you do this right, no-one you'll ever see again."

"Am I in trouble?"

The man nodded.

"Why? What have I done?"

"You've put a story out there that demeans the memory of brave men and women who died in the service of this country."

"I've done what?"

"You heard."

"So it's true?"

"Don't be ridiculous. Those barracks were a coming home base, that's all. Skeleton crew welcoming back traumatised vets ready for reintegration into society."

"Do you really expect me to believe that?"

13

The man shrugged. "Believe what you want, but that's the truth. See, people like you, you're always looking for the 'truth'. But it's always more boring than that. The truth is people died because of a gas leak and explosion. That's the truth. People who had fought in Afghanistan, people who were hurt for this country-"

"For our oil supply more like!"

"Really, Simon? Don't be a twat." The man smiled, but it was a weary smile. Now Simon looked more closely, the man had deep lines around his eyes and he looked exhausted. *Red-rimmed eyes, too, this guy has been crying a lot.* "You're a blogger, Simon, which puts you beneath paparazzi and reporters for The Sun or Daily Mail and way beneath pond scum. You are of no consequence, but you wish there was a story. You want to be successful, but you're writing about the wrong things. Get some naked women on your site and your hit rate will go through the roof. But really, stay away from this. This is not what you think it is."

The man stood and pushed his chair under the table. "Let it go. This isn't a story."

He left the pub, with the other two close behind him. *What the hell was that all about?* Simon took a longer drag from his pint and was dismayed to see his hand shaking. *Easy, it was true, the guy was telling the truth. Not the soldier, the other guy. The soldier was lying through his teeth.* Simon grinned, feeling energised. *This is going to make me.*

His source was staying a short drive away. Jake had come to him a couple of days ago with the most outlandish tale. He claimed to have been part of a group that attacked the base in Kent and that they had been chased off when helicopter gunships had shown up and started firing indiscriminately at them. He had said that they were there to free a man. A man being kept captive against his will. Someone who had supposedly been killed in Devon by a pack of deranged wolves. *Seriously, we're expected to believe this?*

Simon pulled his notebook out and scanned it quickly. Jake had seemed insane. He had, after all, claimed to be able to turn into a wolf. There had been something about him,

14

though, something desperate. His wounds were superficial, but he was covered in them. Somewhere in his rambling, Jake had said a name that Simon had latched on to.

Jack Stadler.

A man that had been reported dead.

Simon finished his pint and walked out of the bar. He got in his car and pulled into traffic. *Time to see my source, get more info. If I'm right, that man was Special Forces. That means cover up and that means there's a story.*

Simon whistled as he drove. For the first time in years - actually since Jay had left - he felt alive.

3

Sergeant Peter Knowles climbed into his own car and waited whilst the other two clambered into the front seats.

"Follow the numpty, then," he said. *This guy is an idiot.*

"He has no clue we're following him does he?" Clarke was the shorter of the two. One arm was covered in a tattoo sleeve that looked ridiculous to Knowles.

"No," Knowles said. "Funny really. These bloggers know everything about hiding where they are posting from, but they have no personal security whatsoever. Makes you wonder why they bother."

"Keyboard warrior," Clarke said.

Knowles looked out of the window, watching the grey streets of Wandsworth pass. *There is nothing of merit here. Why do people do it?* A week ago he had been in the woods in Kent. A week ago everything had been on the up for him.

"Do you think he's there?" This came from Phelps.

Knowles shrugged and kept looking out the window.

"Knowles?"

"I don't know," he said. "I hope not."

Clarke looked over his shoulder, a frown on his face. "It's why we're here. Why would you say that?"

Knowles didn't meet the man's gaze. "If Jack is up there, we don't have enough men."

4

Simon parked a street away. He left the car under a street light, not that it would do much good around here, and with his laptop under one arm, jogged to the tower block. He arrived with a thin sheen of sweat down his back and the remains of his hair sticking to his forehead. Leaning on the frame of the lift, he pressed the button and waited. The doors slid open with a ping and Simon stepped in. He immediately recoiled at the strong smell of urine. The lift was covered in graffiti. As he went up ten floors, Simon pondered the various offers of sex if all he did was phone a number and ask for 'Tony's mum' or 'Candy'.

The door opened again, and Simon walked down the dank corridor, whistling to himself.

5

"Tenth floor," Clarke said into his radio. He was looking at the lights above the lift doors, whilst the others sprinted up the stairs.

"Thanks," Knowles said, breathing heavily. "Come on up then."

Moments later Knowles and Phelps arrived at the tenth floor and peered out into the corridor. Simon was standing in front of a door, but he wasn't looking around.

He isn't paranoid enough.

6

Simon knocked on the door three times, waited, then knocked twice more. He heard a lock turn and the door open. A young man stood there, mid-thirties, shabbily dressed. Simon grinned at him and walked into the room.

The man was holed up in a two bedroom flat. It had belonged to Jay before he'd run away with that waiter. Simon had cried for days, but now he was glad. It had given him a place to hide the story of the century.

"You ok?"

The man nodded. "Yeah, I had a shower. It helped."

Well, you need another. "Good. Now, I need to ask you some more questions, ok?"

16

"It's why I came to you."

Simon smiled again and sat at the tiny table in the kitchenette. Dishes were piled high in the sink, two-day-old food stuck to them. *Does this guy have any personal hygiene? Then, if I'd been through what he's been through. Losing his wife like that.*

"How many helicopters were there?"

"I've already told you-"

"Just fact checking, relax!"

The man snorted. "I am a fugitive from the army. Don't tell me to relax."

Drama queen alert! "Help me out here. Your story is a little-"

"Wild?"

"Yeah, wild. It's my arse hanging out when I go to print."

"I thought this was a blog?"

"Figure of speech, ok?"

The door crashed open, three men entered and the door was closed instantly behind them. Simon leapt up and caught a Taser full in the chest. He hit the floor, legs and arms twitching, drool coming out of his mouth.

7

Knowles didn't move his gun from the other man. Phelps had dropped the Taser and now had his gun out too. Clarke arrived seconds later and started searching the other two rooms.

"Who are you?" Knowles asked.

"I haven't done nothing," the man shouted.

"So by definition, you've done something," Knowles said.

The man frowned. "What?"

"I asked you a question."

"Jake," he said. "Jake Williams."

"Good man. You been talking to this numpty?"

Jake nodded.

"Now, how would you know about all that then?"

"What?"

17

Knowles stepped forward and slapped the man in the face. "Don't treat me like an idiot."

"I don't-"

Knowles slapped him again, harder this time.

"I was there. I escaped when the helicopters came."

Knowles sighed and sat down. "So, why would you tell this guy about that?"

"My wife was killed." Jake started crying. "I want her back."

"So you talked to the press?" Knowles laughed. "That's not going to bring her back."

"I found him in a pub. He'd been writing about how he didn't believe that army base blew up by accident."

"Yeah, I saw that."

"I told him I knew what had happened."

"And what did happen, according to you?"

"We went to rescue that man, Jack," Jake looked at Phelps, eyes wild. "The army had him in prison. He was one of us."

"One of you?" Phelps said.

"Please, let me go, I won't tell anyone."

"No, you're right there." Knowles raised his gun and shot him between the eyes.

8

"Holy shit Knowles!" Phelps had his weapon out. "What the-"

"Vermin," Knowles said and spat on the corpse. A streak of red painted the wall behind Jake. Grey brain matter slipped slowly down the wall.

"What happened?" Clarke yelled, running into the room.

"Knowles just shot this man," Phelps said. Now his weapon was aimed at Knowles. "Just shot him."

"Put your gun down."

"No way," Phelps said. "I'm taking you in."

"In to where?" Knowles said. He put his own weapon on the table. "Ring the major. Do it now, go on. See what he says."

"Knowles-"

18

"Ring him."

Knowles waited, sitting in the uncomfortable chair. He toed Simon's body. The reporter didn't move. He was out cold. Clarke had his mobile out and was dialling the number. Phelps watched Knowles, weapon still aimed at him.

"They killed all my friends," Knowles said to Phelps. "All of them. Do you understand?"

Phelps said nothing.

"Meyers. Carruthers. Scarlet. Jonesy. Claire. Even Starkey and Smith. All dead because of these things."

"I think you should stop talking now," Phelps said.

"You were there. Right afterwards, when they took the bodies away. You saw, didn't you? You read the report. You knew what we were doing here."

"We're looking for Jack Stadler, not this guy."

"Yep. We got lucky. One less of them in the world."

"Do you mean-"

"Yes."

Phelps looked at the corpse. He looked like any regular dead guy, really. Same blood. Same bits of bone and brain. Just what anyone who had been shot with a low calibre pistol would look like.

"You sure?"

Knowles shrugged. "He was there."

Clarke hung up the phone. He was very pale. Knowles smirked at him. "Shall we go?"

"The major said we have to clean it up."

Knowles nodded. "Of course we do."

Chapter 3

1

Bryant woke with a start. He pushed his duvet off and jumped to his feet, heart hammering in his chest. His eyes locked on the door. Nothing moved in the room. It was dark, and the alarm clock showed 04:12. He scanned the rest of the basically furnished room. Everything was exactly as he had left it when he went to bed several hours ago. His window, shut despite how hot it was, remained covered by the threadbare curtains.

What woke me?

He opened the door and peered into the corridor. Harsh strip lighting showed the barracks corridor for what it was: stark, in need of a paint job and empty. Bryant stood in the corridor for a moment, sniffing the air. He could smell the body odour of the men sleeping in the other rooms and dormitories; the semen of a lonely man; the detergent from the common shower room.

Grinning to himself, he turned back into his room. He switched the light on and looked at his hand. There was not a scratch on it. Earlier that evening, when they had returned to base after hours of debriefing, his hand had been throbbing slightly. Now it was completely healed. He hadn't coughed on waking either, and he couldn't remember the last time that had happened.

Bryant climbed into bed and pulled the covers over him. He went back to sleep with a smile on his face.

It had worked.

2

The Wolf raised its head. Belly full of the fox it had caught earlier, it had been sleeping under a tree. The sun was creeping up over the moor, changing the sky from deep black to red in a moment. It could see for miles, eyes darting to and fro, taking in all its surroundings. The Wolf sat up, then stood and padded over to the nearby river. It took some noisy slurps of water and then stopped still.

It scanned the horizon again. Birds were starting to sing. A rustle nearby as a deer turned and fled. The Wolf knew there were more deer just over the crest of the hill and also knew that it could catch them easily. It did not chase.

Instead, its fur ran back into its body, shrinking away, leaving pale white skin. In seconds, a man stood where the Wolf had. He stretched, forcing tension out of muscles that had not been used in a while.

Jack Stadler looked around at the bleakness of the countryside surrounding him. He had no idea where he was, other than Dartmoor. Everything had happened so quickly. Katie and Josh looking at him with fear in their eyes. Knowles shouting as Jack jumped through the window. The soldiers shooting at him as he ran. Fleeing Huntleigh had been hard. The soldiers had given chase, but lost him quickly. As a Wolf, Jack could run much faster than them. He could hear and smell them which made it simple to elude them. Even the helicopter had been easy to avoid – its engine giving its position away, even though its noise had been dampened. He assumed the soldiers had night vision equipment, but they were no match for his enhanced senses.

Jack wasn't sure how long had passed since that frantic escape into the night. He had knowledge of his time as a Wolf, but it was not clear: more like an ill remembered dream. How many days had he watched the sunrise?

All of that was irrelevant. Jack had a sick feeling in his stomach, and it wasn't due to raw meat or the cold. Despite the fact it was summer, the sun had not yet warmed the air enough for him to be comfortable, but he couldn't worry about that now. Something had happened. Something bad.

"There's another one," Jack said.

Bryant woke when the banging started. He staggered out of bed, fighting his duvet off and opened his door. Collins stood in the corridor, a concerned look on his face. The look disappeared as soon as he saw Bryant.

"Mate, put some clothes on."

"What do you want? It's the middle of the night." Bryant stood his ground.

"You were shouting your head off. I just came to see if you were alright."

"Shouting?"

"Yeah. I could hear you clearly through the walls. Sounded like you were having a fight."

"Christ, Collins, it's five in the morning and you got me out of bed for that?"

"I just wanted to check-"

"There was no need, I'm fine. Go back to bed."

"Mate-"

"Seriously, Collins," Bryant squared his shoulders, "I'm going to struggle to get back to sleep now as it is."

"Sorry." Collins looked at his feet, before turning to return to his room.

Bryant sighed and could feel his cheeks burn. "Thanks for checking up on me."

Collins paused. "Anytime. I've got your back, remember?"

Yeah. But this is Kent. It's not Afghan anymore. "Hey, what was I shouting?"

"Nothing much, really. Loads of random shit," Collins shrugged. "Then you yelled 'There's another one' at the top of your voice. That's when I came." He looked like he was going to say something else, but his face broke into a smile instead. "Seriously mate, put some clothes on, it's freezing out here."

With that, he returned to his room, closing the door with a soft click. Bryant looked up and down the corridor, but no-one else appeared. He closed his own door softly and sat on the edge of his bed. *There's another one.* What did that mean? He looked at his hand again, but it was still completely healed. *Didn't imagine it.* Traces of his dream lingered at the edge of his thoughts, but he couldn't focus on them. He could recall a hill, some trees and a river, but that was about it.

Rain splattered against his window and he looked out. Collins has said it was freezing, but he felt fine. Too hot if anything. *Afghan has made him soft. It's not cold here.* Bryant turned to switch his light off, but then, and only then, realised that he had not turned it on.

He pulled his duvet up and closed his eyes. For the first time in months, he slept soundly.

4

Jack crept forward, closer to the wall surrounding the holiday cottage. No light shone from any window, but with the sun now fully visible in the sky, it would not be long before the occupants were up and about. He vaulted the wall and ran across the garden. He pulled some clothes off the washing line, picked up a pair of flip-flops and ran back the way he had come. He stopped by a wooden table that had seen better days and scooped a baseball cap off it, then jumped the wall again.

The cottage was the only dwelling for at least two miles in any direction, which generally made people relaxed about security. The clothes had been left on the line overnight but were dry. Jack pulled on the shorts and t-shirt which were only slightly too big for him. At least the flip-flops were the right size, but he was in no position to be choosy. Once dressed, he slipped back over the wall and jogged in a half crouch to the car - a brand new Honda Civic - in the drive.

He tried the door to the car, but it was locked. *Not that relaxed then.* He moved around it, looking for keys left on the tyres. They weren't there. A flash of colour drew his attention to the back door of the property. A kid's rucksack. SpongeBob SquarePants. *It will do.* Jack picked it up, a momentary pang of guilt flashing through him. In a few years, Josh would have one just like it.

A noise behind him. The door was opening. Jack sprinted for the wall and vaulted it, landing heavily on the other side.

He heard footsteps, then a child's voice shout "it's not there, mummy", and the pang of guilt turned into a sledgehammer.

He stripped off quickly and quietly and stuffed his newly acquired clothes into the bags. It was a tight fit. Jack heard the door close. *I'm sorry.*

The glimpses from the barely remembered dream flashed like images in a flick book. An army base. *What was Knowles up to?* He'd seen signs too. Tunbridge Wells. Maidstone. *Back to Kent then.* The Wolf burst out of him and it looked at the bag, sniffing it before picking it up in its massive jaws. It started to run back to the moor, stretching its legs until the cottage was miles behind.

The Wolf did not stop to admire the scenery. It didn't allow itself to get distracted by the deer fleeing ahead of it or even the ponies over the hill to its left. It followed the scent of engine fumes, heading back towards civilisation.

It had a long way to go.

Chapter 4

1

Knowles stood to attention, waiting for the Major to start shouting. It was more disconcerting that he didn't.

"You didn't have to kill him, Peter."

Yeah, like I didn't need to take a shit this morning. "No sir."

"So why did you?"

Knowles said nothing. The Major sighed heavily. "Sit down, Peter. Sit down and relax." Knowles sat in the only other chair in the office. The Major had the deep tan of someone who had just returned from Afghanistan. His scared eyes matched that too.

"Peter, I'm trying to catch up with things here, so you need to help me out."

"Yes, sir."

"I've read the file and all the notes. It's a pretty hard thing to get your head around."

"Yes, sir."

"Ok, cut the crap, sergeant. You're not on trial and I'm not going to bawl you out." The Major pushed the file away from him and drummed his fingers on the desk. "We need to find Jack Stadler, yes?"

"Yes, sir."

"But *you* lost him."

"Yes, sir." *Not that I had much choice in the matter.* No point in explaining it wasn't his fault. If Jack wanted to leave, then he was going to.

25

"I gather helicopters spent the night looking for him and most of the following day."

"Y-"

"But they found nothing? Not even a trail. Several of our men shot at the wolf." The Major paused and stared out of the window. "An enormous wolf. Our men shot at an enormous wolf and either all missed or didn't manage a kill shot. Explain that to me."

"I don't think he can be killed, sir."

"But the others can? The other wolves died. We have about eighty of them in our morgue, being dissected as we speak. How can that be?"

"I don't know, sir."

"Well, do you have any theories?"

Knowles looked at the other man and regarded him with something less than contempt for the first time. Major Paul Raymond, roughly forty-two, so ten years more experience than Knowles. Slighter build, but very toned. He was not your typical desk Major. *He couldn't be more different to Smith.*

"Sir, during the attack, I spoke with one of the wolves, a man calling himself Callum."

Raymond nodded. "He was the first we looked at. No history on him at all. No trace of the man in any database, here or overseas."

"I think he was their leader. He called Jack 'an Original'."

"Yes, and what's that?"

"I don't know, sir."

"Well did you ask him?"

"No, I shot him after he killed two of our people." Claire. Knowles couldn't remember the young private's name, could barely remember his face. Claire Biddlestone, however, was etched on his memory. Her blank stare after Callum ripped her throat out was something he would take to his own grave.

"Do you think these Originals are different to the others?"

"Yes sir, I do. Also, I think Jack is the only one."

"Why do you say that?"

"They took a big risk attacking our base, sir. They must have known they would take heavy losses." Knowles winced

26

as he said it. Heavy losses didn't quite cover the shocking loss of life on that day: a square in an army base covered with bodies. It had started with two men from the guard post and ended with two helicopter gunships shooting the base to pieces. All base personnel dead. A huge number of the wolves dead. Knowles the only human survivor. The worst day of his life.

"They were rescuing one of their own."

"Sir, with respect, would you do that? If we lost someone, knew they were in the mountains with the rest of Al-Qaeda, what would we do? Would we storm in?"

Raymond shrugged and waved his hand at Knowles. *Carry on.*

"No, Jack was special to them. Callum said as much before it kicked off."

"What did Stadler say to you?"

"Nothing. He had no idea."

"He was fooling you, Peter."

"No, I don't think so," Knowles said. "I think that whatever happened to Jack in that cave was an accident. I don't think he wanted any of this."

"So why did he run away?"

It was Knowles' turn to shrug. "He only just got to his wife in time. He saved her, then legged it."

"But we could have helped him."

"No sir, Major Smith was all for dissecting Jack. He wasn't interested in curing him."

"Well, Smith isn't here to defend that accusation, Peter, so I think we'll keep it between us."

Yeah, ok then. "So, what now, sir?"

"Well, we need to double our efforts to find Jack Stadler. That's our first priority. Secondly, we need to find out just how many of these wolf things there are on our lands."

"And kill them, sir? Kill them all?"

Raymond nodded. "Yes. They represent an unparalleled risk to the security of this nation."

Good.

"Thirdly, we need to clean up the mess with that reporter." Raymond pressed a button on his desk. "Send him in."

Knowles turned and stood as another man entered the room. He was the same height as Knowles, but much stockier. His face was hard, and his eyes black.

"Peter, this is Sergeant Jamie Bryant." The two men shook hands. "He is now working with you on everything to do with the wolves. You will give him a full briefing and the two of you will jointly head up a task force, the mission of which will be to find Jack Stadler. Any wolves you find along the way are to be eliminated. We are not interested in prisoners. We want them gone. Is that clear?"

"Crystal," said Bryant.

"Yes, sir," said Knowles.

"Before you do that, I want that journalist taken care of."

"Sir, after we tasered him, we gave him enough sedative to keep him out cold for twenty-four hours. It would have wiped his short term memory too. He woke on a park bench, probably thinking he'd been on a mad bender. He's not a problem."

"I hate loose ends, sergeant. Dismissed."

2

"So you met Stadler?" Bryant asked. They were sitting in the mess, two mugs of tea steaming between them. Bryant sat with his chair at an angle to the table, slouched with his legs crossed. Knowles sat upright opposite him, his hands on the table.

"Yeah. I was assigned to watch him. Thought you'd read the file?"

"I have," Bryant smirked, a natural look on his tanned face. "I know how much you fucked up."

"I didn't. You have no idea."

"You had him in custody. You flew him to Devon." Bryant spread his hands. "He escaped. You're lucky to still have your stripes."

"Have you met any of these wolves?"

Bryant shook his head.

28

"Then you have no idea what you are talking about," Knowles laughed at Bryant. "This isn't some sweaty Arab hoping you'll walk into his IED or sniper scope. These things will rip you apart before you get a shot off."

"You managed it."

"I was lucky." Images of his dead friends sprang to mind, and he swallowed hard. *I am not going to cry in the mess hall.* "Very lucky."

"How? Why you?"

"That is a pointless question and you know it. You were in Ghanners right?"

"Yeah, but we don't call it that anymore."

"No? What do you call it?"

"Afghanistan," Bryant said with a straight face.

"Fair one. But you lost people right? You know, every time, it could have been you. Maybe a few times it should have been you."

Bryant said nothing, but Knowles could tell from the look on his face that the other man knew what he talking about.

"Do you want me to take care of the journalist?"

Knowles shook his head. "He wrote a blog about three blokes jumping him and nicking his source. Our tech boys were all over it. They posted about thirty reports slating the guy, saying he was full of shit. Each of the posts were from Facebook accounts that can be linked to real people's accounts."

"How does that work?"

"How should I know? I can barely turn a computer on. I think there must be desperate people out there who just say yes to everyone who sends them a friend request." Knowles shrugged. "It helps it go viral. Simon Foster is no longer a problem."

"So, what do we do next?"

"We need to find out just how many more of these wolves there are."

"How are we going to do that?"

"Get out there and look," Knowles said. "Scan police radios, look at press reports. There will be odd events - we go take a look."

"And then what? We round them up?" Bryant snorted. "Keep them in some kind of ghetto?"

Knowles looked genuinely shocked at the suggestion. "No. You heard the Major. We kill them. We kill them all."

3

Bryant sat in his car, watching the rain pour down the windscreen. The darkness outside combined with the rain to make him shiver, even though he was in the dry. He drummed his fingers on the steering wheel. *Come on, where are you?*

He had left Knowles as quickly as he could after their conversation. The man had the look of a zealot, eyes shiny as he spoke. Bryant understood where he was coming from, but did that really justify genocide? He didn't want to think about where that left him.

Footsteps near his door made him look up. The shuffling figure of Simon Foster walked past. Bryant clambered out of the car, slamming his door shut. Foster turned, surprise etched on his face. He met Bryant's eyes and carried on walking, albeit a little quicker now. Bryant could smell the fear emanating from the man and his heart beat a little faster.

"Hey," he shouted. "Simon Foster?"

That got his attention. Foster stopped and looked at Bryant. His belly hung over his waistline in what Bryant's ex-wife would have called a 'muffin top'.

"Do I know you?"

Bryant shook his head. "I have something you need."

Foster laughed. "You have a way to stop the trolls spamming my website? Good luck, buddy," he started to turn away again.

"I can stop them."

"How?" Foster snorted. "Who the hell are you?"

"My name is Jamie Bryant. I'm a sergeant in the army. My current assignment is of great interest to you."

"Did he send you?"

"Who?"

"The man who took my source away. Made him disappear. Did he send you?"

"I have no idea who you are talking about." *Knowles. Too blatant. The trail is a mile wide.*

"What do you want Mr. Bryant?"

"The army is conducting operations in this country that I believe are of interest to the general public. I think they are taking risks with people's lives. Unnecessary risks."

He could see he had Foster's attention now.

"You'd better come up then."

Foster opened the door to the block of flats they were standing outside. Bryant followed him into an entrance hall that had seen better days. Paint flaked off the walls, and the strip lighting made it look as desperate as a Soho nightclub at 4 am. Bryant scanned the corners of the room and a satisfied grunt escaped his lips.

"What's that?" Foster asked. The grunt had clearly been louder than Bryant had intended.

"Nothing. Thought you'd live somewhere nicer is all."

"This is just a stepping stone. The flats are nice, just the management company don't care for the bits we pay them to maintain. I've complained-"

"I don't really give a shit," Bryant said.

"Oh," Foster looked embarrassed. "Sorry. It's through here."

His flat was on the ground floor. They went through a solid looking door with additional two locks and entered Foster's home. Bryant closed the door behind him and quietly engaged both locks.

4

He smashed the top of his alarm clock hard enough to hurt his hand, but still the ringing persisted. *Phone, dumbarse.* He swung his legs out of bed and reached for his jeans. They were in a crumpled heap on the floor next to his bed. His t-shirt lay next to them. *Not like me.* He fumbled in his pockets until he found the phone. Knowles' name flashed at him and he clicked the green button.

"Yeah?"

"Bryant? I've been calling for half an hour."

"What?"

31

"We have a situation. We've got wolves in London."

"What? Wait, what?"

"There was an attack last night. In London."

"How do you know it was our wolves?"

"The body was dismembered, with bits of it eaten."

"Holy shit."

"Yeah. It gets worse. Remember the reporter I told you about? It was him. One of the wolves just killed Simon Foster."

Chapter 5

1

Jack walked past a sign saying "Huntleigh" and felt his stomach knot. He had a baseball cap pressed over his head, peak pushed down to hide as much of his face as possible. The sun still hung low in the sky, which meant it was early. Rush hour didn't really exist in the village, but people would still go to work, or be out and about. It had always been a quiet village and now he was thankful for that. He couldn't risk being seen. He was, after all, supposed to be dead.

At the top of his street, the knot intensified. The houses lined the road on the left-hand side, a thick, well-established hedge bordered the opposite side. Jack's house was the fourth one. Three doors further down sat a house covered with scaffolding. He had a dim memory of the place and the horrific events that took place in it. Tied to a chair, surrounded by soldiers, before being shot. *A lifetime ago.* He had been taken by the army when his son was less than a week old. It had been the end of winter when they had shot him and taken him to Kent. He could remember the cold wet morning when this had all started, but barely remember what his son looked like.

He watched his house. The window to his old bedroom was covered with a large plastic sheet. He felt a pang of guilt at that. A shadow moved in the downstairs window, and Jack pressed himself back into the hedge.

Katie stood perfectly framed by the window. She was holding Josh and was smiling down at him. *He's got big.* Jack felt a lump in his throat and swallowed hard. He knew that a lot of time had passed in Kent, but this was the first time that he actually appreciated just how long. Josh looked huge. Jack started to cry, silent tears running down his cheeks. *I have missed so much of your life, but I will fix that.*

Wiping away the tears, Jack walked back up the street, determined to find the other Original. He didn't really want to think how he even knew about the other one. *Someone who can help me. Someone who can return my life to normal. Next time I come back here, it will be to live with my family.*

2

Katie Stadler climbed out of bed with a sigh. He was crying again. Hungry, always hungry. She picked Josh out of his cot and walked downstairs, shushing him with every step. The plastic flapped in the breeze, but at least it would be fixed soon. The insurance company had eventually agreed to pay out, but only after much arguing. They said a window doesn't just 'fall out'. She stuck to the story, especially as she couldn't tell them the truth.

A giant wolf jumped through the window after killing another wolf. No, definitely couldn't tell anyone that. Especially as the wolf might, just might, be my dead husband.

A quick trip to the microwave and then Josh was feeding, greedily sucking down the formula. He was starting to eat solids now, changing almost every day. Her friend, Karen, had warned her that teething would be starting soon and that was a whole new ball game in terms of sleeplessness. *How am I going to cope with that?*

Bottle finished, Josh giggled and burped as he looked up at her. She smiled back and carried him through to the sitting room. Flicking the TV on, she watched the news with Josh perched on her knee. He stared with large eyes, sucking on his fist. She bounced him on her knee and sang to him, whilst glancing at the television. There was nothing cheerful on the news at all. The murder of a blogger in London was the third story. She tutted. Why would anyone murder a blogger? Nobody takes them seriously after all. But then...

Behind the reporter, going into the building where the murder had happened, a familiar face.

Knowles.

Katie cried out, making Josh jump. He started crying, so she stood and began rocking him, forcing a smile onto her lips.

Knowles is in London. At a murder scene.

She thought back to the night he came crashing into her bedroom, chasing the massive wolf that had just saved her life. He had called the wolf 'Jack'. Later, he had denied it. As the soldiers cleaned her house and the helicopters circled the village, he had continued to lie, claiming she had misheard him. Said that her memory was suspect as the wolf was nowhere near as big as she had claimed. Just a wolf that had been imported illegally and then let go when it had grown too big. *Yeah, right.*

In the morning, on the news no reference was made of the incident. She didn't even mention it to Karen, didn't want to be thought mad, again. There were questions about the window from Karen and her neighbours. They'd also asked about the helicopters, but she said she hadn't seen them. Josh had had a good night, she said, so she slept really heavily for once. Karen, in particular, clearly hadn't believed her, but she understood Katie enough not to push it. Katie would tell her the truth – eventually.

But there he was once more. The mysterious soldier, the one in charge. At a murder scene.

What have you done Jack?

3

Bag in its mouth again, the Wolf ran and ran. It stuck to the tree-line wherever possible and put as much distance between it and Huntleigh as possible. The Wolf ran across fields, through streams and woodland. Every few miles it would stop, sniff and then head off again, having checked that it was still going the right way.

Eventually it came to a freshly ploughed field with a tree at the edge of it and thick hedges running around the perimeter. A large green sign towered over the other side of the hedge, and it could hear the engines of the cars and lorries rushing past.

The Wolf checked its surroundings again. It could hear, but not see, the road - so it was a fairly safe assumption that no-one on the road could see into the field. Given also that the bottom of the sign was in line with the top of the hedge, then provided it stayed in the shadow of the hedge it would not be seen.

Moments later, Jack opened the bag and dressed in the stolen clothes. He pulled the flip flops on then tugged the cap over his unruly hair. Then he walked along the hedge until he found a big enough gap to squeeze through and he was standing next to a dual carriageway.

Traffic whizzed by, not yet at the height of summer standstill. The green sign said that Exeter was ahead with Okehampton to his left. The A30: the main road through Devon for holidaymakers. The road that led east. In a few hours, he would be in London and then on to Kent. *Easy.*

Jack started walking along the road with his thumb out.

Chapter 6

1

Knowles surveyed Simon Foster's flat with increasing despondency. Foster had clearly been a clean man. His flat was the most organised he had ever seen for a civvy. The bookshelves in the living room were neatly stacked, with books firstly sorted by size, then by author surname. Mostly highbrow literature, but a few copies of Stephen King, Stephanie Meyers and JK Rowling in there also. The Harry Potter books were in adult jackets, which made Knowles cringe.

Bryant stood next to him, frowning. He was holding an unopened sandwich pack in one hand.

"You going to eat that?" Knowles asked.

Bryant shook his head. "Not hungry. You want it?"

Knowles nodded and took the packet. His stomach was rumbling. "The police got anything?" he asked between mouthfuls.

Bryant shook his head. "No CCTV in here. They're checking the street, but they're not hopeful."

"No?"

"Cameras at the end of the street are broken and have been for some time."

"Ok, we need this secure. No press in, at all. I don't really want the local coppers in here either."

"Working on it, the Major is pulling some strings."

Knowles finished the sandwich and checked his watch. *Only 0900. Going to be a long day.* "Well, whoever did this is long gone."

"Do you think it's Stadler?"

"No," Knowles said. "Last time I saw Jack he could control it. This-" he gestured around the room. The blood covered walls, the lumps of torn flesh splattered on the carpet and the remains of the body. "This was an animal. This was out of control."

2

An hour later they were driving back to the base. Bryant was silent, watching the world go by. Knowles drove, lost in his own thoughts. He didn't dwell on the bollocking he had received last week – that had come with the territory. He had defended himself against the accusations. It had been Smith who had put the base to a skeleton crew and luckily the orders had been agreed up the chain. He could not explain why he was the sole survivor. *Luck. Pure, shitty luck.* Knowles swallowed hard, blinking tears away. *Not again. I am done crying.* He had been surprised – clearly as surprised as Raymond – they had kept him on. He'd known people canned for less. And now, here he was, covering up another murder. *When is this going to end?*

The road blocks around Devon had been his idea, the cover story of an escaped convict enough to keep the public quiet. It was only a matter of time before they caught Jack, or better, more of the wolves. The brass had decided to keep him on, mostly because he was the only survivor and, therefore, the only person who had any idea what they were up against.

Knowles was a pragmatic man. Staying on this op meant he could find the wolves and kill as many of them as possible. Revenge for Carruthers, Meyers, Knowles, Scarlet and of course, Claire. Who knew what could have happened there? Probably would eventually have gone the way of all of his relationships, but damn it would have been a fun few years first. The wolves had taken that away from him. He hadn't even kissed the woman.

He tapped a rhythm on the steering wheel. Bryant looked at him with cold eyes. "Sorry," Knowles muttered. The other man resumed staring out through the window. *This is going to be a long op unless he learns to lighten up.*

Knowles didn't mind really. Bryant had seen recent action, everything about the way he carried himself screamed that. Six months ago, Knowles had been much the same himself, but he had his mates to pull him through. The same mates that were now dead. *Who knew that Devon was so dangerous?* A wry smile creased his lips, but Knowles was a long way from finding anything about this situation funny.

Six months ago the scorching heat of Afghanistan. The constant threat from IEDs and insurgents. Now, what? The dreariness of the British weather with the constant threat that anyone you meet could actually be one of the wolf things. Throat ripped out in seconds by a creature that shouldn't exist.

Of course, underneath all that was Jack. Just a normal guy, a dull civvy with a pretty house and prettier wife. Punching above his weight in that regard. Jack was alright, really, just wanted to be with his family: to return his life to normal.

Kill them. Kill them all.

Maybe then, he could return Jack to his family.

3

"Roadblock," Tom said. There was a hiss as the airbrakes kicked in and his thick forearms held the wheel tight. Jack watched him closely. The truck driver had stopped soon after he started hitching, for which Jack had been grateful as the rain had started. No sign that he recognised him. *Of course not: you don't get pictures of dead people in the papers. Have you seen this man? Whereabouts unknown, but last seen in a morgue.*

"What?"

"Where you been living, mate?" Tom grinned. "Someone escaped from Dartmoor prison. Someone dangerous apparently."

"Rubbish," Jack said. "They don't do dangerous prisoners in Dartmoor anymore. I thought they were closing it down."

"Not rubbish," Tom said. "It were on the news last night."

"What's he look like, this guy?"

"Bit like you really. Same sort of height. Darker, longer hair and a beard, though." Tom glanced over at Jack, eyes widening slightly. "Ah, shit."

"I'm not going to hurt you." *Goddammit, they* do *put pictures of dead people on the news.*

"You a little on the small side to be thinking along them lines, mate." Tom's smile had returned.

If only...

"I am not an escaped prisoner."

"I'm not interested. You need to get out of my cab."

"I need to get to London."

"Whatever, not in my cab." Tom looked directly at Jack. "Out."

"Whatever they say I did, I didn't do it."

"Let me count the number of fucks I give. Get out of my cab."

Jack looked out the front of the cab, counting the number of cars to the roadblock. Five. If he jumped out now, he would clearly be seen.

"Please-"

"Save your breath. Out."

"But-"

Tom opened his door and jumped onto the tarmac. "Hey!" he shouted as loud as he could. At the roadblock, Jack could see the soldiers turn and look.

"He's here! He's in my truck!"

Jack opened the passenger door as the soldiers started running towards the lorry.

"It's him!" one of them shouted. Jack sprinted to the side of the road and jumped the barrier between the dual carriageways. Traffic screeched to a halt as he ran. He could hear the soldiers shouting, hear them sprinting, smell their fear. *How much do they know?* He doubted they knew everything. Perhaps they'd been told the escaped prisoner story too – perhaps even believed it.

A shot whizzed past his ear. Jack upped his pace. He knew that if he changed he could outpace them all, but this was far too public for that. All the holiday makers and their kids, he couldn't give them nightmares. *If you don't change they'll catch you.* Jack ignored the voice. Another shot rang out and he stumbled. Searing pain roared up his leg and he stumbled. CRACK! Another shot. This one caught his shoulder and he hit the tarmac. He tried to push himself up, but his legs felt heavy.

Jack rolled over in time to see two of the soldiers approach with rifles raised. He raised his hand, watching his fingers turn into claws. *Got to get away.*

Two guns fired simultaneously.

4

Knowles sat alone in the canteen, mopping up the remains of his egg with a cardboard piece of toast. He had finished his paperwork from the morning and sent all the required emails regarding the death of Foster. A team would now liaise with the local police and essentially cover it up. The exact nature of the death would be played down to the media, and it would be pinned on an internet loon who was now safely behind bars. All lies, of course, but necessary ones.

It had been one of the grimmest scenes he had ever witnessed. What he couldn't work out was why. It was clearly the work of the wolves, but why? Foster's posts had been about the attack on the base, and the cover-up surrounding that. He hadn't mentioned wolves, probably for very sensible reasons. His murder didn't make much sense.

Unless it's us doing the killing and making it look like something else.

The thought came from nowhere, but he immediately kicked himself. Had Raymond ordered Foster's death? He 'hated loose ends' after all. Bryant carried himself like a Special Forces operative, all hard stares and long silences. *A walking cliché.* He could easily have driven to London and killed Foster and got back in time for Knowles' early morning call. Rip the body apart to make it look like a wolf had done it.

Knowles swallowed hard. If Bryant was capable of that, then what else what he capable of? Was any man really capable of that level of bloodshed? Knowles had spent enough time in war zones to know the answer to that was an emphatic *yes*.

It still didn't answer the 'why' though. If Bryant was Special Forces, he had to know a hundred ways to kill a man without raising this level of suspicion. If Bryant had done it like that, then Raymond was now either extremely pissed off or talking to the brass about escalating the nature of the threat posed by wolves.

Was that it? Was Raymond planning to have more troops on the wolves? If so, then he was playing with fire. Their existence had to be kept secret – the consequence of panic amongst the public was too great to contemplate.

Knowles pushed his plate away. It was time to pay the boss a visit.

5

Jack woke in an army tent. A blanket had been pulled over his head and he was momentarily disorientated. He sat up, fighting with the fabric for a moment before he pulled it away from his head. A soldier stood in the entrance to the tent, looking out at a road. Beyond him, Jack could see more soldiers packing up the roadblock. Traffic was moving, slowly but steadily, out on the road.

Jack stood as quietly as he could. He looked around, trying to see a way out. The only exit was blocked by the soldier.

Canvas.

He looked at the lining of the tent. Quickly he knelt by the back of the tent. His (stolen) t-shirt had two burn holes in the front of it, causing it to hang loosely on his frame. Bullet holes, not burn holes. Jack concentrated on his hand and watched as his index finger turned into a massive and razor sharp claw. Using the claw, he pierced the canvas and dragged it down cutting the canvas with a loud ripping noise.

Oops.

The soldier turned and shouted. Jack pushed the ripped canvas open and stepped through without looking. The soldier raised his gun and shouted again.

Jack nearly made it out before he fired.

6

Knowles stood to attention in front of Raymond's desk. The major waved for him to sit down.

"What can I do for you, Knowles?"

"Sir, did you order Bryant to kill Foster?"

"What?"

"Did you ask him to make it look like the wolves had done it?"

"Have you lost your mind, Knowles?" Raymond put his pen down and stared at Knowles. "Explain yourself."

"Sir, I think Bryant killed Foster. I just need to know why. Foster was not our enemy."

"Foster was trying to inform the general public of the truth behind the events that you are the sole survivor of."

Not sole. "But we had discredited him."

"Yes."

"So why kill him?"

"Knowles, you are way out of line here. I did not order Sergeant Bryant to do anything of the sort. As far as I know, Sergeant Bryant was here when Foster was killed."

Knowles sank back in his chair. He had been sure he was right. "You didn't ask him to-"

"Don't finish that sentence Knowles," Raymond said. "I fought for you to remain on this op. Should I have let them throw you to the wolves?" He winced at his poor choice of words but maintained eye contact with Knowles.

"No, sir."

"Good, then cut the crap about Bryant. He's a good soldier and a good man to have on your side if things go south. You are suggesting that he ripped apart a man on my orders? I could have you canned for even thinking that."

"Sorry, sir." It wasn't enough, not nearly enough. Knowles brushed at the sweat beading on his brow. "Guess I'm not thinking straight, sir."

"Jesus Christ Knowles." Raymond was close to shouting now. "How could you think that I was capable of this? What would I gain from it?"

Knowles remained silent.

"For God's sake, Knowles. I want this problem resolved, not made public. What you're suggesting is ridiculous. This island will be free of wolves before the end of this year. We will stamp them out. Do you understand? We will work together, not concoct bullshit conspiracy theories. Now get out of my sight."

As Knowles stood, the phone rang. Raymond listened intently then shouted at Knowles to close the door. He covered the mouthpiece.

"They found Stadler. A couple of guys shot him dead at a roadblock."

"He's not dead."

"I know, he's just been shot again trying to escape."

"They need to tie him up, with chains if they can."

Raymond nodded and repeated the instructions. He hung up and looked at Knowles with a sour grin on his face. "Looks like you could be useful after all. Get Bryant, get a bird, go get Stadler."

"Sir, Bryant asked for some personal time this afternoon. Seeing a doctor, I think." *Shrink probably, but no soldier would ever admit that.*

Raymond swore to himself.

"Sir, Stadler trusts me and knows me. I can go alone."

After a moment, Raymond nodded. "Don't cock this up, Sergeant."

Chapter 7

1

Bryant slowly stripped off and put the green plastic nightgown over his head. Neatly folding his clothes, he placed them in the locker next to his bed. Once done, he sat on the edge of the bed and waited.

This would be the last time he would come here. Of that, he was certain. The small private hospital was only three miles from the base, but it was the dictionary definition of discreet. When he had started coughing up blood, it was the only place he even considered going to. The diagnosis had been bad, and the prognosis worse.

Six months.

Bryant had come to terms with his own mortality years ago: most soldiers did. When you see death on a daily basis, you have to. He had not expected to go like this, though. In his head, it had always been in a storm of bullets, hopefully saving the life of someone in his team in the process. Not this. Months of chemo and a cocktail of pills large enough to count as a three-course meal.

Drastic times require drastic measures.

Now, Doctor White had asked him to stay a little longer. Bryant knew that his blood tests had been analysed already, why else ask him to stay? All he had to do now was come up with a convincing reason for his miraculous recovery. Somehow, impaling himself on a magic bone would not really cut the mustard.

The door opened and White came in, holding a clipboard. He shook Bryant's hand.

"Jamie, I have some really remarkable news." White's face creased as he smiled. It made him look even older.

"Yes?"

"I cannot find any tumour markers in your blood."

"What does that mean?"

"I don't know! I've never seen anything like it," White paused. "A tumour marker allows us-"

"Doc, seriously, I don't care. Just tell me what it means."

If White was offended by his interruption, he didn't show it. "I cannot find any trace of cancer in your blood sample."

"So, that's good news, right?"

White nodded. "It's marvellous news, Jamie. I've never seen anything like it and I can't explain it."

"Who cares, right?"

This time, White laughed. "The medical profession, Jamie. You're a miracle."

Bryant looked at the ridiculous gown. "I don't feel like one."

"I have to run some tests, see if I can get to the bottom of this."

"No."

"What?"

"You heard."

"But," White looked shocked. "But, whatever has happened might lead to a breakthrough in cancer treatments. You might be the key to curing this once and for all."

"I don't care. You're not running more tests." Bryant stood, heading for the locker.

"Jamie, please-"

Bryant ignored him. White started breathing hard.

"Jamie, this is not reasonable behaviour. Please reconsider."

Bryant opened the locker.

"Well, at least sign this so the blood tests can run. Please."

He closed the locker. "What tests?"

46

White waved the clipboard at him. "The army are looking for miracle cases. I have sent your blood to them."

Bryant felt his head start to throb. "You shouldn't have done that."

"It's done. All I need is your signature and my secretary can send the package off. It's all done, you don't need to do anything."

Shit.

"Where's the package?"

"It's on her desk, ready to go. Please, just sign this." White looked at him hopefully, eyebrows raised and a smile on his lips. The smile wavered as he saw the expression on Bryant's face. "What's wrong?" White heard the tremor in his own voice and didn't like it. He had treated servicemen and women before, including lots of Special Forces people like Bryant, but none had looked at him like that.

Bryant arched his back, making it pop audibly and then he pointed a finger at White. "You shouldn't have done that."

White started. The voice didn't sound like Bryant and he started to back away, realising that he really had made a terrible mistake.

2

The door opened and a nurse ran in. The wolf snarled and then leapt at her. Its jaws closed around her neck, severing her head in one bite. A corridor led away from the consulting room, two doors either side. One of those opened now and a doctor peered out. The wolf ran towards her, the screams energising it. The doctor tried to close the door, but the wolf was too big, too strong.

The door flew off its hinges, smashing the doctor on the head. She fell to the floor and the wolf was on her, biting through her clothes and into her stomach. The doctor screamed and screamed until she died. The wolf heard a sound behind it and turned in a jump.

Another nurse stood in the doorway, her mouth open in shock. She was frozen to the spot. The wolf snarled, breaking the spell and the nurse fled. With another jump, it landed on her back and bit into her neck, ripping her throat out.

The wolf was now in another short corridor. A flicker of deeply hidden memories came to the fore and it knew that the door ahead of it lead to reception and from there, the car park. It jumped at the door, bursting through it. Reception appeared to be empty. The wolf sniffed. *Yes, there.* It jumped onto the desk, then hopped to the other side. Underneath the desk, the receptionist was hugging her knees, shaking in terror.

"Please," she got as far as saying.

3

Bryant stepped into the car park, feeling more alive than at any other moment in his life. Energy coursed through his veins, his cock almost painfully hard. He looked around the car park. His car was the only one there. *Good.* Less to cover up. He had, in wolf form, smashed the whole of the hospital to pieces. Every computer, desk and camera had been destroyed. In human form, he had double checked for safes or backup computers. He had also destroyed every single blood sample he could find.

Satisfied, he had then dressed. The gore surrounding him hadn't bothered him in the slightest. In fact, it had turned him on even more. Now, he was free.

He walked to his car, whistling to himself, but then, something made him turn to the tree line at the edge of the car park. A woman stood there, calmly watching him.

A witness.

He stood still. The woman waved, and he realised she was naked. Bryant grinned. She turned into a wolf and watched him.

Bryant sauntered over to her. *This is turning into a great day.*

4

The female wolf turned and ran as he approached, but stopped about ten metres away. He jogged towards her and she ran away again. *I haven't got time for games.* She stopped again, same distance away. They were now in the woods that lay behind the doctors' offices. Bryant ran towards her, his lust overcoming his annoyance at her game playing.

She looks like a wolf and I still want her. I am one sick bastard. He laughed to himself. Full belly, hard cock, no morals. A twig snapped behind him and he turned, assuming a martial arts stance immediately. A man stood behind him, watching him intently. The man was also naked. From a tree next to him, another man stepped out, then a woman and so on around the clearing until he was surrounded by naked people. The original wolf turned back into a woman and put her arm around the biggest man.

Damn.

"What do you want?" Bryant asked.

"You," said the man. He patted the woman on her bottom and stepped into the clearing. "We have come to help you."

"Do I look like I need help?"

"No," the man smiled. "Your work was most impressive."

They watched that? They sat back and watched those people get eaten? "Don't get any funny ideas, mate, I'll happily do the same to you."

"We have not come to fight you."

"Well, what do you want then?"

"We have come to worship you."

Bryant looked at the faces surrounding him. He counted twelve people in all. Their faces were hard, bodies toned more than most soldiers he had served with. Despite the hard looks, there was a fervour in their eyes.

"Why worship me?"

"Why do you need to ask?" The man looked shocked.

"Worship is a strange word." *Respect I could live with. Blind worship tends to get people killed.*

"You are the most powerful of all of us here. This is my pack, gathered from the survivors." He watched Bryant, looking for understanding. "I give it to you."

"You are crazy mate. You know that?"

"I am not the person who followed a naked woman into the woods, even though she turned into a wolf."

Bryant laughed. "Fair one."

"My name is Carl Rogers."

"Jamie. But call me Bryant, everyone else does."

A buzzing sound came from Bryant's pocket. He pulled out his mobile and scowled. "Nobody make a sound." Without waiting for assent, he pressed the answer button. "Knowles. I'm busy."

Rogers watched him as he listened. Something about the man's demeanour really irritated Bryant. "Ok, I'm on my way. I'm an hour out."

"You have to leave?" Rogers raised an eyebrow. He looked like a hairy version of Roger Moore.

"That was my boss. Sort of."

"You no longer have a boss. You are in charge of yourself."

"Ok, mate, I don't really have time for some mickey mouse zen crap, so I'm just going to go now."

"When will we see you again?"

This was from the woman that he'd followed. Rogers looked irritated that she'd spoken, and the look intensified when Bryant smiled at her.

"You found me once. Guess it won't be hard for you to find me again." *Besides, I can smell you, so pretty sure you can smell me.*

He turned and started to head back to the car park. One of the men stepped into his path.

"Ryan-" Rogers said.

Bryant felt his mouth change. One minute he was smiling at Ryan, then his whole face changed into a wolf's and he roared at the other man. Ryan jumped back, face pale, eyes wide as Bryant changed back, the same grin on his face.

"Next time, I bite."

Bryant walked out of the woods, once again whistling to himself.

Chapter 8

1

Jack opened his eyes and tried to sit up. He couldn't move. *Here we go again.* He concentrated on his arms, forcing the change into them.

"Really, Jack, don't bother."

The familiar voice broke his concentration and he felt the power ebb. He craned his head towards the speaker. Knowles waved with his left hand. The gesture was almost sarcastic. In his other hand, Knowles was loosely holding a revolver, not quite pointing it at him.

"Hi, Jack." Knowles smiled. "You really could use a shower."

"Untie me, Knowles."

"Nope."

"I can just break these you know."

"Carbyne chain? I doubt it."

"A what?"

"You should be flattered, really Jack. That stuff holding you down is based on carbyne. This could well be the only chain of the stuff in the UK and it's being used to keep you tied up." Knowles shrugged, indicating that he didn't know what carbyne was either.

"Where am I, Knowles?" *We'll see about the chains.*

"Kent. Different base, but back in Kent. Turns out it's where they launched the helicopters from." Jack did not feel better with that knowledge. The last time he had seen

51

helicopters, they had been used to look for him. The time before that, they had been used to blow a base to pieces.

Jack groaned. "Why am I in chains?"

"You tried to escape. My boss wants you tied up, so you're tied up."

"I had to go, Knowles. You know that."

Knowles shrugged. "Yes. I understand Jack, but I still have to follow orders."

"I thought they'd have fired you."

"It was close."

"All I wanted was my family, Knowles," Jack said. "You know that. I never wanted to hurt anyone." He looked at the ceiling, feeling tears well. "But I was going to put them in danger."

"I know. But you should've come back with me."

"And let them cut me open?" Jack raised his eyebrows. "We both know that's what eventually would've happened."

"You'd have healed."

"Maybe. But that's not really a chance I want to take."

"Where have you been anyway?"

"Away."

"Very good Jack, you can play it like that if you want," Knowles said. "I am your friend remember?"

Jack turned his head away from Knowles. It was true that Knowles had shown him kindness. He and the female medical captain. They were the only ones who had been nice to him. Even when he'd shown he could control it, the others had still been wary of him. When the base had gone to a skeleton crew – even then – he had not been trusted. He had been a prisoner he realised now, and no amount of cooperation would have got him home to his family. *What was her name? Clara? Claire? Something like that.* She was gone however, Callum had seen to that.

"What happened at that base wasn't your fault Jack."

"Then whose was it?"

"You're a good man, Jack. Not like those other things."

"I've killed people, Knowles, you know that."

"Not for months."

Another memory swam into his mind. The wolf bearing down on Katie and Josh just before Jack's jaws tore its throat out. A few more seconds and he would have been too late.

"That's not strictly true."

"It is. You've not killed a person for months."

This time, Jack didn't miss the emphasis. *So that's the way of it.* "Knowles, I am one of them, you know."

"No, you're different."

Jack laughed. "How? There is a beast in me."

"Which you can control. You are not like the others."

"How do you know the others can't control it either?"

Knowles stayed silent, staring at him until Jack turned away.

What have you done Knowles? "What happens now?"

"I take you to see my boss. He decides from there."

"And if he wants me dead?"

Knowles grinned. "I'd kinda like to see him try."

"Before we go, there's something else."

"What?"

"I was coming to you, when they caught me. I was trying to find you."

Knowles looked surprised. "Why?"

"There's another one. Like me. Callum called me one." Jack saw Knowles shudder at the mention of that name. "An Original. There's another one."

2

Knowles sat next to Jack, mouth agape. *Another one.* "How do you know?"

Jack shrugged. "I don't know. I felt it."

"You a Jedi now, Jack?" There was no mirth in Knowles' voice. When Jack didn't answer, Knowles pressed on: "What does it mean?"

"I don't know," Jack said again. "But, I can't help thinking about when this happened to me. I could have used some help."

Knowles nodded. He didn't need reminding of how bad it had been when he and Jack had first met. Knowles still awoke some nights in a sweat. Sometimes it was the blood-smeared floor surrounding the corpse of a young doctor, other times it was some street thugs in Barnstaple getting ripped apart. They weren't thugs, though, not really. Just some drunks who had, quite literally, bitten off more than they could chew in taking on Jack.

"Do you know how to find him?"

Jack shook his head. "But I think I'll know when I'm close to him – or her."

"How close?"

"I don't know."

The radio on his belt buzzed at that moment. Knowles unclipped it and walked away from Jack's bed. "Yeah?"

"It's Bryant. I'm back."

"About time. Where have you been?"

"Personal time, Knowles. None of your damn business."

Knowles let that slide. He would deal with Bryant later. "Alright. Where are you now?"

"I'm with Raymond. He wants to meet the package, now."

"Package is secure. Raymond-"

"Who's Raymond?" Jack said, from beside him.

Knowles whirled around, reaching for his sidearm. Jack couldn't hide the smile on his lips. "Relax, Knowles, if I wanted to escape I could've ages ago."

Strongest stuff in the UK, my arse. He spoke into the receiver again. "Scratch that Bryant, we're coming to you. Stand to." He switched the radio off and turned to Jack.

"Jack, you can't just break free like that. People will shoot you."

The chains were on the floor next to the bed. Jack had broken them and lowered them to the floor without Knowles hearing. He was getting more powerful.

"Stand to? That mean assemble the troops?" Jack said. He still had that same smile on his face.

"Something like that," Knowles muttered. In one moment, Jack had proved who was really in charge. *Just how much has he changed?*

"Come on then. Let's go meet the boss."

54

3

Moments later, Knowles led Jack out into bright sunshine. Four soldiers stood in a rough semicircle around the door, guns aimed at Jack.

"All this, just for me?"

"Jack, for once, just shut it, ok?"

Jack looked at the soldiers, laughed, then followed Knowles. A path led past three buildings, each one taller than the previous. A jeep sat outside the last one, a large machine gun squatting in the back of it. The soldier standing behind the gun was staring at Jack with something close to hatred. *A few months ago, I would have been terrified here. Now...* Jack kept his eyes away from any soldiers. He kept focused on Knowles' back. He knew he could kill everyone here and escape. That would be the end of ever seeing Katie and Josh though.

Suddenly he stopped. Sweat broke out on his brow, and he started to tremble. Jack looked around at the soldiers surrounding him. Something was wrong, but what? He held his hand up and claws appeared, just for a moment, and then disappeared. *What the hell?*

Knowles kept walking, until he spotted the machine gunner turn the barrel towards him. He turned to look at Jack.

"What's wrong?"

Jack shook his head. The feeling had passed now, as quickly as it had come. "Nothing. Keep going."

Knowles held his hand up at the man on the jeep. Jack caught a slight almost imperceptible shake of his head. Then, Knowles opened the door to the largest building and ushered Jack inside.

4

Bryant stood to attention in front of Raymond.

"Relax, Bryant," Raymond said, although his voice held a trace of irritation. "I don't mind the personal time, I just object to the timing."

"Yes, sir." *Get this over with, you pompous overpaid twat.*

"The journalist needed our full attention. Tracking his killer could be a matter of national security."

"Yes, sir." *Every time you open your mouth you sound like a cliché.*

"All leave, even for a few hours, is to be preapproved by me, understood?"

"Yes, sir."

"And spare me the crap, Bryant, you did not get where you are by being a yes man."

"No, sir."

"Are you ok? You're sweating."

"Yes, sir." *No, I feel awful.* He could feel his arms and legs trembling.

Just then, there was a sharp knock on the door.

"Come!" Raymond barked. The door opened and Knowles walked in. Behind him came a man dressed in very loose combat fatigues, clearly at least a size too big for him. A few days' worth of stubble graced his chin, and he had the dark skin and smell of someone who had not seen a shower for a long time. The stench of raw meat and stale sweat assaulted his senses. Bryant met the man's eyes and before he knew what was happening, Bryant let out a guttural shout and changed.

5

Jack didn't have time to react beyond pushing Knowles out of the way. The soldier changed in front of him, bursting out of his clothes and leaping in one movement. Thick black fur erupted along his body as he jumped and then it was on top of Jack, jaws apart, drool hanging lower than its tongue.

Jack changed, just as the jaws snapped close, missing his face by millimetres. The Wolf bit back, aiming for the other's neck, but it moved its head and body out of the way. The Wolf pushed up, using its back like a lever and catapulting both of them into the air. The other wolf banged into the doorframe, splintering the wood, causing the door to hang loose.

As soon as they landed, the Wolf spun on top, trying to bite the other. A popping sound filled the air and both wolves realised they were being shot at. Bullets tore into the Wolf and it yelped and crashed to the floor. The other wolf sprinted for the outside door. A soldier had pulled it open and now the wolf barrelled into him, knocking him clean off his feet. Almost as an afterthought, it ripped the man's throat out, before running across the camp outside.

The Wolf yelped once more before its fur started to run back inside its body. Jack grunted, holding his shoulder where the bullet had torn into it.

"Knowles, it's him. It's the other Original," Jack said, then passed out.

6

Knowles swore loudly as he jumped to his feet.

Behind him, Raymond was standing slowly, surveying the mess in his office. Files scattered all over the floor from where Knowles had hit the table. The door hanging off its hinges.

"Knowles, what the hell is going on?" he roared.

"No idea, sir. Stay here." Knowles sprinted down the corridor, leaping over the dead soldier in the doorway. Blood coated the walls, arterial spray covering every surface in sight. Outside, the man on the jeep - Bryant's man, Collins - was firing 50mm large calibre rounds across the base. Other soldiers were running towards Knowles. Every single one of them looked petrified. *I'd almost forgotten what this was like.*

"Where is he?" Knowles yelled at Collins, who waved in the direction the wolf had run. Knowles followed the gesture. The wolf -Bryant- was crawling towards the fence. Its back legs had been shredded by the machine gun, but it still dragged itself forward. Knowles ran towards it, feeling relieved when some of the other soldiers followed him.

Bryant was two hundred yards away, and a hundred yards beyond him was the fence. More soldiers were running from the right now, heading to cut off its route to the fence.

Got you.

Even as the thought formed, even as he saw the inevitable capture of Bryant, Knowles saw more wolves gather at the fence. He counted at least ten, all howling and snarling. Even at this distance, their teeth gleamed in the sunshine, ready to snap down on human flesh. He watched in despair as one of the wolves tore a hole in the fence with its mouth. The other wolves pushed past, through the hole and into the base. In seconds, they were amongst the troops, biting and taking them down. The soldiers were too shocked to retaliate and suddenly Bryant was at the fence. The wolf at the fence made the hole bigger and then dragged Bryant through.

Why isn't that electrified?

Knowles would worry about that later. The other wolves were now sprinting to the opening. Knowles managed a few rounds, but without time to aim, they went wild. Soldiers were also shooting, and he heard the satisfying thump of some of them hitting home. Wolves yelped, and made for the hole in the fence. None stumbled, none fell and as suddenly as it had started, the base was quiet.

The wolves were gone.

Bryant had escaped.

7

Chaos reigned. Soldiers ran in every direction, some carried wounded men to the infirmary whilst others ran to the hole in the fence. They were armed, some of them heavily, but they all looked scared.

This is a hell of a thing, especially the first time. Knowles surveyed the base. Aside from chunks of grass where the 50mm had torn up the turf, the base itself was undamaged: a marked contrast to the last time Knowles had seen the wolves attack a base.

Raymond stood next to him, a scowl on his face. "Explain what is going on, Knowles."

"Sir, I think Bryant might be one of the wolves."

"Funny, Knowles, real funny. How did that happen and how the hell did those other wolves find him?"

"I don't know. But the last time a base was attacked, it was a lot more organised than this." *And lethal.*

"Conclusion?"

"I think this was opportunistic."

"They just happened to be passing?" Raymond nearly shouted this. Knowles winced. He knew how weak his suggestion had been.

"Where is Jack?"

"He is under lock and key in the brig, four men watching him."

Knowles nodded, trying not to let his face show what he was really thinking. *That's not enough. Not nearly enough. If Jack wants out, he's getting out.*

"Is he still unconscious?"

Raymond nodded.

"Then we should speak to him as soon as he wakes. I'm not sure what just happened, but he might know."

"Do it, Knowles. I want to see you as soon as you have discussed this with him."

"Yes, sir."

"In the meantime, I want every inch of those woods covered. I want Bryant in custody before nightfall."

Chapter 9

1

Bryant pulled himself free of Rogers' grip. "Let me go, I can walk."

"You can't walk: look at your legs. We have to run so let me help you," Rogers said. He looked over his shoulder as the rest of his pack crashed through the undergrowth. Some kept going straight past him, two of them still in wolf form. They were in the woods, not far from the base, but surrounded by tall trees and thick bushes. Sunlight dappled thought the leaves overhead, and birds took flight to avoid the sudden commotion in their home.

"It's the army, Rogers. Where exactly are you going to run to?"

The other man smiled. "We have a plan for that."

"I'm screwed," Bryant said. He fell to the ground now he had no support. His left leg was missing below the knee, but he felt nothing. His right leg was bleeding but not severely. He could put his weight on it. *Healing already.*

"Not yet."

"They will hunt us down."

Rogers nodded. "Yes, but they only know what you look like. The army do not know who we are. Please, Bryant, trust us."

Bryant snorted. "Trust? We just met and I'm supposed to trust you? Anybody I trusted is either dead or back there, shooting at us."

"That was the old you," Rogers said. "Please," he repeated, "we have to keep going. You do not need them."

They both turned as they heard shouts behind them. Sounds too, of men coming closer. Bryant could smell their sweat. His men. His friends. Maybe Knowles too. Knowles, who would now kill everyone he was with.

"Ok, let's go, but only until I can figure out how to get out of this mess."

Rogers smiled then turned back into a wolf and ran. Bryant changed, marvelling for a moment at how easy that was, and started to follow Rogers. He tumbled to the ground and it was then that he realised he only had three legs. *You can't run enough. Stop and kill them all.* The thought was not his – not entirely anyway. It came from deeper within him. The wolf shook his head, trying to clear the thought.

Turn around and kill them.

The wolf pulled himself up unsteadily and turned to face the men chasing him.

2

Collins crashed through the undergrowth, rage boiling inside him. Close behind came Parker and Wills. All three carried L85A2 assault rifles, each with thirty rounds in the mag. Wills' rifle had a grenade launcher underneath it and he carried three grenades. *I hope we don't need them.*

Collins stopped suddenly and held up his hand. The other two made weapons ready and stopped running immediately.

"The wolves get it big time, but Bryant comes home with us – got it?" Collins hissed. The other two men nodded, grim-faced. Collins pointed at Wills and then left, before repeating the motion to Parker but to the right. The men disappeared without making a sound.

Collins walked forward slowly, hunched over, making himself as small as possible. He was sure he had heard something. A twig or a branch snap. It meant they were close. He leaned around a tree and froze. In a small clearing, the largest wolf Collins had ever seen stood stock still. It was the same wolf he had seen running from the major's office on the base. It was holding its left hind leg up off the floor. On

61

second look, he saw that, actually, the leg was missing below the knee. *Do wolves have knees?*

Bryant. It's not a wolf. It's Bryant.

No sign of the other wolves. Bryant was on his own. Collins peered around the tree again, this time gazing down the sights of his rifle. Ever since the spiders in that cave, Collins had read and reread the file on Jack Stadler. As a soldier, he had been trained to believe his eyes and the situation that unfolded in front of him, not some hypothetical bullshit from the training ground. He could accept that his friend was now a wolf because that's what was happening right now. Rationalising or saying he didn't believe in this was for later.

"Bryant," a voice called. The wolf's head whipped round. Parker had stood up and was shouting at the wolf. "Bryant, hey, man! It's us, what're you doing?"

Oh shit.

The wolf leapt at Parker, jaws wide. Parker realised his mistake a fraction of a second too late and the wolf was on him. A tearing noise could be heard above the screams.

"Parker!" Collins yelled and opened fire. Bullets tore into the wolf's flank and it lifted its head in pain. Blood flew out of its mouth in the motion and it spat a chunk of flesh onto the grass. It turned towards Collins, its own blood pouring out of its side. Its three legs were shaking, but it growled all the same. Then Collins heard a pop, had a second to realise what it was and then he leapt to the ground, dropping his gun and covering his ears with his hands.

The explosion came first as a loud bang followed closely by a heat wave. Lumps of earth showered down around him, as he gathered up his weapon and turned back to the wolf. It was lying in the crater caused by Wills' grenade. Now both hind legs were missing entirely.

Wills nodded at him and they walked slowly towards the wolf, both with weapons raised. *Good, he's read the report too.*

"Parker?" Wills asked. Collins shook his head, but he knew that wasn't why Wills was asking. This was about trying to return to normality.

"Is he dead?" Wills nodded at the wolf. Again Collins shook his head.

"If he's like Stadler, then no."

"So, let's get him back to base, yeah?"

Collins nodded. "Yeah."

They looked at the wolf for a moment longer. "So how we going to do that then?" Wills asked.

Collins looked at the bleeding stumps of the wolf's rear legs then at the massive head and jaws. "I'll take the head."

"What so I get covered in its blood? No way, man."

"Alright, I'll take the legs."

"What so I get the head? Have you seen those teeth?"

"For Christ's sake, Wills!"

"Just messing with you man. Jesus, lighten up." Wills grinned and Collins chuckled, despite the situation. *Just letting off steam.*

"Come on then, let's get out of here before those wolves come back."

Wills stood by the head so Collins went to the back of the wolf. It really was massive.

"Ok, on three, lift," he said. "Holy crap!" The wolf was heavy. *It's a long way back to base.*

3

Rogers watched in wolf form as the two soldiers lifted the body of the Original. Their arms were straining under the weight and he knew they wouldn't get far before having to stop. His ears still rang slightly from the explosion, but other than that he was unharmed. Ryan appeared next to him, impressing Rogers with his silence. The big wolf looked at him with sad eyes.

Rogers nodded his head to the soldiers.

We follow and we wait for the right moment.

They didn't have to wait for long. The soldiers had managed fifty yards before one of them gave a shout and dropped the wolf.

4

"His fucking leg grew back!"

63

Collins leapt back from the wolf, hitting a tree as he did so, but he didn't care. Wills also dropped the wolf and ran a few yards away. He stopped and looked at Collins. "You're kidding me."

Collins shook his head. "No, I felt something scratch my arm, and man there it was. A leg."

Wills walked slowly back to the wolf. He raised his weapon and looked down the sights. "Shall we pop a few more in him, just to be sure?"

The wolf moved. Its eyes snapped open and it launched itself at Wills, jaws wide. Wills squeezed the trigger, but it was already too late. The jaws snapped around his legs and Wills toppled backwards, screaming. He kept firing his weapon, bullets screaming into the air, ripping apart the trees above them. Leaves showered down around them, bringing autumn to July. The wolf moved again, this time biting down on Wills' stomach. His screaming stopped.

Collins didn't move. He was frozen. Fear coursed through him, loosening his bladder and making his legs jelly. Something hit him from behind and he crashed to the floor, dropping his weapon. As he rolled, he saw what he already knew. The other wolves were here.

Please God, someone must have heard the shots, someone must be coming.

One of the wolves bit his leg, tearing a chunk out of his calf. Collins screamed and fumbled for his weapon. *No-one is coming. You're on your own. Deal with it!*

A hand swatted his weapon away.

"Don't," a voice said. Deeper, rougher somehow, than usual.

Collins blinked away tears of pain and looked up at Bryant. The man was standing naked, leaning slightly on his right leg. Two wolves stood either side of Bryant, teeth bared and snarling. Without another word, Bryant turned into a wolf – it looked like it exploded out of him, consuming him completely – and all three wolves crashed away through the undergrowth.

Seconds later, Collins heard more noises, but this time it was heading towards him. *The cavalry. At last.* He knew he should be tying a tourniquet, but he couldn't move. All the drills, all the training, deserted him when it was needed most. Collins sank into unconsciousness.

Chapter 10

1

Jack woke with a start. He was strapped to the table again. The unmistakable sound of a gun cocking clicked loudly next to him and he strained his head to look. A soldier who looked about twelve was aiming a wavering gun barrel at him.

"Don't move!" he snarled with a deep voice that was completely incongruous with his looks.

"Ok, keep calm. I won't do anything," Jack said.

"I see so much as one hair grow on your body, I will put you in the ground."

One hair? Really? "Message understood, mate. Where's Knowles?"

"Who?"

"The guy in charge, your boss."

"That's Major Raymond."

"Oh, right," Jack said. Army ranks had always been a mystery to him. "Please, could you stop waving that gun at me?"

"No, sir. I have orders to make sure you don't move."

"Well, that's great," Jack said. He forced himself to relax, resting his head back on the table. "By the way, call me Jack. Only the kids call me sir."

The soldier looked confused. *Well, he could have been taught by me last year.* Jack didn't want to think about all that had changed in the last year. Less than six months ago he had been happily married with a kid on the way. A secure job in a nice school in Devon. Now, well, now he wasn't.

"Private Patel." The new voice belonged to a stern looking man in a smart uniform. He wore a lot of medal strips on his shirt and a crown was stitched into a patch on his shoulder.

"Yes, sir," Patel snapped to attention, dropping his gun to his side as he did so.

"You may leave us."

Patel looked confused.

"You heard the major," Knowles said, appearing from behind the man. "Oh, and *I'm* Knowles. You might want to remember that."

Patel blanched, then half marched, half fled from the room.

"Why am I tied up?" Jack said.

"I need to ask you some questions," Raymond said, his voice as stern as his face.

"You know I can break these, right?" Jack wiggled his arms, making the chains rattle and clink against the metal table. *Not a table. This is a bed. No wonder army folk are always so miserable.*

"Yes, Mr Stadler, I do." Raymond pulled a chair from next to the bed into view and sat down. "However, it would go a long way to impress me if you would allow this. A charade maybe, but a necessary one."

"Jesus Christ, seriously? Knowles?"

Knowles shrugged, inclining his head at Raymond. The look said: *he's in charge.*

"I need to know if I can trust you, Jack."

"I *could* eat you now if that makes you feel any better." Jack scowled at Raymond. The man was about the same size as Knowles, maybe a couple of inches taller. He looked quite young to be a major, maybe late thirties, but then Jack didn't really know how old someone was to be a major. *The age of some of these men, maybe twenty is old to them.*

"Jack." The warning in Knowles' voice was unmistakable.

"That's not funny, Mr Stadler," Raymond said.

"Look, face facts, your chains would not keep me here. Your bullets would only stop me for a moment. If I wanted to, you and all your men would be dead, so cut the crap, ok?" Jack flexed his arms and they rippled for a second. The chains pinged off, crashing to the floor but not before Jack had leapt to his feet to stand toe to toe with Raymond.

At the noise, the door burst open and four men ran in, all brandishing weapons. Knowles had his hand on the pistol in a holster on his belt. All the colour drained from Raymond's face. The men were shouting and aiming their guns at Jack.

"Stand down!" Raymond roared. The men glanced at each other but didn't drop their weapons. "Now!" With a grumble, the weapons were lowered. Knowles relaxed his grip on the pistol. "You win, Mr Stadler, point made. Please, sit down."

Jack looked at Knowles, then sat down. His heart was hammering in his chest, but he was trying not to show it. He knew that he could do all of those things, but also that if he did, then part of him would be lost forever. *Empty threat, it was just an empty threat. Yeah?*

Why did you break the chains then?

He tried to keep his face neutral but he wasn't sure he was being entirely successful. The voice was back. The *other* voice. The one that had taken charge in the hospital in Barnstaple and had made him kill that poor doctor. The one he hadn't heard for a while now. Jack wiped sweat from his brow without taking his stare from Raymond's.

Raymond waved his hand and the soldiers filed out of the room, more uncertainly than when they'd entered.

"I want to see my wife and boy," Jack said.

"We've been here before Jack," Knowles said. "It didn't end well."

The look of fear on Katie's face. Josh's big sad eyes. The blood over the walls. No, that was pretty much the dictionary definition of not ending well.

"Knowles, I want my life back. I've thought about this. I came here because I knew there was another Original. Someone who could help me." Jack paused. "That can't happen now."

"Why not?" Knowles said. His hand was no longer over the gun at his waist.

"That man was as clueless as me. He's as new to this, probably newer, than I am."

"Then what are you suggesting Jack?" This came from Raymond.

"I help you catch him, you help me get my old life back."

2

Knowles ran his hand through his hair. He knew that Jack's thought process was close to his, but also how impossible that would be. There were two of them now, two Originals. How many more were out there? Hundreds of wolves had attacked the base a week ago. Over eighty were killed immediately, but that still meant there were more out there. The Originals were really dangerous, but so were the ordinary wolves.

Ordinary wolves. Jesus. Knowles knew they had to get this situation under control and quickly. They had to recapture Bryant and ascertain the true nature of the wolf threat: just how many were there? Jack was vital to both parts of that: he and Bryant were linked somehow. Whilst the wolves were a very real threat, Jack would not be allowed to see Katie: Raymond could not allow it.

"Jack," Raymond said, "I don't think we need your help."

"Wait a second, a minute ago you were asking if you could trust me."

"Yes. I think you can give me information, but I don't need your help. This is the British Armed Forces, - we are the best in the world. We don't need the help of," Raymond paused, searching for the right word, "of a teacher."

"I don't think you can class me as a teacher anymore," Jack said, with a rueful smile. "My students and my boss think I'm dead."

"How did you know that Bryant was an Original?"

"I didn't. I saw him and just knew, there and then, like I could sense him."

"You changed immediately, like you had no control. Do you think it would happen again?" Knowles asked.

Jack shrugged. "No idea. It didn't happen with the other lot." No-one needed to ask him what he meant by that. "So I assume it only happens with Originals. It happened a few nights ago too. I woke up and knew there was another one."

"What?" Raymond barked. "When?"

"It was about three, maybe four nights ago," Jack said. Raymond and Knowles exchanged a look. "What?"

"Bryant was part of the team that went into your cave."

"Not my cave," Jack said.

"You know what I mean. Anyway, Bryant found the skull of the thing you landed on."

"Knowles," Raymond said, "I want you to interrogate his team from that night. Did any of them see anything? Find out what they know."

"Yes sir," Knowles said, "but I think they are part of the team chasing him."

"Ok, then they are all in custody the minute they set foot back on this camp. Get a message to the others. Bryant's team are to return to base immediately."

"Yes sir," Knowles said. He stood and started to march towards the door when his radio buzzed. He listened for a few seconds then turned back to Raymond. *This is bad.*

"Sir, that was from Clarke. They are calling everyone back to the base."

"What? Why?"

"It's Bryant's team. They're dead sir, all except Collins and he's been bitten. It's not good, sir."

3

Knowles sat opposite Raymond, Jack next to him. Behind them, two soldiers stood relaxed but even so gave the impression that they could have their weapons ready in a moment's notice. Raymond was listening on a telephone, saying little until he eventually hung up.

"They have amputated Collins' leg," Raymond said.

Poor bastard. "We should just kill him," Knowles said. Jack looked at him, mouth open in disgust.

"Why? It's not his fault," Jack said.

"He's one of them now," Knowles said.

"So am I."

"Quit it. Knowles, no-one is killing Collins, clear?"

"Sir," Knowles started to say.

"No, Knowles, Collins is here. He's under lock and key and he has our medical staff looking after him. If Collins has any surprises for us, we're ready for him."

"May I speak freely, sir?"

"Yes, Knowles, you usually do. I don't think I could stop you."

"This is a mistake, sir. I've seen what these things can do."

"So have I, Knowles."

"With respect sir, not like I have. I've been in battle with these things. I am the sole survivor-"

"Not sole," Raymond said, inclining his head at Jack.

"You know what I mean."

"I'm still in the room," Jack said. Knowles turned to him, a scowl on his face. "Don't look at me like that. I am one of these *things* or have you forgotten?"

"Yes, but you're not like them."

"What, I'm OK for one of them?" Jack sneered. "I didn't have you down as a casual racist, Knowles."

"I'm not."

"Some of my best friends are wolves?" Jack imitated Knowles' voice.

"Fuck off, Jack," Knowles said.

Silence descended on the room for a moment, both men glaring at each other.

"What happened to you?" Jack said.

Knowles opened his mouth, but the words would not come out. *Claire. Claire happened to me. And the others. All my friends died in an afternoon.* Eventually he said, "The wolves are dangerous. You, of all people, know that. We need to eliminate that threat."

"What if we join together? Me and Bryant? The wolves think we're gods, that's what that Callum fella said, remember?"

Knowles nodded. He remembered Callum, but they were not good memories. *His jaws closing around Claire's neck, severing her arteries in a heartbeat.*

71

"We could get the wolves to follow us. We could stop the killing, on *both* sides," Jack looked pointedly at Knowles, "and then I could go back to my family."

"How do we stop Bryant?" Knowles said. "That is more pressing than anything else."

"You can't," Jack said. "He's like me. If you shoot him, it'll only stop him for a while. Then he heals and, well, he's back again."

"Ok, Jack," Raymond said, "how did you control it?"

Jack shrugged. "I don't know."

"So how is Bryant going to control it then?"

"I don't know that either."

"Well that's very helpful," Raymond snorted.

"It took Jack a few goes," Knowles said. They had been testing him for weeks, putting him under pressure. Each time it had gone wrong and had required more and more tranquiliser to put Jack down. Then, one day, the Wolf had gone crazier than usual. It had chased Claire into a courtyard. In his head, the scene was crystal clear: the Wolf approaching Claire whilst he was too far away to help. He had never felt so helpless before. Luckily, Jack had not eaten her. It turned out that Claire and Katie, Jack's wife, shared a taste in perfume. It had saved her life. *Or at least, gained her another month.*

"I killed at first," Jack said, a sudden tremor in his voice. *Edwards. Doctor Baxter. The drunk blokes in Barnstaple.*

Knowles nodded. "But you are essentially a good person Jack. How many times, before all this, have you been in a fight?"

"School," Jack said, "when I was about fifteen."

"Exactly."

Raymond was nodding now. "So, we have a problem then, because Bryant is a trained killer."

4

Patel came in carrying a folder which he placed on Raymond's desk. He saluted smartly then left, still looking nervous.

"Now what," Raymond muttered, opening the folder.

Knowles glanced at Jack. He looked so calm, so very different from the person he had first met in a pub in a sleepy village in Devon. *Who wouldn't be changed after all that?* Jack met his gaze for a moment, then turned back to Raymond. His eyes were darting from Raymond to the desk. *What are you thinking Jack?*

"It appears we have a problem," Raymond said. He held up a photograph. It showed a room covered in limbs and blood. Knowles felt his stomach lurch.

"More attacks?" Jack asked. "That's not normal."

"Where is that?" Knowles said at the same time.

"It's local. A few miles down the road." Raymond handed Knowles the folder.

Knowles flicked through the photos, each one increasing the sick feeling in his stomach.

"This isn't normal," Jack said again.

"Damn right it isn't," Knowles muttered.

"What do you mean, Jack?" Raymond said.

"The wolves have been hidden for years, centuries even. Why attack now? Why be so public?"

"This isn't public," Knowles said. "This is a private hospital. I've driven past this place every day for the last week and I had no idea it was there."

"It was Bryant," Raymond said. Knowles flicked to the last photo and saw a naked man standing amongst the blood and carnage. He was grinning in the grainy image, and it was clearly Bryant.

"Where did these pictures come from?"

"The hospital had a private security contractor. They wired up their CCTV and monitored it remotely. The company have released these images to the web, which is where we found them."

Knowles reached the last page in the folder. It described everything Raymond had just told him. The images had been blocked by the web team, but it was only a matter of time before they surfaced again.

"This will go viral," Knowles said.

Raymond nodded. "We've closed it down, but I don't know if anyone has seen it before we did that. We will close

73

them all down, but it will rapidly become a game of whack-a-mole." He mimed hitting imaginary moles on the head.

"Use it to your advantage, then," Jack said. The two soldiers looked at him sharply. "Look, the wolves have been secret all this time. They do not want their existence becoming public."

"Why not?" Knowles said. "What's stopping them?"

"I don't know," Jack said. "This is as new to me remember? I think that the wolves are terrified of being discovered. People will hunt them down and kill them." He gave Knowles a pointed look. "They don't want this."

"What about Callum and those others that attacked us?" Knowles said. "He said they wanted to rule us. You've changed everything, Jack."

"How so?"

"They want you to rule them because they think you're an Original. What will they do if they find out there are two? What if they don't need you?"

Jack laughed. "Most of the wolves that know I exist are dead. The others are terrified and running for their lives."

Knowles shook his head. "No, I don't think that's right. They knew about you before you knew what you were. They found you."

"So what?" Jack said. "They are pretty much all dead."

"No-one to spread the word," Raymond said. "But what if Knowles is right? What if they do know about you? Know about Bryant? Know what he is?"

"Then we're screwed."

"Yes," Raymond said, "we are."

"So we have to stop him," Jack said.

"No shit, Sherlock," Knowles said, "but how? How do you stop a god?"

"Release the image," Jack said with a smile. "Let it go viral. Get everybody looking for the sick bastard that mutilated a poor nurse."

"Are you nuts?" Knowles said.

"No," Raymond said, nodding slowly. "He's right. Make it so the public will scream if they see Bryant. Give a reward for information, maybe the people who took him in will turn on him."

"No reward," Knowles said. "A reward will bring the nutcases out. We'll be chasing false leads from now until Christmas."

"Maybe," Raymond said. "I'll get a press release ready."

"Sir, with respect," Knowles got as far as saying.

"Don't finish that sentence, Knowles," Raymond said. "I might be giving you free reign around here, but that doesn't mean you can question my every judgment."

"Yes, sir." Knowles' face betrayed his real thoughts, but he stayed quiet.

"Good. Now find out why Bryant was at that hospital. Collins might know." Raymond looked at Jack. "And take him with you."

5

Collins looked deathly pale as he slept on the hospital bed. Jack couldn't take his eyes off the weird way the blankets fell around Collins' legs. *Or lack of.*

"When will he wake up?" Knowles asked the doctor, who shrugged.

"He could wake any time. Everyone reacts differently to this op." The doctor paused. "We don't normally knock people out, but he was extremely agitated."

I bet he was.

"Did he say anything?" Knowles asked.

The doctor shook his head. "Only that he'd been bitten."

"Who found him?"

"Phelps' team. They are back out looking for those things." The doctor glanced at Jack when he said that. It was only a flick of the eyes, but it was enough.

"Ok, thanks, Doc. Let me know if he wakes," Knowles said and left the room without another word. Jack jogged to catch up with him. They walked down many identical corridors, talking all the way.

"Nobody trusts me, do they?" Jack said.

"No, they don't."

"Why?"

"Do you really need me to answer that?"

"Knowles, I'm on your side. *You* know that, right?"

"Yes Jack, I know you think you are."

"What does that mean?"

They opened a set of double doors and stepped into bright sunlight. Knowles stopped walking, looking at the chaos outside. Soldiers were patrolling the fences whilst others set up large calibre weapons to cover the exposed areas. Lights sat on the backs of flatbed trucks, their enormous bulbs illuminating the immediate perimeter and beyond to the edge of the wood. A team was welding the fence shut again. The noise was incredible and, as if it wasn't loud enough, a helicopter roared overhead.

"We had Bryant contained, Jack," Knowles said. "He was there, in Raymond's office. You turn up and all hell breaks loose."

"That wasn't my fault, Knowles, and you damn well know it." Jack shook his head. "You didn't even know what he was until I showed up."

"What if Bryant was getting ready to turn himself in?"

"What if he wasn't? What if he was going to kill you both at the first opportunity?"

"He had plenty of opportunities, Jack. So why didn't he do it?"

"I don't know," Jack said. The helicopter made another pass, making conversation pointless for a few seconds. "Maybe he still has a conscience."

"Like you?"

Jack shook his head sadly. "Knowles, that's out of order."

"Probably."

"Probably?"

"Since I met you Jack, an awful lot of people have died. Now Collins has lost a leg, and probably a lot more too. Raymond knows the score, he gets it, like I do."

"I've lost you, Knowles."

"No, Jack, you understand. We are not safe. None of us. Not whilst those things are out there."

"Where does that leave me?"

"I honestly don't know."

"Should I go?" There was a hint of panic in his voice and Jack didn't like it.

"Would you join them, Jack? Become like them?"

"I would never join them."

"Never say never."

"I don't get this Knowles," Jack said. "I have done nothing to you."

"No, not directly," Knowles said. "But I can't help thinking that if you hadn't fallen in the cave then none of this would be happening. Maybe those things would stay hidden and maybe a lot of people would still be alive."

"It wasn't my fault," Jack whispered.

"No? Then whose?"

Chapter 11

1

Bryant sat on the damp ground and surveyed the group in front of him. Rogers and Ryan sat on a log on the far side of the clearing, deep in conversation. Every thirty seconds, like clockwork, Ryan would glare at him.

He'll be first.

Bryant sighed heavily and looked at the others. The woman, Jenny, watched him with a slight smile on her lips. She would smooth her hair whilst the others twitched by her side. Bryant tried to smile back, but images of Collins, Wills and Parker kept forcing the smile away.

What have I become?

The remaining two wolves were Joe and Henry: brothers, nearly identical. They stood watching the tree line for signs of their pursuers. Both looked on edge and one of them had facial twitches that Bryant had seen before. *He won't sleep tonight. Not for long anyway.* Bryant pitied him: he had seen many good soldiers with that same look in Afghanistan. They were usually killed or shipped home shortly afterwards.

"The longer we stay here, the more chance they will find us," Bryant said.

"We have a place," Jenny said. "A little way from here. A roof to hide us from helicopters."

"You have a house?" Bryant said, clearly surprised.

"Did you think we lived in forests? On the moors? The remote places?"

"Well, yes."

"Some of us do," Rogers said. "The more esoteric of us. Many of us still have jobs, lead fairly normal lives."

"Do you?"

Rogers shook his head. "We have everything we need: we are provided for." He rested a hand on Jenny's leg and patted it with a smile.

So she's the provider. I have to keep her on side.

"We need to go, before the army finds us," Joe said, his arm around his brother, who was shaking slightly. Not enough for the others to notice, but Bryant saw everything now.

"They will not attack us again," Rogers said.

"Why do you say that?" Bryant said.

"We have you."

"I can't protect all of you," Bryant said.

"They are scared of you, Jamie," Rogers said.

"Don't call me that," Bryant snapped. *Only my friends get to call me that.*

"Apologies, Bryant, I meant no offense."

"Can we go?" This came from Jenny, who looked as frustrated as Bryant felt. "It's a long way."

"We just need to get to the cars," Joe said.

"This way, then," Ryan said. His voice was nasally and with an accent that it took Bryant a moment to place. German. Something tugged at the back of Bryant's mind. Something about the accent. *It will come to me.* Bryant followed the others into the woods.

2

No roadblocks were set up by the time they reached the cars. Bryant could hear a helicopter in the distance, but the engine noise did not get louder. Two cars, both nondescript normal family saloon cars. Bryant was impressed: nothing to draw attention to them here.

The drive was short, traffic light. The Kent countryside passed in all its green glory. Wheat fields and oast houses stood as wealthy reminders of a former life. They were soon driving down a long lane, and came to a stop outside a five bar gate with pillars flanking it. Henry shuffled out of the car to open the gate and they drove along a tree lined driveway up to a large house.

It was a red brick building, with ivy clinging to the outside. Two more Roman style pillars marked the porch to the house. 'Porch' was not a good enough word for what he was looking at. The house was close to a mansion, and in this part of the world, that meant money. A lot of money.

"Whose place is this?" Bryant asked as he stepped out of the car.

"Mine," Jenny said. She led the way up the short steps and pushed open the front door. Bryant followed, the twins behind him. They were in a large hallway complete with long sweeping staircase and Bryant upped his – already large - estimation of how much this place was worth. A deer's head watched him from its mount on the wall.

"My first kill," Jenny said, then walked into the next room. *Is she joking?* He didn't have time to ask as the others entered the house behind him. Ryan scowled at Bryant.

"There has been a development," Rogers said. He did not wait for Bryant but left the hallway by the same door as Jenny. The way he walked away was full of demand: he expected Bryant to follow him. *Things need to change.*

"Best go," said Joe, the non-shell shocked twin. He patted Bryant on the shoulder, but it was a friendly pat. There was a nervous smile on the man's face. He went into the room, pulling his brother gently with him.

Bryant followed - he didn't have much choice after all. Predictably enough, it was a large room, dominated by a table that looked like it cost more than Bryant's flat: a marble top supported by solid oak legs. As he looked more closely, he could see signs of wear – a few scratches in the polished surface, ring marks from wine glasses and coffee cups. Ten leather chairs were neatly placed around the table, four on each side and one at each end. Rogers sat in one at the head of the table, Jenny on one side, Ryan the other. Joe and Henry sat the halfway point of the table and Bryant took a seat opposite them.

"What's going on?"

"This," Rogers said. He lifted a remote control and a section of the wall behind Bryant slid down, revealing a large TV. It flickered to life, and Rogers changed the channel to a news programme. The presenters were talking about yet another horrendous situation in Afghanistan, but it was the ticker tape that caught Bryant's eye.

... Violent and dangerous ex-army sergeant Jamie Bryant is at large tonight. He has killed at least three people, including a mother of four at a hospital in Kent. More to follow.

Bryant swore but kept watching. After a few minutes, one of the anchors turned to the camera and started talking about him.

It was not good.

Photos of him walking out of the hospital, a big smile on his face. Photos of him in his uniform, sitting in Afghanistan with a weapon resting on his lap. Pictures of the dead people from the hospital. A live shot of the four children crushing their father with hugs at the school gates. All the while, the reporter spoke as if talking about someone else. Bryant felt sick to his stomach.

"This is a problem," Rogers said.

No shit.

"Why have they released this?" Jenny asked. "What will they gain?"

"Everyone will be looking for me," Bryant said. "They're thinking that I cannot go out in public as I'll be recognised."

Rogers nodded. "Yes, they want you to go into hiding."

"Why?" Ryan asked.

"Reduce the opportunity for me to kill," Bryant said.

"But if you are spotted and recognised, won't this force you to kill?" Jenny asked.

"That seems to be the chance they are taking," Rogers said.

"I'm not an animal," Bryant said.

Ryan burst out laughing. "You are. Or at least half of you is."

"You know what I meant," Bryant said, with a scowl.

"They're offering a reward," Joe said. "Look." He pointed at the screen. The reporter was saying that the family of the murdered doctor was offering a reward of £500,000 for information about Bryant's whereabouts.

"That's a lot of money," Ryan said.

Bryant glared at him. "What will you spend that money on? A bag full of bones?"

"Enough," Rogers said, holding up a hand. "This place is secure. No-one knows we are here, thanks to Jenny. We can hole up for a few days, keep safe until the search dies down."

"Then what?" Bryant asked. "I am wanted for murder."

"Please, Bryant, be patient. We lie low for a few days, then see where we are."

"The others might be here by then," Jenny said.

Rogers nodded. "I hope so, Jenny. I hope so."

Others? What others? Bryant looked around the room but saw only grim smiles. *Now what?*

3

Bryant did not sleep easy. The house was large enough for them all to have a room to themselves. The twins elected to share, but that would be Joe making sure his brother was ok. Jenny went upstairs with Rogers, with Ryan following close behind. Bryant had got himself a glass of water then found an empty bedroom and clambered into the bed.

Suddenly weary, he fell asleep immediately. Something niggled away in his subconscious. He kept seeing the doctor's face as he bit into his neck. The nurse - *mother of four* - running from him, face white and tears streaming down her cheeks. *Extra salt, mmmm.* Bryant tossed and turned, sweat covering his sheets. The reporter, Simon whatever, screaming as he started to change. Bryant sat bolt upright, a moan on his lips.

Something felt off.

He looked down, saw the hairs running back into his arms. *Changing in my sleep now.*

No, it wasn't that.

He could hear voices. Low, clearly whispering. Two men. Arguing. *Stadler was right about the hearing.* It was so clear.

Rogers and Ryan.

They were coming for him.

4

"He is a liability," Ryan said. He was talking quietly, but the anger in his voice was clear.

"No," Rogers said. "He will lead us to a new age."

"Now you sound like Callum," Ryan said, with a grimace. "That did not end well, did it?"

"Callum's plan was flawed."

"You didn't say so at the time."

Rogers snorted. "Nobody stood up to Callum." He drummed his fingers on the table. "Bryant is a soldier. He is used to leading. The others will follow him."

"Callum said the same about Stadler."

"Yes, but Stadler didn't want to join us," Rogers said. "Bryant knows what he is. It's different."

"The entire British army is looking for Bryant. The police too, judging by that news broadcast. It's only a matter of time before they find us."

"How long have we stayed here?"

"Yes, but-"

"How long?"

"Three years, approximately."

"Right," Rogers grinned. "So I think it's safe to say that no one knows we're here."

"That was before we took a murderer in."

"You've killed people. We all have," Rogers said. "Bryant is no different."

"That hospital was different. That was a bloodbath."

Rogers shook his head. "Yes, but he is only now coming to terms with his powers."

"You are joking?" Ryan laughed. "He knows what he is, yes. He knows what he can do, yes. He has studied Stadler. He is revelling in this and he is a liability."

Ryan slapped his hand on the table, the sudden bang making the other man jump.

"Shh, you'll wake everyone," Rogers said.

"He is a liability with, as Americans are fond of saying, a price on his head."

"What are you saying?"

"You know exactly what I'm saying."

"So, we turn him in, get the reward and live out the rest of our days in secret?"

"Yes."

"The army knows about us now. How long do you think before they decide to find us? How long before they decide to kill us all?"

"They did not kill Stadler."

"Because they can't! What part of that do you not understand?"

"We cut his head off. Now, whilst he is sleeping." Ryan's eyes were bright, his cheeks flushed.

Rogers paused, a second too long. A second that would prove costly.

"So, who's going to do the cutting?"

The voice from the doorway made them both start. Ryan leapt to his feet, spinning round. Bryant stood in the doorway, filling the frame. Behind him, Jenny was walking down the corridor, wiping sleep from her eyes. Joe's pale face could just be seen behind her, which meant Henry wasn't too far away.

"Bryant," Ryan got as far as saying. Bryant leapt forward, changing as he did so. His pyjamas - given to him by Jenny - ripped, falling to the floor in tatters. He landed next to Ryan and bit hard on the other man's leg. In one bite, he severed the limb. Ryan screamed and fell back against the table. The wolf swung its head, still with the leg hanging out of its mouth, and hit Ryan with the limb. The blow connected with his face, and Ryan grunted. The wolf swung again and again, each blow thudding into Ryan's head. Fresh blood mingled with that flowing from the severed leg. The wolf spat the leg out and changed back to Bryant, who rained further blows on Ryan's head, this time with fists. Bryant's roar became louder than Ryan's groans and cries until eventually Ryan stopped making a noise. Then, Bryant changed his hand into a wolf's paw and punched through Ryan's rib cage. He withdrew his human hand seconds later, holding Ryan's heart. He flung it at Rogers who hadn't moved the whole time. Rogers turned his face as the heart hit his cheek with a wet slap.

"Your turn," Bryant snarled. He twisted Rogers head, snapping his neck with a loud crack. Rogers crumpled to the floor instantly and was soon covered in Ryan's blood.

Bryant turned back to the doorway. Joe and Henry had disappeared and Jenny stood in her dressing gown, chewing her lip. He found it an extremely erotic gesture.

"They wanted to kill me," Bryant said.

She nodded.

"Who's side are you on?" he asked.

She slipped the dressing gown off. Bryant grinned.

Chapter 12

1

Bryant woke with a start. Jenny had a leg draped over him and he pushed it away. He stood by the window, letting the sunlight warm him. *An interesting night.*

Today he would bury the bodies of Rogers and Ryan. Now that he was in charge, it didn't seem wise to leave the evidence of his coup lying around. Jenny could tell him more about the 'others' who were supposed to be joining them later. He was still none the wiser as to who these people were. Would they be happy that he had killed the man in charge? In the meantime, he would make peace with Joe and Henry, make sure they were on his side.

I am very persuasive now.

The sudden thought chilled him: would he kill the twins if they didn't accept him being in charge? A metallic taste filled his mouth, but he didn't feel sick. Quite the opposite in fact: he turned back to Jenny, not wanting to waste the feeling. She was awake-

-pity-

-and sat up in bed, making no attempt to cover herself. She smiled at him, eyes travelling down his body. She slid over the sheets, lowering her head. He felt the warmth of her mouth and then grunted. He grabbed her head, forcing her to take more. She started to gag and slapped at him with her free hand.

-yeah, you love it-

He held her there, relishing the warmth of her mouth. She hit him harder and harder. He yanked her up and slapped her hard enough to knock her back to the bed. Before she could move, he was on her, pushing her legs apart. She started to yell at him, but he didn't stop-

-fight a little, I like that-

-he pushed himself into her and the only sound in the room was the slapping of his thighs and her sobs. He slapped her twice, growling "shut up" in a voice not quite his own.

-what the fuck am I doing?-

Bryant jumped off the bed, staring at Jenny with horror. She crawled away, pulling the covers up over her body, sobs still wracking her, shoulders heaving with each anguished cry.

"Jenny," he said, "I'm sorry. I don't know what happened."

"You bastard," she said. Her hand disappeared under the sheets and came back bloody.

"Oh god," he said.

"I liked you, Jamie. You didn't need to do this." She wiped the blood on the sheets. The stain caught his eye wherever he looked.

-oh yes, smell that, it's fresh-

"Jenny, I think you should leave," he said. He could feel the blood rushing in his ears, feel his heart beat faster.

"It's my house!" she yelled. "You leave!"

"This isn't me," he said, "I can't control this." He was breathing hard, then, "Please."

She looked at him with bright blue eyes. Even through the tears, she was beautiful. *What have I done?* He didn't know what she saw, but without another word, she grabbed her clothes from the floor and left the room. As soon as she was gone, he leapt on the bed and started licking the blood, smearing it around his mouth.

I've gone crazy.

A noise made him stop. It was a door slamming. He ran to the window, licking his lips. Jenny was marching to the car, gravel crunching under her feet. Joe and Henry were close behind. The wheels spun, kicking stones up, and then they were gone.

Swearing, he turned away from the window and caught sight of himself in a full-length mirror on the wardrobe. Blood was smeared all around his mouth, his hair was bedraggled and his eyes were yellow. He stepped to the mirror to have a closer look, and his eyes faded to their normal brown. He blinked and they alternated brown and yellow. He shook his head and they stayed brown.

This is not good.

"I need help," he said to the empty house.

2

Bryant stood outside the front door of the house. He had dressed and was now holding a hot mug of tea in one hand and the house phone in the other. It was warm, despite the early hour. The quiet was almost eerie and he felt another pang of remorse at what had happened with Jenny.

What have I become?

The questions kept going round and round in his head. This life, when he had first read Stadler's file, had seemed the right choice. The way Stadler had learnt to control the Wolf. It had all seemed so easy. Now he was a mass murderer and a rapist. This was not going the way he had intended.

Better than the alternative.

Maybe. The thought wasn't his: he was getting better at knowing the Wolf.

Without me, you'd be dead.

Bryant dialled a number quickly and raised the phone to his ear before he could change his mind. It rang several times, and then a familiar voice answered.

"Don't hang up," Bryant said.

3

Knowles had just emerged from the shower when his phone rang. His skin was still tingling from the shower gel and he hoped to God someone had allowed Jack to shower. He picked it up just as it stopped ringing. It said 'Unknown' under missed calls. Having dried quickly, then dressed, he was about to leave the room when his phone rang again.

"Hello," he said.

"Don't hang up," a familiar voice said.

"Bryant? Jesus, what are you doing?

"Where are you, Knowles?"

"You know where I am," Knowles snorted. "I'm about to go and visit your mate, you know, the one whose leg you bit off."

"Not that you'll believe me, but that wasn't me and the one who did it is dead."

"You're right, I don't believe you and I don't care. You need to come in."

"Why? So you can lock me up and study me? Cut me up like you planned to do to Stadler?"

"That was not *my* plan."

"I don't care, Knowles, it ain't happening to me."

"We will find you, Bryant."

"Maybe. Maybe not."

"Come in, Bryant," Knowles said. "We can help you."

"I was dying, Knowles. Did you know that?"

Knowles said nothing. His heart was beating hard in his chest.

"That skeleton was my only chance. Cancer. I had a few months left, according to the doctors. Strange though, I felt fine. Then I started coughing up blood every morning and knew I had to do something. I don't want to die, Knowles."

"So instead you've become a killing machine?"

"No." Bryant's voice was deeper now. *Jack used to do that. When he was strapped to a chair in Huntleigh, after being shot enough times to stop an elephant. The Wolf, making itself heard.*

"It's quite a body count you've got so far, Bryant. You ok with that? Everyone dies so you can live? Seems pretty shitty to me."

"I want to talk to Stadler. He with you?"

"No, Bryant. It's first thing in the morning. I don't sleep with the guy."

"I'll call back in thirty minutes. I want to speak to him. Your phone. Keep it on."

Knowles opened his mouth to say more, but Bryant was gone.

4

Bryant roared in frustration and threw the phone to the ground. It bounced and skittered across the floor. He could hear the Wolf at the back of his mind, laughing at him. *Stadler.* How had he – a civilian – managed to control this? Bryant thought of his own mental toughness. Alone in the desert, waiting for high-level targets to cross his sights. Killing insurgents and wiping out families. All of that was nothing compared to the grip of the Wolf.

Whatever I do, it's there.

You can't get rid of me.

No, but I can control you.

Why do you want to? You love it. Deep down, you love it.

No.

Yes.

Bryant flung his mug at the wall and it shattered. Splinters from the mug hit his face, drawing blood and adding to his frustration. He looked around the floor and picked up the phone. Twenty minutes until he could ring Knowles back. Twenty minutes to keep the Wolf at bay. Bryant put the phone on the wall next to him and then started to run. He ran around the house, going faster and faster until he was moving almost at a blur. Round and round, faster and faster until the Wolf burst out of him. He kept running in Wolf form, enjoying the feel of the wind on his fur. Enjoying the smell of the birds in the trees. The smell of the grass all around him and the flowers in full bloom.

He stopped by the front door and stood as he changed.

You love it.

He did, he really did.

5

"Why is he doing this?" Jack asked. It was not, in Knowles' opinion, a bad question.

"Maybe he's had a change of heart, wants to come in," Raymond said.

"I told him to give himself up," Knowles said.

"We're set up in here," Raymond said. "Your team ready?"

Knowles nodded. Four men, heavily armed and covered in Kevlar were sitting in a Lynx helicopter outside the building. Next to it sat an Apache helicopter, smaller, sleeker but loaded with weapons. As soon as the call was traced they would be in the air. Jack had been impressed with how quickly this had all come together.

"How long do I have to keep him talking?" Jack asked.

Both Raymond and Knowles looked surprised. "Christ, Jack, it'll be traced before you get the phone. It takes less than thirty seconds," Knowles said.

Holy shit. "Oh, ok," was all Jack could come out with.

The phone rang, and Jack jumped.

"Bryant," Knowles said. He listened for a moment, then said, "He's right here." He handed the phone over, and Jack took it. A computer screen behind him showed a circle getting smaller. Tunbridge Wells sat on the circumference of the circle.

"Go," Raymond mouthed. Knowles ran for the door. Raymond nodded at Jack.

Jack raised the phone, hoping his hand was not visibly shaking. He felt sick to his stomach; sweat was forming on his brow.

"Hello," Jack said. Bryant started to speak, but Jack roared. He felt his face change, his mouth elongating. He tried to speak, but it was too late.

The Wolf was coming.

6

Bryant heard something as Knowles said "He's right here." Something in the background that he would have missed a week ago. Something under the surface noise, something he was not supposed to hear.

"Hello?"

Go. Someone had said go.

91

7

Raymond watched with horror as Jack's head changed into a wolf. "Everybody out, now!" he screamed. The soldiers on the computers turned at the sound.

Jack dropped the phone and fell to all fours. His clothes started to rip, thick black fur pushing its way through the tears.

"I have the location, sir!" One of the men shouted.

"Send it to Knowles, now, then get out," Raymond barked. Two of the soldiers were already rushing to the door, pushing each other in the hurry to get away. Raymond turned back to Jack and his breath caught in his throat. A huge wolf - no, Wolf, the reports were right - stood where Stadler had been. It looked right at him, drool pouring out of its enormous jaws.

"I've sent it sir," the remaining soldier said. The Wolf's head snapped to him. Yellow eyes narrowed as it looked at him.

"No sudden moves, Singer," Raymond said. The Wolf turned back to him. It opened its terrifying mouth and howled.

"RUN!" Raymond yelled. Singer jumped up and ran for the door, a distance of fewer than five metres. The Wolf started to move and Raymond stood in front of it.

"No," he said. Raymond was used to being obeyed. From Officer Training through to the poppy fields of Afghanistan, even in the shithole that was Helmand, when he spoke, people listened. More than that, they obeyed.

The Wolf roared.

8

Knowles looked at his team with trepidation. Sure, everyone knew what they were dealing with now. It wasn't like Smith and his team. Kevlar covered the men, and helmets with full visors protected their heads.

It's not enough.

Each man carried an SA80 with grenade launcher attachment. They also had four hand grenades each, and enough ammunition to kill everyone in Tunbridge Wells several times over. Knowles glanced at the pilot, whose eyes flicked around the instrumentation. GPS showed them seconds away from the house. It also showed the large urban area of Tunbridge Wells.

A lot of people live there.

Knowles smiled at his team. All had been in Afghanistan. All had seen combat prior to today. They were, in Raymond's words, 'good men'.

Just like my old team.

"Thirty seconds, sergeant," the pilot said. Knowles nodded.

Everyone in my old team is dead.

A voice he didn't recognise came on the radio. He was shouting and screaming something about a wolf. Knowles felt his blood go cold. He was not taking chances anymore. Back at the base, everyone could be dead already. *Jack has lost it.*

"Change of plan," he said to the pilot. "New orders. Blow the house up."

9

Raymond stared at the Wolf. Fear was crippling him. He had been in tight spots before, faced potential death before, but this made those situations laughable.

The Wolf was much, much bigger than him. It dominated the room that seconds before had been a hive of activity. Singer had made it to the door, yanking it open and fleeing into the morning air. Now, with any luck, soldiers would be running towards him, ready to help their CO out.

My life is in the hands of other people. The thought did not calm him. He had not survived Afghanistan by handing his fate to others. Trust them, yes, but never complete control. When he had stepped in front of the Wolf, he had thought that it would be his last act. Now, the Wolf was watching him and he dared not move. He racked his brains about the things Knowles had said. Jack could control the Wolf, he had definitely said that.

He wasn't in control then, on the phone.

Raymond wished that part of his mind would shut up. The seconds stretched into a minute and still the Wolf watched him.

We could be here all day.

"Jack," he said. Raymond always thought he had a good 'command' voice. A deep timbre, firm yet warm, a voice full of trust. One he could use on Radio 4 when he made it further up the chain. Now, though, under the Wolf's baleful glare, his command voice deserted him and library voice took over. The Wolf cocked his head, reminding Raymond of a dog he had had as a boy. The gesture was almost comical.

Almost.

"Jack," he tried again, and this time a little of his command voice made it through. He drew his service revolver but the weight of it in his hands did little to calm him. The weapon was tiny compared to the Wolf and he knew it would have little impact on it. Raymond raised the weapon and was pleased to see his hands weren't shaking.

"Stand down, Jack."

He knew it was ridiculous: did Stadler even know what 'stand down' meant? The Wolf was snarling at him, but not moving. *Shoot it, now, before it decides you are on the menu.* Raymond took a deep breath.

The fur on the Wolf started to recede, running back into shortening limbs. The animal was shrinking too until Jack stood naked in front of him. He was panting and a light sheen of sweat could be seen on his brow.

"Sorry," he said.

It wasn't nearly enough.

10

Rage ripped through Bryant, but it wasn't solely hearing Stadler's voice. Something else too, something about the way he spoke. Bryant had never felt anything like it: the sound was like nails on a blackboard and it had sent shivers down his spine. He felt the Wolf take hold and he roared down the mouthpiece. His face changed first, and then the change ripped through his body. The borrowed clothes he was wearing fell to the floor in tatters and the phone clattered to the floor. It jumped around the room, knocking the expensive table over despite its weight. It started to rip up the chairs, but then stopped, a long strand of leather hanging from its mouth. The Wolf padded through the house and out onto the porch where it sniffed the air.

Adrenaline pumped through its veins as it realised, from the dark pit of its mind, what the noise meant. The Wolf took flight, sprinting for the boundary of the gardens. It vaulted the fence, clearing it easily and kept running for the trees.

It could hear the helicopters coming. The *pop pop pop* as missiles launched. It was long gone before the first one hit.

11

Hellfire rockets streaked away from the Apache, screaming towards the house. Knowles was impressed by the mansion, sitting in the middle of its own grounds and looking like something the Bronte sisters might have dreamt up.

It's not going to look that impressive for very much longer.

The house exploded as the missiles smashed into it. Clouds of dust and rubble shot into the air. Glass shattered in every window in the house and the west wing collapsed instantly.

"Again," Knowles ordered. More hellfires instantly spat towards the house, this time smacking into the east wing. This, too, collapsed under the fire, sending more detritus into the air. The devastation was complete and the house, so impressive a moment ago, was now a pile of rubble.

"Put us down," Knowles said.

Moments later, he was surrounded by his team as they walked slowly towards the ruined building. As soon as they were clear, the helicopter took off again and joined the Apache in circling the airspace above the house. The team did a full circuit of the house, scanning the building and the tree line as they went. Unsurprisingly, nothing moved: even the birds had gone.

"We need a full team here," one of the men said. Knowles had to agree: searching through this rubble would take hours, if not days.

"Do you think they were here?" the man asked.

"Can't see how they escaped if they weren't," Knowles said, with a shrug. "It's been less than five minutes since the phone call put them here. I don't think even the Originals are that fast."

The team were beginning to relax now that they knew nothing was going to jump out at them.

"We need to find Bryant's body, ASAP," Knowles said, "before he can regenerate or whatever it is they do. Call it in."

12

The Wolf returned to the edge of the woods once the explosions stopped, panting hard. It surveyed the ruined house from a distance, keeping low in the undergrowth. The Lynx helicopter had landed and soldiers stood around the ruin. It recognised the formation, had once stood like that itself, a million lifetimes ago.

The man barking orders was familiar. Of course he was. The way he stood, the way he carried himself. The Wolf felt anger burn through it, coursing through its veins like the heroin it had tried when the diagnosis came through.

Knowles.

Disappointment was an alien feeling for the Wolf: a distinctly human emotion. Nevertheless, that was what it felt now. Knowles was in charge here, that much was obvious. He had ordered the destruction of the house, signed the death warrant of anyone inside.

It was sheer luck that they weren't all dead now. Of course, Knowles would be expecting him to be alive, expect him to heal. But what of the others? Jenny. The twins.

Snarling, the Wolf stood up. Could it charge them? How many would it kill before they shot it enough to trap it? A twig snapped behind it and it whirled around, ready to pounce. Anger had distracted it long enough for someone to get close, but that someone would regret it.

Another wolf stood watching it, with two others flanking it. The wolf started to stand up, fur running back until Jenny stood before it.

96

"Don't," she said. "Come with us, meet the others."

Bryant stood up.

"You came back."

Jenny said nothing.

"I don't know how to say sorry. That wasn't me."

She shrugged. "I know."

How can you know? You only met me yesterday.

He returned his gaze to Knowles and his team. "I will kill them all."

"Yes, but there are too many today. Come with us, get help."

"I'm sorry," he tried to say again.

Jenny looked away. "Come with us, Jamie."

She turned into a wolf and padded away into the woods. Bryant looked back across the field to the house. The soldiers were sifting through the ruins. Despite the devastation to the house, they would surely find the bodies of Rogers and Ryan soon. Maybe they would assume him dead too. *That's a pretty big maybe.* Bryant knew he had bought himself a couple of days' breathing space at most.

I don't want this, not any of it.

Think of the power.

Bryant turned away from the house and started to run after Jenny and the twins, changing mid-stride, travelling fast to catch them up.

Chapter 13

1

"You're sure?" Katie asked for the umpteenth time. John smiled at her, also for the umpteenth time.

"Just go, Katie. Me and the little man will be fine." He gestured to the cot, where Josh was fast asleep. "I'll just watch some TV. Bound to be a film on somewhere."

"Thank you, John." Katie started to put her trainers on. She was dressed in shorts and a t-shirt for a band that had broken up last decade.

"Karen's waiting for you. She's a bit nervous - thinks you'll leave her behind."

"I haven't run in ages, John. She'll be fine."

"Still, she's nervous."

She's not the only one. Katie looked at the sleeping Josh and felt tears well in her eyes. This would be the first time she had ever left him: the first time they would ever be apart.

It was barely a week since the wolves had attacked her home. Several days of sleepless nights - for her, not Josh. She knew they would be back, and they would be coming for her. This irrational fear would reduce her to a quivering wreck in the middle of the night, but it was still there in the daytime, gnawing away at her subconscious.

Katie still had the shotgun; the police had not confiscated it, nor even asked about it. She had shot one of the wolves that had entered her house and had tried to shoot the other one. But then, as the wolf bore down on her and Josh, a huge wolf had arrived and killed it. She shuddered at the memory.

Those were the facts from the evening. Everything else... The wolf had looked at her and seemed to focus on Josh. There had been something very familiar about its eyes.

Something that was also absurd.

She had not told anyone about her thoughts. *They will take my baby away.* The shotgun was only the first part of her plan to keep them both safe. The second involved getting fit again. Katie had run three times a week, every week since finishing university. Horrified at the weight she'd put on over the course of her studies, she'd set about losing it all. In the process, she'd become addicted to running, and had run the London Marathon twice before she met Jack. She'd run through the first six months of pregnancy but then stopped. Running with a growing belly had just not been fun. Fitness had been important to her then and was even more so now: being fit might literally mean the difference between life and death.

You can't outrun a wolf.

She pushed that thought aside. She could certainly try, and if it came to it, she didn't want her lack of fitness to be an issue. She leant into the cot and planted a gentle kiss on Josh's forehead. An Elbow song immediately sprang to mind and she smiled. *I plant the sort of kiss that will not wake a baby. Something like that anyway.* One of Jack's favourite bands, when he was in a mellower mood and not listening to those awful rock bands he also liked.

"Go on, Katie, we'll be fine," John said.

She hugged John tightly, gave Josh one last yearning look, then went downstairs and out into the street. Karen had parked directly outside her house, and she waved hello as Katie got in the car.

"I'm a bit nervous," Karen said as she pulled away.

"Me too."

"First time you've left him?"

Katie nodded.

"It gets easier."

"I'm not sure I want it to."

The rest of the short journey passed in a comfortable, companionable silence.

2

The sign read 'Huntleigh Woods' and underneath listed the walks you could do around it. There were further signs announcing that the land was owned by the Forestry Commission and not to block any gates. A conspicuously new sign informed readers that certain areas of the woods were currently out of bounds and not to trespass.

The women walked past the signs and stood at the top of a track. They had two choices, left or straight ahead. The circular track ran around the outskirts of the wood, so it didn't matter which route they took.

"Which way do you want to go?" Karen asked.

"Jack always went left," Katie said. She lifted her left ankle behind her, stretching her thigh.

"So," Karen copied her and nearly lost her balance.

"It's the easier run. The hills are steeper, but you end on the flat. Go the other way and you have a really long hill to finish."

"Do we have to run up the hills?" Karen looked even more nervous.

Katie laughed. "Not today, but we will eventually. You'll be surprised."

"I will," Karen muttered.

They started jogging, Katie setting a slow pace down the hill into the woods she hadn't visited since her husband had fallen into a hidden cavern so many months ago.

3

Karen was out of breath before they'd gone more than two hundred yards. Katie was surprised with how good she felt to be running again. Ahead of them, the track levelled out for a while before dropping down further into the trees. It was darker here: the large trees cast everything in deep shadows. The temperature fell too, although they were both warm enough.

The track started to head up for the first short hill, and Karen stopped almost immediately. She walked up the hill. Katie ran on, pushing herself to reach the top. They had not run far, no sense walking yet. At the top of the hill, she stopped and jogged on the spot whilst waiting for Karen to catch up.

"You love it don't you?" Karen said, breathing heavily as she approached.

Katie shrugged. "Yes, always have."

"I hate it," Karen said.

Katie burst out laughing and stopped jogging.

"This was your idea," she said.

"I know, I know," Karen said. She patted her stomach. "I love cake too much. Now I'm in my forties, I've got to do something."

"You could stop eating cake."

"That's the most ridiculous thing you've ever said."

"Just a thought."

"It's a miserable one."

Katie laughed again and set off at the same slow pace she had started with. Karen sighed then followed her, running quickly to catch up then slowing to match her friend's pace.

"So, they given you a date for your window?" Karen asked, between breaths.

"Not yet. They've agreed to do it, though. I need to get three quotes and then they'll sort it out from there."

"So how did it happen again?"

"I don't really want to talk about, Karen."

"Is that because you've been lying about it?"

Katie stopped running so abruptly, Karen was five paces ahead before she realised. "What do you mean?"

"Katie, sorry, but you really are a terrible liar."

"I-"

Karen laughed. "Windows don't just fall out, Katie. What happened?"

"You wouldn't believe me if I told you."

"Katie, you're my friend. Whatever is happening with you, I've got your back. You know that right?"

"A giant wolf, that looked like Jack, jumped through it and ran away whilst a soldier shot at him."

"Girl, you're nuts, you know that right?"

Katie laughed again. It felt good to laugh again, but then Karen had always been good company. She had always found ways to make Katie smile.

"So what really happened?"

Katie held her gaze.

"Seriously?" Karen had her hands on her knees, breathing hard. Sweat was beading on her forehead and had started to trickle down the side of her face. She looked at her friend, not quite sure whether she was having her leg pulled.

Katie nodded, slowly but definitely.

"Christ."

"Yes," Katie said. "Now do you see why I don't want to talk about it?"

"Those wolves all got burnt in that fire."

"That's what they told us. There are more of them, though."

"How many more?"

"I don't know," Katie said. "There's at least one more."

"That looks like Jack?" Karen shook her head. "You know that's you projecting right?"

No, I'm not projecting. I know what I saw, both in my house and in the hospital on the night Jack died. He IS the wolf. It's real, all the stories and the myths. And he's still out there.

Instead she said, "Yes, I know that. I miss him."

"We do too."

"My boy needs a dad."

Karen hugged her long enough for tears to well in Katie's eyes. "Come on, let's finish this stupid run then go find some wine to drink."

"It's not even ten yet Karen."

"It's six o'clock somewhere, right?"

They ran on.

4

Five minutes later they were at the bottom of a big hill: the biggest in the circuit. Karen took one look at it, swore and started walking. Katie smiled and ran on, waving over her shoulder. A piece of advice about running she'd been given years ago spurred her on. Never stop on a hill; always get to the top, then walk for a bit to get your breath back.

Halfway up the hill, her legs were burning. *I am so out of shape.* She looked back at Karen and instantly felt better, but she saw something out of the corner of her eye. She turned towards it and stopped running.

Police tape was tied around the trees to her right. Plastic barriers formed a rough circle around a hole in the ground. The barriers were emblazoned with signs declaring 'Danger' and 'Keep Out'.

Katie took a deep breath and walked towards the barriers. She heard her name being called and ignored it. She touched a barrier with a shaky hand. Five metres away the pit yawned, black and threatening even on this glorious day.

A hand touched her on the shoulder, the touch gentle yet firm. "You ok?" Karen asked.

Katie forced herself to nod. "I've not seen this before."

"You ok?" Karen repeated after a moment.

"I-" Katie stopped. "This is where it all changed for us."

"I know."

Katie shook her head. "You don't. No-one does. Except maybe that soldier."

"Soldier?"

Katie waved her hand, a gesture to mean *nothing, never mind.*

"Come on, it's just a hole in the ground."

"Jack fell in there. Imagine that, Karen, he was in there for hours until they rescued him. He must have been so scared."

"Yes, but they did rescue him. He even got to you in time for Josh's arrival."

"It must have been so dark in there," Katie continued as if Karen hadn't spoken. "He saw things in there. A stone slab, that's what he said. Covered in carvings. A man, with horns."

"Yeah, John told me."

"It was dark, though, Karen. How did he see all that in the dark?"

"Um, it was daytime? The sun?"

103

Katie shook her head. "It's dark here, with all the trees. Sunlight wouldn't get in there, would it?"

Karen shrugged.

"How did he see the carvings, Karen? Even with light, there wouldn't have been much, it would've been like dusk. Not enough light to see any details, surely."

"I don't know, honey, your eyes adjust, don't they?" Karen said. Her brow was creased, and she had her hand back on Katie's shoulder. "He's gone, Katie. I'm sorry."

Katie gently lifted her friends hand off her shoulder. "I know." *No he's not.* "I didn't think through coming here. Can we run somewhere else next time?"

Karen grinned, relief apparent in her face. "Of course, we can run anywhere you want. Particularly if it's near a pub or somewhere we can get prosecco."

"Deal." Katie started running again, faster this time until she heard Karen grunt behind her. She slowed down, letting her friend catch up and she forced a smile onto her face. Katie didn't make eye contact with Karen until they were back at the car, and Karen didn't force the issue.

I will find out what happened here.

Chapter 14

1

Knowles stood to attention in Raymond's office. *Only twenty-four hours since I last stood here. Jesus. Just a day since Bryant went AWOL.* Raymond had been yelling at him for a full five minutes now, but Knowles didn't care.

"Our cover story won't hold you know. Nobody is going to believe a gas main exploded under that house. People will have seen the helicopter. What were you thinking?"

It took Knowles a moment to realise that this time Raymond was actually asking him a question. "Sir, I had received a message from Private Singer. He sounded terrified, sir and I felt that strong action was required."

"Strong action?" Raymond spat the words. "Well, it doesn't get much stronger than blowing a house up."

"No, sir."

"Do not underestimate me, Knowles. You have created a very serious situation for us."

"Sir, I made a judgment call. If I had the time again, I would still do it. I believe it was the right call."

"Christ, Knowles."

"Sir, a ground assault could have led to a slaughter. We didn't know how many wolves were there. Bryant, by himself, could have taken us all out. I watched these things take out a police squad in Barnstaple. I was there when they wiped out our base."

"And you came out without a scratch on you. Very commendable, sergeant."

No scratches you can see. I can't remember the last time I slept through a night.

"Sir, we can't take chances with these things. If we get the chance to wipe them out from the air, then we take it."

"What if there were civilians in the house Knowles?"

"There weren't."

"What if? What then?"

Knowles shrugged. "Collateral damage."

"You are a hard man, Knowles."

"No sir, I am a survivor."

Raymond chuckled at that. "Yes you are, sergeant. I had another look at your file. I couldn't work out why you are still a sergeant. Today, that became abundantly clear. Do you go out of your way to piss off your superior officers?"

"Yes, sir." Knowles sighed inwardly. *This is nothing I haven't heard before.* "I mean, sorry, sir, no, sir."

"You are lucky that you're not in jail right now Knowles. The people upstairs are not happy with you, not happy at all. Neither am I." Raymond paused. "Your actions today could have seriously compromised this mission and led to the deaths of civilians. Any repeat of this and you will be dismissed from Her Majesty's forces. Am I clear?"

"Yes, sir."

"I managed to persuade the boss that you could be useful. You are still the only person that seems to understand the threat these things possess. Smith wanted to weaponise them didn't he?" Raymond didn't wait for Knowles to nod. "Well, trust me, that boat has long sailed. The wolves present a threat to the security of this country, the like of which we have never seen before. You could still be useful to us Knowles: your knowledge of Stadler and the wolves is second to none. You still have your job due to the Devon op; maybe you should be grateful for that. Dismissed."

Knowles marched out, past the two MPs who were looking seriously annoyed. *I will never be grateful for going to Devon, you arsehole.*

2

Jack was in chains, with two armed guards stood at the door to his cell. He raised his head when the door opened. The sudden streak of light blinded him momentarily, and he jammed his eyes shut. When he opened them, Knowles was in front of him.

"Come to laugh?"

Knowles shook his head. "You know there is nothing I can do about this." He gestured to the chains and the heavy door. It was still open, the two guards flanking it with guns ready. "You brought this on yourself."

"It wasn't my fault," Jack said.

"So you keep saying," Knowles said. "You scared the shit out of Raymond."

"I couldn't help it," Jack said. "I heard Bryant's voice and lost control."

"Twice."

"What?"

"Twice. You've lost control twice. First when you met, then again just from speaking to him."

Jack nodded. "It's not my fault," he said again.

"How will you help him if you can't control it yourself?"

Jack remained silent.

"I can't get you out of here Jack, even if I wanted to."

"I could free myself."

"Yes, but how far would you get? You could kill me, the guys there, but then what? There are over one hundred people stationed here, and after the events of the last twenty-four hours, they're looking for an excuse to bag themselves some wolf."

"I would heal."

"Yes, but at what cost? How sure are you that a stray bullet wouldn't hit anything vital? We still don't know the limits of your healing. What if someone decides that your head would look good in the mess? How sure are you that you'd recover from that?"

Jack stayed silent. He knew that Knowles had a point, knew that he was no closer to Katie and Josh. What could he do?

"You said 'if you wanted to'," he said eventually. "What do you mean? Am I stuck here?"

"For now, Jack, yes."

"Have you changed your mind about helping me?"

Knowles was silent for so long that Jack thought he wouldn't answer. "Yes. You're dangerous. I didn't think you were, but now I'm not sure. Bryant has changed things for you. I don't trust you. You're a dangerous man, possibly the most dangerous I have ever met."

3

Knowles left the makeshift prison, a sick feeling in his stomach. The look on Jack's face as he left haunted him. Throughout his army career, Knowles had been told to be honest. The truth is the only way to deal with people, particularly when you are going to be in life-threatening situations with them. Jack was dangerous, that much was clear, but was telling him the right thing to do? Would it make him more dangerous? More volatile?

Knowles wasn't sure, but he also didn't know how Raymond would respond now. Raymond had a ruthless streak - would he order Jack killed? Knowles grimaced and ran his hand through his hair. *This is a mess.*

He stepped into the sunlight and squinted. Around him things were returning to normal. Soldiers were completing PT on the ruined grass; mechanics were working on the vehicles; others were patrolling the fence line. It looked like a normal day on an army base, but it was as far from that - to Knowles' eyes, at least - as possible.

Knowles nodded hello at a small group who marched past him, and then realised his phone was ringing. Unknown caller loomed large on the display.

"Hello?" he said, clicking receive.

"You missed," said a familiar voice. Then the line went dead.

Knowles swore loudly, drawing looks from the men and women nearest him. He turned and ran to Raymond's office.

"Where is he?" Raymond roared.

"I don't know, sir," Knowles said. "I've given my phone to the tech team and they are trying to trace it."

Raymond nodded.

"The phone doesn't need to be in use to be traced," Knowles said.

"I'm not an idiot, Knowles," Raymond said. "I'm more interested in why he rang. Why let us know he's alive?"

"He was always alive, sir," Knowles said.

"Which makes your actions earlier all the more mystifying. You are assuming that a direct hit from a hellfire wouldn't kill him?" Knowles didn't answer so Raymond pressed on. "In which case, why fire them?"

"I took out the threat from his followers," Knowles said, "and tried to incapacitate him so we could get him in custody."

"Right," Raymond had a grim smile on his face that Knowles had never seen before. "Bryant has removed all doubt in the matter that he is alive. It would have taken days to check that rubble. It doesn't make sense for him to make this easy for us. I don't like this, we don't know enough about our enemy."

Knowles could see where this was going.

"I want to know what's going on," Raymond said. "I want Stadler cut open."

Knowles lay on his bed staring at the ceiling. It was dark now, but he'd been lying on his bed for hours, not sleeping. Raymond's words were deeply troubling. Jack was a civilian, and despite what Knowles thought, a man who was stuck trying to do the right thing. It wasn't Jack's fault that Bryant had turned into a homicidal maniac. It wasn't Jack's fault that so many were dead. *Apart from that doctor and those thugs in Barnstaple.*

So, Jack wasn't entirely blameless, but this recent turn of events was definitely not his fault. The dead were Bryant's responsibility and his alone. He should be strapped to a table tomorrow and cut open. *He* should be held to account for his actions.

Knowles turned over, yet again, but could not get comfortable. They had traced the phone call made by Bryant. They found the phone lying on the ground on the edge of the M20 – clearly tossed out of a moving vehicle. The road snaked through the middle of Kent: M25 and London one way, the coast and Dover the other. Bryant could be anywhere. The ports were on high alert, as were the airports, but Knowles didn't think it would matter. Bryant would not leave the country, or at least not yet. Whatever was happening between him and Jack was not over. Jack remained the best person to find Bryant, he was sure of it.

Knowles mulled over the two encounters between the men. Despite the fact that one had been over the phone, the outcome was catastrophic. Jack had lost control. That had not happened for months, even with Callum and the events of that final, horrendous day on the old base. Was it possible that the Originals couldn't exist together? Was that why they had died out? Did they all lead their own little tribes of wolf things, carving out their own patch?

If that was the case, then how big a 'patch' did they have? With Jack in Kent, did that mean Bryant had to go elsewhere? Essex? Surrey? Further? And if the patch covered the whole of the UK? What then? Would Bryant come looking for Jack? The man's actions so far would suggest this.

The more he thought about it, the more cutting Jack open seemed a bad idea. If Jack were free, maybe he and Bryant would be naturally drawn to each other. Maybe. *They could attack each other, maybe solve the problem for us.*

Raymond needed to hear this. Knowles dressed quickly and left his room. He jogged through the barracks and out into the cool night air. The stars were out in force above him, but still only a fraction of what could be seen in Devon. Knowles jogged to Raymond's office, but he could see the lights were out. A solitary soldier marched past. It was Patel.

"Any idea where Major Raymond is?" Knowles asked. Patel shook his head.

"Gone home I think, sergeant." Patel turned and continued to march across the green, heading for the barracks.

Knowles swore softly to himself. Raymond would return in the morning, but that would be too late for Jack. Without realising he was doing it, Knowles walked to the block where they were holding Jack.

A plan was beginning to form.

6

Knowles walked past Jack's cell and down another flight of stairs to the rooms being used as a makeshift hospital. A guard stood outside the double doors that led through to the rest of the wing. The guard nodded at Knowles as he walked in. He was surprised to see it was Evans.

"What are you doing here?"

"Watching, waiting," Evans said.

"You served together right?"

Evans nodded. "I've known him for years. We met in basic."

"How did you get here then?"

"Bryant needed a driver. Collins volunteered me. Seemed a cushy op."

It was Knowles' turn to nod. *Been caught out like that myself.*

"They cut his leg off. The man has done two tours of Afghanistan and loses his leg in Kent." Evans shook his head. "Makes no sense."

Knowles had no answer for that, so he pushed through the inner doors without another word. He was now in a long corridor, with rooms leading off either side of it. Two soldiers stood flanking the last door on the right. Knowles approached carefully and greeted the two guards.

"He awake?"

"Yes," the younger of the two men said. "He's in a lot of pain."

"I want to talk to him. You got a problem with that?"

The soldier shrugged. "Are you armed?"

Knowles nodded.

"Just in case," the other man said.

"Any sign?"

Both men shook their heads.

"Maybe he's waiting for a full moon," Knowles said. No-one laughed. Knowles pushed the door open and entered Collins' room.

He was strapped to the bed with the same chains that Jack had broken. Another guard stood in the corner of the room, silently watching Collins. Knowles waved at him before pulling up a chair and sitting next to the bed.

"Collins," he said.

The big man looked at him with haunted eyes. A drip fed into his arm and a small breathing tube was hooked under his nose. His leg had been cut off just above the knee.

"My foot itches."

"You want me to scratch it, cos you know-"

"Not that foot, sergeant. The one that's in the bin."

Actually in a lab, being looked at by the docs. You can't bin something like that. Knowles didn't voice the thought. He didn't think Collins would appreciate it.

"How are you feeling?"

Collins just stared at him. The tubes, pipes and beeping of the heart monitor reduced the effectiveness of the stare, but it was enough to unnerve Knowles anyway.

"Sorry," Knowles said. "Force of habit."

"Sorry isn't going to bring my leg back."

"I promise you we will get Bryant," Knowles said. *Never promise anything.* That was a mantra he had lived by in Afghanistan, but that was then. Modern Britain, security cameras everywhere: Bryant would be found sooner or later.

"Bryant didn't do this to me," Collins said.

"Well, you can't kill the doctors," Knowles said.

"No, I don't mean them. Bryant didn't bite me; it was one of the others."

"Bryant killed Wills and Parker though, yes?"

Collins nodded.

"So, with respect, it doesn't matter. We need to get him and soon."

"I want to see him," Collins said.

"What?"

"When he's brought back here - him, and anyone else you get - I want to see them."

"They won't let you shoot them you know."

"I want him to know, Knowles. I want him to see what he's done."

Knowles nodded.

"I served with him, you know, in Afghanistan. I thought we were mates."

Knowles was beginning to get a serious case of déjà vu. It wasn't the first time the wolves had created rifts between tight people.

"So what about you? Anything happening?"

"If you mean have I turned into one of those fucking things, then no." Collins smiled ruefully. "You don't get to shoot me after all."

7

Knowles left Collins and stood outside Jack's cell. "He awake?" he asked the guard, who shrugged.

Knowles tapped on the door softly and waited. No noise came from the cell.

"You can't go in there," said the guard.

"Are you going to stop me?"

"Sir, I have orders."

"Don't worry, son, I'm only messing with you." Knowles grinned at the man, who visibly relaxed. "I have no intention of visiting Stadler." He tapped the door again.

"Can I help you with something else then?"

"What time is he scheduled for the vivisection?" Knowles said.

"Nine o'clock."

Knowles nodded. "So, they'll come to sedate him at what, about eight thirty?"

The guard nodded. "Are you going to be there?"

"This man is the reason that a lot of people are dead," Knowles said with a grimace. "Damn right I'm going to be there."

Jack heard Knowles march away from his door. He heard the soldier on guard sigh and return to his post. Having been woken by a tapping sound, he had heard the entire conversation

What is Knowles playing at?

He thinks I'm dangerous.

Knowles was not an easy man to read and was full of contradictions. Earlier he had seemed scared and wary of Jack, but now he was warning him. It was only a few weeks ago that Knowles had sneaked beer into Jack's room. Only a few weeks ago that he'd spoken to Jack like a friend.

So much has changed.

Now, Knowles' friends were dead. One of his colleagues - Bryant - had also become an Original, apparently deliberately. Jack could not understand why anyone would do this voluntarily. The Wolf's voice murmured away deep inside him and he ignored it. *I will control you.*

Jack sat up and rolled his legs so he was perched on the side of the bed. According to Knowles, he had about eight hours to figure out how to get out of this place. If he didn't, then tomorrow he would be cut into little pieces so the army could figure out how he worked. If he didn't, then Katie and Josh would never know he was still alive.

Katie.

Josh.

He had come to find Knowles as he was the one who could help him. Now that was not looking likely. If Jack wanted his family back, then he could only count on himself. He had to get out; had to let them know he was alive. Everything else could be dealt with after that.

His main problem was that he didn't have the first clue how he was going to escape.

9

Knowles lay in bed watching his clock change agonisingly slowly. Morning was now just a few hours away. Had Jack heard him? Had he done the right thing?

Thoughts went round and round in his head. Ever since his first tour to Afghanistan, Knowles had slept with headphones on: music helped him to sleep. It had not helped tonight. He was on his second full album, and would not have been able to say what he had listened to so far.

Jack is a good man.

Jack is dangerous.

He needs his family.

He needs to be killed.

Every time he felt like he had reached a resolution, the other thoughts came back countering every argument he had. The arguments in Jack's favour were that he hadn't killed anyone in months. It was not exactly a ringing endorsement of the man.

There was also Bryant to consider. Bryant definitely was dangerous, but he too kept giving them clues to his location. Raymond was right: Bryant had not needed to let them know he was alive, so why had he? Was Bryant fighting the Wolf, like Jack had when they first met? Jack had beaten the Wolf - could Bryant?

Knowles eventually drifted off to sleep, but nothing in his head was resolved. He slept fitfully and shallowly. By the time the morning came, he still didn't know what was for the best.

It was not long before events overtook him and forced his hand.

Chapter 15

1

Bryant stared out of the window. Greenery whizzed past, broken up by lorries, cars and other vehicles travelling on the other side of the motorway. Joe was driving, focussed entirely on the road. They were keeping pace with the rest of the traffic, therefore speeding, but not by enough to gather attention from the police. Henry was in the back with Bryant, staring out of the other window. He hadn't said a word the whole time Bryant had known him.

Jenny was in the front, ignoring Bryant but not really talking to Joe either. The whole car was heavy with an atmosphere of mistrust and depression.

I am a monster.

No.

I have killed so many people.

Yes, but that was before you met me.

That was war.

Keep telling yourself that. We both know different.

Bryant shook his head, trying to clear it. The beast was getting stronger, taking control.

Joe started to indicate, and minutes later they were parked outside a service station. Bryant climbed out of the car and surveyed his surroundings. Service stations all looked the same: concrete nightmares with a tiny bit of grass. A dog walked forlornly around this patch now, but it was hard to tell who looked the most disgusted: the owner or the dog. A large building squatted at the end of the car park, a sign outside

116

advertising the pleasures held within: a Costa Coffee; a M&S food hall; a Moto cafe and a WH Smith. *This place wasn't even good enough to warrant a KFC. What a shithole.*

"This way," Jenny said, heading towards the building. She had not mentioned the events of the previous night. The way she moved her arse as she walked away from him could have been taken as a sign of forgiveness. He watched her for a moment and didn't notice Joe next to him until he spoke.

"Yes," he said. He nodded at Jenny's retreating back, also admiring the way she moved. "Good work."

"Pretty sure she doesn't think that about me," Bryant said.

Joe shrugged. "She made us come back for you. You must have done something right."

"Did she say anything about last night?"

Joe shook his head. "Listen, Carl was an arsehole. He was a religious nut, obsessed with the Originals." He shrugged. "Not my bag really. Me and Henry were waiting for a chance to bug out when this all kicked off."

"What do you know of the Originals?"

"Same as everyone else. Nothing." Joe could see Bryant wanted more. "Seriously, nothing. Until Stadler and you, no-one even believed in them. There was talk of one in Germany, but that turned out to be bollocks."

"So how did you find me?"

Joe shrugged again. "We all knew. I can't explain it. It was like a light had gone on and there you were by the switch."

Joe looked up and saw Jenny standing by the entrance to the building. He started to follow her, then paused as if he had forgotten something. Joe turned back to the car, opened the door and gently coaxed his brother out. Henry shuffled alongside him, not looking up and letting himself be guided by Joe's arm on his shoulder.

We are a right state. Bryant set off after them, worried about what the others would think when they walked in.

2

The Moto cafe was open plan and noisy. Despite the early hour, it was also packed. Everywhere he looked, Bryant could

117

see groups of people staring at him. Dotted around these groups, sitting at various tables were families where harassed parents were trying to keep their children calm. The families were oblivious to the groups around them, all wrapped up in their domestic hell. Yet, judging by the speed they were eating, at least two of the families knew something was up.

Jenny was talking to a heavy set man who was stood next to a large group of people seated at a table. He was dressed in jeans and a shirt, looking like a man about to go on holiday. He stared at Bryant throughout the conversation with Jenny.

"That's Michael Smith," Joe said. "He used to live with Jenny. Be careful."

Great.

"What happened?"

"As far as I know, he made Jenny." Joe shrugged. "He killed some people, so he had to leave."

"You've killed people, Joe."

Another shrug. "Guess I'm more careful."

Jenny beckoned them over. Now all six pairs of eyes at the table were on them. Three women were all different sizes, with one looking like she was carrying at least four extra stone. The smallest looked like she would snap in a stiff breeze. The men were all about the same size, all wiry but none looked like a challenge. *This is why Michael is in charge.*

"I'm Michael," he said, offering his hand.

Bryant looked at it, then looked at the table. Joe sucked in a heavy breath.

"Jenny has told us everything about you," Michael said.

"Everything?" Bryant glanced at Jenny, then resumed staring at Michael. "Weird. She's never mentioned you."

"Yes." The way he said it suggested that, yes, she probably had told him everything, including what happened last night. "You are in charge now," Michael continued, ignoring Bryant's barb. "This," he gestured around the cafe, "is your clan now."

"You're giving it up, just like that?" Bryant scanned the room again. The people watching him seemed different now he looked harder. Their faces were expectant, full of hope.

118

"Yes," Michael said. "Why would I deny an Original?"

"I've been in charge of men before," Bryant said. "In my experience, when someone new comes in, it never ends well for the old guy."

"This is not the army."

"I don't think that matters."

"I am not you. I am happy to serve."

"Is everyone here in agreement with that?" Bryant looked around the table. The fat woman looked away, but the others held his gaze.

"What if I don't want to rule?"

Yes you do. Power, Bryant, more power.

"It is your birthright."

Bryant laughed. "I wasn't born like this."

"Irrelevant," Michael said. "You are the most powerful one amongst us. That means you are in charge."

"Again, what if I don't want to?"

Michael shrugged.

"How do you know I'm the most powerful? There is another Original."

This time Michael nodded. "We have plans for him too. He will either join us or die."

"I thought Originals couldn't die."

"There are ways," Michael said.

Bryant smirked. "You threatening me, Mikey?"

"Not at all. Just stating a fact." Michael returned the smirk. "Originals can be killed. How do you think they all died out in the first place?"

"Ok, Mikey, it sounds like a threat, and I don't respond well to that," Bryant said. "Also, to be honest, you lot don't look all that."

"Do not be fooled by how we look, Bryant."

"Yeah, ok, whatever," Bryant said. He tapped Jenny on the arm, "Come on, let's go."

"Would you like to see what we can do?" Michael said.

Bryant turned back to him, a sick feeling rising in his stomach. He looked around the service station, at the families sitting around them.

119

Michael stood and clapped his hands. The fat woman responded first. She giggled and started to undress. Fat fingers started to unbutton her blouse, a strangely sensual movement.

"Hey," a man shouted. He was dressed in the blue uniform of a security guard but it was too big for him, making him look ridiculous. "What are you doing? Stop it!"

A teenager started laughing and pulled out her phone, filming the fat woman with it. Other people were pointing. The family nearest them stood, their meal half eaten in front of them. The father scooped up the youngest child and hoisted him onto his shoulders. The mother put her hand over the other child's eyes and steered them towards the door.

The security guard walked past them, heading for the fat lady. He didn't see a man stand in the family's way and block the door. The father said something and tried to step past the man, but his way was blocked again. He dropped his shoulder and barged into the man, pushing him out of the way. Bryant heard a snarl and knew that the father would never barge anyone again.

The fat woman was topless now and laughing. The teenager was also laughing, phone still held aloft.

The security guard was nearly at their table.

The rest of the service station seemed still, everyone transfixed by the slow strip of the fat woman.

It meant that most people didn't notice the others starting to take their clothes off.

3

Harriet Miller tutted and sighed without taking her eyes off her mobile phone. Her dad was so embarrassing. His jokes would shame cracker joke writers, yet her mum just about pissed herself laughing at every one - even the ones she had heard a million times before. He always said he had funny bones. Harriet thought they'd been broken a long time ago.

Not like Jake, now he *was* funny. All those other older boys, farting and burping to try and get her attention without realising that it really wasn't nearly as impressive or hilarious as they thought. They weren't funny either. No, Jake was sensitive and kind and she hadn't minded when he put his hand up her top. He hadn't minded when she'd stopped him moving his hand further down. His last text had said as much. Her last text had promised that he could do that when she got back from this stupid holiday.

"Hey, look at that," her dad was saying now. "That fat woman is taking all her clothes off."

"Good one, dad, but I'm busy." She continued to fiddle with her phone: reading Facebook and texting Jake.

"You're so funny Tony," her mum said. Her idiot brother nodded whilst sucking his coke noisily through a straw.

"I'm not kidding," he said, pointing behind Harriet. Her idiot brother started sniggering, then laughing out loud. *This better not be one of those "funny bones' things.* She turned and her mouth dropped open.

She texted quickly: YOU ARE NOT GOING TO BELIEVE THIS. SOME FAT BITCH IS TAKING ALL HER CLOTHES OFF.

A second later her phone beeped: NO WAY! TAKE A PICTURE.

I CAN DO BETTER THAN THAT. She clicked the video symbol and held her phone up. Her mum was so shocked at what she was seeing, she didn't even do her customary tut.

4

Jake looked at his phone again. I CAN DO BETTER THAN THAT. The girl was crazy. Good crazy though, the kind that made him look twice; the kind that made his stomach go every time he saw her in the corridor at school. He couldn't believe she had let him kiss her, let alone touch her. The next two weeks were going to drag.

His phone pinged and a video popped up. Harriet waved at him and then panned her phone across. Even in the low resolution, he could see the table full of serious looking people and then he saw the fat woman. He started to chuckle as her blouse came off. Then he caught a movement in the corner of the frame. Something that Harriet hadn't noticed because she didn't move, didn't change the camera focus.

"Holy shit," Jake said. "Harriet, run!"

She couldn't hear him, didn't see the coming danger. "Oh Christ, no!" Jake shouted.

Then, from his phone's tiny, tinny speaker, came screaming.

5

Harriet didn't know what was happening. The fat woman finished taking her clothes off, then everyone was screaming. She lowered her phone and looked around. She couldn't believe what she was seeing: her brain refused to acknowledge the events unfolding around her.

Wolves. There are wolves here.

The doors to the carpark were blocked by two enormous wolves. A security guard was rolling on the floor, apparently fighting another wolf. The fat woman had gone, replaced by the biggest wolf of them all. As she watched, the wolf threw back its head and howled.

Then she felt a hand grab her T-shirt and pull hard. Her dad was dragging her backwards, away from the table and away from the wolves. He had her idiot brother in his other hand.

"Tony," his mum said and Harriet heard a tone she had never heard from her mother before.

"Shh," he said. "No sudden movements."

"The door," her mum said. Her dad nodded.

"Toilets," he muttered. "Now."

They backed away slowly. Around them more and more wolves were appearing and grabbing people. The tiled floor was slick with blood. Harriet felt her bladder go but didn't care. Her phone was in her hand, still recording.

Off to her right, near the table where the fat woman had sat, a man watched her. He had a strange expression on his face. *Not a paedo expression, something else.*

"Tony," her mum said.

They were 10 metres from the toilets.

"Babe, please, be quiet."

8 metres.

"That man," her mum said.

7.

Her dad looked over at the man. His face was changing now.

"Holy shit," her dad said. He never swore. Even when she had spilt a whole glass of red wine over the new carpet. It had been her mum's fault – she shouldn't have put the glass on the floor so Harriet could knock it. Even then-

5.

Her dad pushed her idiot brother towards the toilets entrance and swung Harriet after him.

"Harri, RUN!"

4.

An enormous black wolf hit her dad in the back, sending him flying forward, skidding on the tiles. Harriet ran past him, past her mum who was hitting the wolf, past her idiot brother - *Will, his name is Will* -

2.

She stopped by the toilets and turned back to her brother. "Will, come on!" She reached out her hand and felt his little hand grab it.

Then it was wrenched away and she fled into the toilets.

6

Jake watched even though the motion of the video made him feel sick. The man Harriet had been filming had turned into a wolf. A wolf. A real bonafide wolf. *Holy shit.* He nodded to himself, accepting the truth. Now the screen was shaking wildly, confusing shots of Harriet's jeans and the floor meaning that she was running. *Running for her life.* He heard her shout for Will, heard her gasp as he was taken from her. The phone was muffled whilst she pushed past people who were running out of the toilets and then he heard her lock a cubicle.

That isn't going to help.

Jake listened to her sobbing for a moment, knowing that she was still recording. Then he did something that he hadn't done for years.

"Mum! Help! Harriet is in trouble!"

7

Bryant looked at the three bodies at his feet and felt a pang of guilt.

No.

Just a kid. He was just a kid, can't have been more than ten and now he was dead.

Having fun yet?

Fun? You call this fun?

Not the first time you've killed innocent people.

Bryant pushed the voice away. He looked at the kid one more time. His mother lay beside him, throat torn out. Her eyes were fixed on the boy, her expression torn between terror and horror. *Last thing she saw was her son being eaten alive. Fuck, I want cancer back.*

No you don't. This is better than dying Bryant, you know it.

"Bryant."

He turned away from his part in the slaughter and saw Jenny and Michael. All around them, wolves were feasting. Smaller packs were sniffing around the other shops, looking for survivors. As he watched, a small wolf gave a yelp as a man burst out from behind a counter. He made it five metres before three wolves pounced on him. Soon more blood flowed across the marble floor, mixing with the rest.

"Bryant," Michael said again.

"You're crazy."

"You wanted a show of power. This is on you."

"On me?" Bryant roared and grabbed Michael by the throat. The other man stared at him and the blankness in his eyes scared Bryant more than anything else he had seen that day.

You could kill him.

Bryant let him go. "This is nothing to do with me, and you do anything like this again and I will kill you. Am I clear?"

"Crystal," Michael smirked. "Do you doubt us now?"

124

"You won't get away with this," Bryant said. "This is too big. The police will be on their way, and then the army will get here. Trust me, you don't want to be here when they find out."

"What will they do?" Michael sneered.

"They will blow this place to pieces. They won't take any chances."

"They've done it once already," Jenny said. "I used to have a house."

"How will they know we're here?"

Bryant sighed. *A psycho and an idiot.* "There are cameras everywhere, and how long do you think it will be before a car comes in here?"

"That's already taken care of," Michael said.

"They've blocked the entrance to the services," Jenny said. "Two police cars."

Bryant grunted. He didn't bother to ask where the police cars had come from. It was irrelevant.

"Stop killing people," Bryant said, surveying the scene again.

Michael laughed: "Why?"

"We might need more food, depends on how long we're staying."

Michael nodded. He walked away, barking orders at the others. Bryant felt someone take his hand and turned to Jenny.

"We can rule them all, you know," she said.

He nodded. "We need Jack Stadler. With him, then we can." *And with him, maybe I can stop you all.*

You don't want to stop us, Bryant. You want to rule.

No-

Yes.

8

Joe and Henry sat next to Bryant, backs against the foodhall wall. It was made of glass with a frosted bar across the middle. A handprint was perfectly visible in the middle of this wall. *How the hell did that get there?* Bryant shook his head. Carnage surrounded them and yet he paused to wonder

125

about a handprint? The human brain had such a way of dealing with traumatic incidents.

You're not human anymore.

Fuck off.

"We need to get out of here," he muttered to Joe. Henry nodded, eyes wild. Dried blood decorated the side of his face like a goth kid's mascara.

"We just got here," Joe said.

"Michael is nuts," Bryant said. "I've seen guys like him before, and they only succeed in getting everyone killed."

"He's put you in charge."

"I know, but I want nothing to do with this." Bryant gestured around him. "This will not end well."

"They have policemen on the entry ramp. This place is closed to the public. No-one knows we are here."

"Yeah, right." Bryant pointed to the ceiling, where the black dome of CCTV cameras hung at regular intervals. "Where do they go? Who's watching?"

"I don't know."

"Me neither, but I guarantee that someone knows we are here."

"What do you suggest?"

"Look, I need to know what's happening to me," Bryant said. "There is only one man out there who can help me."

"Stadler," Joe said.

"Yep," Bryant nodded.

"You attacked him."

"True, but I don't know why. I still think he's the only person who can show me how to control this."

"He won't help you. He's with the army. They will kill us all," Joe said. Henry started rocking when he heard the words 'army'.

"I need leverage. I need to make him help me."

"How?"

"He has a family."

9

Jenny sat down next to Bryant, her arrival stretching the pause that had resulted from his declaration.

126

"What are you three planning?" she asked with a smile. "You look as thick as thieves."

"Bryant wants to leave," Joe said.

She looked at Bryant, eyebrows raised.

"It is a death sentence to stay here," he said. "Look around you Jenny. The military won't let this slide."

"Michael won't want you to leave," she said.

"Tough shit."

"Where will you go?"

"Devon. I'm going to persuade Stadler to help me."

"Then I'm coming too."

"This isn't a fucking picnic, Jenny."

"I'm not stupid. Michael is dangerous, that's as obvious now as when-" She didn't finish the sentence; didn't need to. "He will not let you walk out of here, though."

"He won't be able to stop me."

"No, but he can stop *us*."

Henry whimpered at this point. Joe hugged him and pulled him close.

"We need a diversion," Joe said. "Can't stop us if he don't know we're leaving."

Bryant remembered the girl, running into the toilets, fleeing her dead family.

"Find us a car and wait outside with the engine running," he said to Joe.

"How?"

Bryant gestured around them. "No-one here is using their car anytime soon."

"What are you going to do?"

"Get Michael's attention diverted."

Joe nodded and walked away. He stopped at a few corpses, went through their pockets and then headed out to the car park. The services themselves sat between two large areas of concrete. The door nearest Bryant led to the car park, but at the opposite end was a door to the lorry park. Michael and some of the others were standing near there.

In front of them, on their knees were five humans, heads bowed. Several were crying. *He's gathering the food, like I asked.* Five humans were not going to last this pack long: there were at least fifty of them.

Bryant stood and stretched. He grabbed a passing man. "Hey, anyone checked these toilets?" He pointed at the ladies toilet in front of them.

"Not yet."

"Mind if I do it?"

"Of course not." The man stopped, and Bryant could see recognition in his eyes. "Sorry, mate. I'm Scott, you want help?"

"Do I look like I need help?"

"No, no, no," Scott held his hands up. "No offence."

"Good, get lost."

Scott hurried away, his face crimson. Bryant strode to the toilets whilst behind him, Jenny helped Henry to his feet and they headed for the same exit as Joe.

10

Harriet looked at her phone and realised it was still filming. She turned the camera to face her, sobbing quietly as she did so.

"Jake, if you're watching this, please help me."

She clicked off. The home screen of the phone sat waiting for more input from her. All the icons arranged in a neat grid, inviting her to press them - including the envelope with the smiley face on it. *Of course.* She opened up the messaging app and started typing all her friends' names in. Texting was quiet and she didn't want to risk making more noise than necessary. When she was done, she put her head on the cubicle wall and tried to calm down.

Think.

How the hell am I going to get out of here?

She knew she should ring the police. Every time she raised her phone to do just that, she started to shake. What if one of those things was outside, waiting for her to make a noise? *Someone else would have rung the police. Definitely.* There were loads of people in this service station. Hundreds, probably. One of them would be ringing and help would be coming now. She just had to wait, be patient.

Jake would ring them. Or his mum would. Jake would be her hero and she would let him do what he wanted. Yep, no doubt about that at all. Then, if she were ever in this situation again, at least she wouldn't die a virgin.

Ever in this situation again? Jesus Harriet.

What if no-one else was ringing? What if she were the only one left alive? What then? What if Jake had stopped watching? Got bored and started playing FIFA? What if he hadn't seen the fat woman change?

Then you will die here.

Tears started to roll down her cheeks again. At this rate, she would die of dehydration before the wolf things got to her. She smiled to herself: that was the sort of joke her dad would have made.

Which made more tears come.

Get a grip. Ring the police.

Harriet took a deep breath and raised her phone to dial. It started buzzing in her hands: replies to the texts were coming in. She gripped it tightly, trying to stop the noise.

HA-HA, GOOD ONE HARRI.

NOT FUNNY.

WHY ARE PIRATES CALLED PIRATES?

Three different people, none of them helpful. With a finger that was trembling way too much, she dialled the emergency number and then the door to her cubicle was ripped off its hinges.

She started to scream, but a hand covered her mouth. It was the man. The one who had stared at her dad and then-

"Do not scream," he said. "If you want to get out of here alive, do not scream."

He released the pressure on her mouth slowly, waiting to see what she would do.

"Good girl," he said. "Does that have a camera on it?"

It took her a moment to realise he was talking about her phone. She nodded.

"Film this," he ordered. She started to shake her head, but he stared at her. Her teachers stared like that sometimes: well, not *exactly* like that. She pointed the phone at him.

"Stadler, I'm coming for you," he said and grinned. Then he took the phone off her, pressed share then put it next to the sink outside the cubicle. "Come on," he waved an arm at her and after a moment she stepped out of the cubicle.

"What's your name?"

"Harriet."

"Hi, I'm Jamie. Listen, we're going to go outside in a moment. I will create a diversion and you can run away, clear?"

She shook her head. "Why are you helping me?"

"Harriet, I've done some bad things. If I can save you, then maybe it will help balance my books."

She didn't understand what he meant, but she focussed on 'save you'. This man was going to save her life.

"Wait here," he said. "I'll come and get you as soon as I know it's clear."

She started to protest, but he left anyway. She sank against the wall, feeling fresh tears in her eyes.

11

Bryant stood outside the toilets and surveyed the scene. This was a hastily put together plan, which meant it had holes. *It will have to do.*

The services were essentially a long corridor. The toilets were roughly half way along that corridor. On his left were the gents, then WH Smiths. Opposite him was the food hall where he had sat with Joe and Henry and next to that a phone shop. Adjacent to the phone shop was the cafe, where he had first met Michael. If he carried on to the left, then he would reach the car park; if he turned right it would be the coach park.

Most of the wolves were in the cafe, telling jokes and tall tales. The aftermath of any conflict was like that, even when it was as one-sided as this. He counted three groups of wolves sniffing around the shops. A flight of stairs sat opposite him, between the shops. One of the groups went up these stairs, presumably looking for more survivors.

130

Michael had moved from the exit and was now talking to the fat bitch that had started this madness. Kneeling next to them were the five survivors. *Good, this might work after all.*

He slipped back into the toilets and found Harriet slumped on the floor, tears rolling down her face. She wasn't making a sound, though. *Tough girl.* He helped her to her feet and grinned at her. For a moment, he saw the gorgeous woman she wouldn't become.

"When I say, you run out of here, turn right and keep running. You will reach the coach park, but head left towards the grass bank. The motorway is the other side of it. The state of you, someone will stop. OK?"

"I'm not very fast," she whispered. She was looking at her clothes, and the expression on her face showed she had just realised she was covered in blood.

"You don't need to be," he said. "Just keep running."

She nodded.

"Ready?"

She nodded again.

"Ok then." He looked out of the opening for the toilets, then turned to her and said, "Now!"

12

Harriet ran. She tried not to look and just sprinted for the door.

-dead bodies-

It looked so far away, like a zoom shot in a cheap horror film.

-so much blood-

She heard a shout behind her and knew they were coming. From somewhere deep inside, she found more pace: a burst of speed that her PE teacher would have been both proud of and surprised at.

She crashed through the doors, flinging them open and stumbling into daylight. Lorries sat in parallel lines, dwarfing her as she sprinted towards them. *This isn't right. He said there would be a bank, a way to the motorway.* Fresh tears streaming down her cheeks, she ran on. Her legs were burning, her lungs screaming for air. Then her legs gave way, and she tumbled to the asphalt. The skin on her palms and knees ripped away, but she didn't care. The pain was irrelevant anyway. Her parents were gone. Her brother was gone. She would never see her friends again. Jake would move on - would he even remember her in a year?

The wolves got closer: she heard their breathing, could hear the pad of their feet as they approached.

She closed her eyes and waited.

13

The girl ran with surprising speed. Bryant watched her go and grinned as the wolves gave chase. The ones standing with Michael all watched the commotion and started shouting orders at the rest of the pack. Bryant strolled the other way, towards the car park. No-one stopped him or challenged him, until he reached the door.

"Hey-"

He heard the shout behind him and then ran through the doors and out into the car park. Unlike the girl, he could run for a very long time if he had to. A car pulled up in front of the entrance and the door flew open.

"Come with me if you want to live," Joe said with a grin. Bryant leapt into the car and they were moving before he shut the door. He looked in the wing mirror and saw the wolves coming out of the service station and running for the car. Three of them, closing fast.

"Go faster," he said. Joe pressed his foot down and the car lurched forward with a growl.

"German engineering," he said with another grin. "They know fuck all about wolves, but you gotta love their cars." He patted the BMW sign in the middle of the steering wheel. The car was soon clear of the car park and hurtling down the slip road and straight onto the motorway. No police cars blocked their way here and it took Bryant a moment to realise that there was no need. The barricade only needed to be on the entrance slip road. Joe sounded the horn as he went across two lanes. Horns were sounded in return, and brakes screeched, but somehow no-one crashed. After a couple of miles, Joe slowed down to a more normal pace and moved into the middle lane.

"So, we still going after Stadler?"

Bryant looked out the window for a moment. "Yes," he said. "Take us to Huntleigh."

Chapter 16

1

Jack stood, watching the door. They were coming for him and coming soon. *They are going to cut me open.* He knew it was the sensible course of action for them and really, if it was him, he would do the same, but that didn't make him feel any better. *Will I heal?* Knowles had reminded him that there was so much unknown about being an Original. *If they slice me up, will I put myself back together? What if they cut into my brain? What then?*

He watched the clock tick towards 8:30 and the anxiety grew. Deep inside him, the Wolf sensed this. Jack tried to keep calm: he controlled the Wolf, not the other way round. Nonetheless, the nerves fed the Wolf.

The soldiers were coming at 8:30, that's what Knowles had said. *Was he helping now? Does he want me to escape?* Jack swallowed hard. He could hear men talking outside the building, but even with his hearing, it was too muffled to be clear. *If I run where will I go? Can I find Bryant?* Jack was sure he could. *Find Bryant and then what? Persuade him to give himself up?* Jack snorted: Bryant did not seem like the 'give it up' type. But what choice did he have? He had to try. He took a deep breath, getting himself ready.

They were coming now.

2

Knowles stood outside the detention block and watched the squad come towards him. They were dressed from head to foot in Kevlar and looked more like a bomb disposal team than escort detail. He knew Taylor by reputation. He was a man going places. Taylor had led some teams on tough anti-insurgency patrols. Rumour had it he had taken out some high-ranking Al-Qaeda member, but it was *just* a rumour. Tellingly, Taylor had arrived after Bryant's escape. He carried himself with an arrogance that irritated Knowles instantly. *Wait until you get your arse kicked by these things, mate.*

"He will be waiting for you," Knowles said to the man at the head, stepping calmly in front of him.

"We have our orders, Knowles, move," Taylor said.

"He will kill you all."

"No, he won't." Taylor pointed at his team and gestured to the many weapons they all carried.

"They didn't work last time," Knowles said.

"So how are you still with us then?"

Knowles didn't answer.

Taylor laughed. "Everyone knows you like the guy, Knowles. We all know you'd do anything to keep him alive. After all, he saved you didn't he?"

"Is that what you think?" Knowles snarled.

"We all know, Knowles."

"All you really know is that you are taking a man - a civilian, a teacher, for fuck's sake - to be cut open."

"Just following orders, Knowles. Now move."

Knowles stepped to one side, glaring at the man. The rest of the squad trooped into the building. *Maybe one of them now has more doubts about what they are doing.*

Knowles leant on the wall of the makeshift prison. His weapon sat in its holster, its presence heavy on his hip. *How far are you going to go?*

3

The key turned in the lock, the mechanism groaning as it slid back. Jack winced at the sudden loud noise. The door swung open quickly and Jack just had time to see four guns aimed straight at his chest. The Wolf started to burst out of him just as all four guns went off.

Four tranquiliser darts smacked into its chest and with a whimper, it skidded to a stop in the doorway.

4

Knowles watched as four men, straining under the weight of the massive Wolf, came out of the cells carrying a stretcher. The Wolf was far too big for it, which made the whole thing somehow comical.

"Your pet dog thought it could attack us." Taylor was smirking, but sweat was beading on his brow.

Knowles said nothing, just watched the men struggle away. *So he did change, but they were prepared. Shit.*

He was trying to think what to do next when his radio burst into life.

"Knowles, Raymond's office immediately."

Swearing again, Knowles jogged across the base. He marched in and saluted smartly, but was surprised by how grim Raymond's face was. *Now what?*

5

"We have a situation in Kent, Knowles," Raymond said. "A service station is under attack from wolves. A video has been released to the web. This is not good."

He turned his laptop screen so Knowles could see it. The image was grainy and shook slightly, making Knowles feel nauseous. A fat lady was taking her clothes off, which would have been bad enough, but what happened next was becomingly increasingly familiar.

"When was this?" Knowles asked.

"It was posted about an hour ago. Police were called about ten minutes before that. They have cut off the service station and have set up a perimeter around it."

"Deaths?"

Raymond nodded. "No idea at the moment; potentially a couple of hundred."

"Jesus."

"Quite," Raymond said. "I have sent a team to advise."

But not me. That hurt - a surprising amount.

"The team should be there any minute and will be in contact as soon as they have more info."

"Why not-"

Raymond laughed, cutting him off. "You think I should send you? Despite the fact that the last time I did so, you ended up blowing up a house that could have been full of civilians?"

"But it wasn't, sir."

"You got lucky, Knowles. You are too twitchy around these wolves. You could cause a blood bath."

"With respect sir, it looks like there's already been one."

"Yes, and I don't want that situation any worse."

"Do you want me to leave?"

"Resign?"

Knowles swallowed hard. "I don't want to resign sir."

"Then what are you offering?"

Knowles paused. It was an excellent question. If he left, then they would kill Jack. If he stayed, then Jack would probably be killed anyway. If he left, then maybe he could get his career back on track. Maybe.

"Sir, killing Stadler is not the answer to this problem."

"I never said it was."

"No, but if you cut him open, that's not going to stop this." He gestured at the laptop, at the scenes of slaughter that were on a loop.

"Know your enemy, Knowles."

Raymond stared at him until Knowles dropped his eyes. "I have delayed the vivisection. This needs my attention." He waited until Knowles returned his gaze. "But know this, we will look at Stadler. We will know what's inside of him."

Knowles nodded. He had a few hours at most to think of something else.

"Is Bryant in Kent sir? Did he do this?"

Raymond watched the loop for a few seconds before answering. "He's not in this video." He blinked several times and for the first time, Knowles had an inkling of the strain he was under.

"This is somebody else."

6

Knowles spent the next two hours watching the screen. Raymond had it split in two: one half was dedicated to footage from his team on the ground, the other to the breaking news on the BBC News 24 channel. Every time they showed the grainy footage of the attack, Raymond swore. The journalists had tracked down the boy who had posted it: a sporty looking teenager with a quiff that Elvis would have envied. He spoke well, even if he was in a state of shock.

Raymond had his net experts tracking down the footage and destroying it as soon as it appeared, but the fact the BBC had it was a major problem. A cover story was being put together now: a cover-up involving a film production company. It would buy them some time to cover the actual cause of death of the people in the service station. The girl's phone footage was more of a problem, although social media reports showed that most of her friends had thought she was joking.

"I should be there," Knowles muttered, not for the first time.

"Shut up, Knowles."

Raymond's phone rang at that moment. He scowled at it before answering.

"Raymond," he said then listened intently for a moment. "Yes, go ahead. Bring the survivors here." He hung up.

"They're going in?" Knowles asked.

Raymond was silent for so long that Knowles thought he hadn't heard him. "Yes, they're going in now. Hopefully, we can resolve this without more civilian deaths."

7

Jack awoke and discovered that he was strapped to a table. He looked around, surprised that he was still alive. Around him were many monitors and medical machines. He recognised some from the medical dramas that Katie liked to watch, but he had no idea what any of them did.

Next to his bed was a table covered in white plastic. On top of the table lay enough scalpels and saws to have made the Spanish Inquisition wince.

"Shit," Jack said.

"He's awake!"

The man who spoke sounded panicked. Jack heard footsteps running towards him.

"Wait-" he got as far as saying before another load of tranquiliser darts smashed into his chest and the world disappeared again.

8

Knowles looked at his watch. An hour had passed since the phone call. He knew that was bad: these sorts of operations should be over in a matter of minutes. He was just about to voice this opinion when both his and Raymond's radios squawked.

"We have the survivors coming in now sir."

Raymond held his unit up. "How many?"

"Sir, we have Corporal Wallace on the gate. He has two lorries full of survivors. When they hit the building, it was chaos. They didn't know who was who, so they used tranquillisers and brought everyone here."

"Why did he not report in sooner?" Raymond barked.

"Sir, he felt radio silence was the best policy. Too many journalists trying to listen in."

Raymond looked at Knowles with eyebrows raised.

"Could be legit," Knowles said. He spoke slowly, the need for caution clear in his words.

"Could be bullshit," Raymond said. He raised the radio to his mouth again. "Bring them in. Set up a perimeter around the trucks. I want everyone fully armed, plus tranquilliser darts. Let's take no chances."

Raymond looked at Knowles. "I don't like this."

"Me neither, sir."

"Let's go. If there is any doubt, we kill everybody."

9

Jack awoke with a start, but this time he was wise enough not to make a noise. He was still strapped to the bed, but he was unsure how much time had elapsed. *Not much, Jackie boy, their drugs aren't working as well as they used to.*

Jack tried to ignore the Wolf, but he knew it was true. When he had first arrived in Kent, months ago, a couple of darts had been enough to stop him. Now it was four, and that hadn't put him out for long. It felt like minutes since he had last awoken.

I can keep you awake, Jackie boy...

The Wolf was starting to sound like Gary Edwards, the first man he had killed. *But not the last. Remember that-*

Jack forced himself to recite prime numbers, pushing the Wolf back down.

2...
The doctor
3...
he tasted
5...
good.
7...
And that woman
11...
What was her name?
13
17
19...
23...

Jack breathed out slowly. *Silence.* He looked at the tray full of scalpels again. *If I stay, I am a dead man.*

He raised his head slightly and saw two soldiers standing by the door. Neither were looking at him and both stood in a way that suggested they were relaxed. *They think I'm out for hours.*

Jack flexed his arms, forcing them to change, biceps growing until the straps holding him popped. They flew off him, whistling through the air until they hung impotently by the bedside. At the same time, Jack ripped the straps off his feet and he leapt for the soldier nearest him. He changed mid

140

jump, hitting the surprised soldier before he had a chance to raise his gun. The soldier crashed into his friend, sending them both tumbling to the floor.

The Wolf did not hang around. It burst through the doors and ran. Another two soldiers dived for cover as it emerged from the hospital room. One of them raised his gun and fired. A dart smacked into the Wolf's hind leg, but it ran on. Down a short corridor and then it leapt at another door.

This door exploded off its hinges, flying into the courtyard. The Wolf recognised it from earlier, but now the scene was chaos. Two large trucks sat in the middle of the parade ground. They were surrounded by about twenty armed soldiers, but the soldiers had their backs to the Wolf, aiming at the trucks.

The backs of the trucks were open and people were staggering into the sunlight. One of them was enormously fat, and another was looking right at him. The Wolf howled: it recognised a kindred spirit. Several of the soldiers turned as he burst into the courtyard.

The Wolf saw Knowles marching across towards the trucks. Saw his mouth open in surprise. But it was far too late. The wolves were here, and no-one was getting away this time.

10

Ten people got out of the trucks and stood in a line. Three of them looked wildly around, whilst the others all stared at the ground. Michael was one of those staring at the ground. He looked up and saw they were surrounded by soldiers.

He glanced at Sally next to him. Her corpulent frame was now clothed again and she was playing the part of terrified victim well. The plan had been hatched quickly once they knew Bryant had run away. Michael knew the police would be involved, but he hadn't factored how quickly. The army had arrived soon after, their different scent clear on the breeze.

Michael had moved quickly. He had stripped some of the bodies, mixing and matching intact clothing. Not much of it had been clear of blood, but that didn't matter. The army would execute anyone who was either in wolf form or naked. Several of the others, including Sally, cottoned on to what he was doing and joined in. The others, either drunk on the blood and feast they had had, or else too stupid to think they had any chance of surviving, had been shot by the soldiers as they stormed the building. Some had run away, but he didn't know how far they'd managed to get.

Two of the five surviving humans had been killed in the assault. The other three were with them now - all in a state of shock. The rest lined up were wolves, and now Michael was waiting for the opportunity to attack. As soon as those rifles were lowered he would give the command. With surprise, the soldiers would not have time to react. Each wolf could take down two soldiers in a matter of seconds.

They just needed to time it right.

The door to a building off to his right exploded outwards, buckling and shattering as an enormous wolf burst through it. *No, not a wolf. The Wolf. It's Stadler.* Michael grinned to himself as he made eye contact with the enormous beast.

Several of the soldiers turned at the noise, and Michael knew that it was time.

11

Knowles marched alongside Raymond. They were moving quickly, although Knowles was fairly certain that wasn't needed: the prisoners were going nowhere.

When they neared the courtyard, Knowles could see it was chaotic even though they were still over a hundred metres away. Ten civilians in a line, surrounded by twice that many soldiers. *If the press sees this, we're in trouble.*

"Shit," he said, "how do we know who is human?"

"Quite," Raymond said. "We need to contain this until we can test their blood, look for the same anomaly that was in Stadler's."

"The press are already all over this."

"Don't state the bleeding obvious, Knowles. Unless you have a solution keep your mouth shut."

142

At that moment, the door shattered and the Wolf jumped into the courtyard. Knowles felt his mouth open in surprise, but then the chaos multiplied exponentially.

A soldier - Patel, Knowles saw - stepped out behind the Wolf and shot it with his rifle. The tranquilliser dart hit it in the rump and it howled. It turned and swiped at Patel with a massive paw. The man flew against the wall, blood pouring out of a number of gashes in his face. Even at this distance, Knowles could see the skin hanging off the man's cheek. Patel had not been a good looking man before but now he would actively scare people.

The Wolf turned back to face the group around the truck. Even though he was half expecting it, Knowles was still surprised to see seven of the group change instantly. Each jumped at a different soldier, biting hard at the exposed necks. Immediately, each wolf turned to the next man and suddenly the air was filled with the screams of the dying.

"Fuck!" Raymond roared. He fumbled for his radio but dropped it. Knowles pulled out his weapon and took aim down the sights. One of the wolves' head exploded in a shower of red and he took aim again. More rifles popped and Knowles heard shouts of men running.

Another wolf collapsed in a heap as bullets tore into it, but Knowles couldn't tell where the bullets had come from.

Raymond now had his radio back in his hand and was barking orders into it.

"Sir, we need to get you to safety," Knowles said.

The Wolf looked straight at him, but then its attention was diverted as a bullet ripped into its side. The Wolf howled and leapt towards the man who had fired. Taylor. It charged him with head down and the force of the blow sent him crashing into the side of the building. Taylor lay on the floor in a crumpled heap.

Knowles could smell the blood, death and cordite in the air. *Not again.*

No-one stood in the original circle of twenty soldiers: they were all dead or dying. The three civilians were also down. One of the wolves had turned back to a human and was starting up one of the trucks.

"Let's go!" he roared.

Knowles aimed at him, but then the Wolf ran across his sights. Knowles lowered his weapon for an instant, then aimed again, but the truck was moving now and the shot had gone. The smaller wolves were running for the truck and jumped into the back. The last one in turned into a man who spun around as soon as he landed in the truck. The man held his hand out to the chasing Wolf.

"No," Knowles roared and he fired three rounds in quick succession. No bullet found its target.

Other soldiers arrived, some firing at the retreating truck, others rushing to help fallen friends. The Wolf ran after the truck, keeping pace with it easily. Bullets hit the Wolf, knocking it off its stride for a moment. But only for a moment.

"It's shielding them," Knowles muttered. *What are you doing Jack?*

"They will be stopped at the gate," Raymond said.

"No, they won't."

Knowles was right.

12

The truck bounced along the track, throwing the people in the back around like marbles in a sack. Michael grabbed hold of the side of the truck and stared out of the back. The Wolf was still running behind them, blood coating one side of its body. He held out his hand, but the Wolf ignored him. *It's covering us, letting the bullets hit it, not us.* He marvelled at the thought - despite what he had heard, the Wolf was on his side.

"Yes!" he screamed.

The Wolf suddenly sped up and ran past the truck. Michael risked looking forward, hanging out of the truck. Sally shouted his name, but he ignored her.

The gates of the base were rapidly approaching. An armoured car sat in front of the gates, with four soldiers aiming guns at them. A fifth man was on the car, aiming the large machine gun at them.

"Get down!" Michael roared as the man opened fire.

He jumped into the back of the truck, lying as flat as he could in the bouncing vehicle. High calibre rounds tore the cabin of the truck to pieces. The driver didn't stand a chance. Bullets smacked into the slowest of the wolves, the impact carrying his body out of the back of the truck.

So close.

13

The Wolf leapt at the man on the Armoured Personnel Carrier first. Its full weight hit the man on the side and he flew off the back of the car, hitting the ground with enough force to be knocked out cold. The Wolf stood where the soldier had been, the gun hanging impotently from its stand next to him. Four men turned to face the wolf, but one of them dropped his weapon and ran.

The other three took aim, but then the truck hit the armoured car. Metal screeched as the vehicles collided. The Wolf jumped to the side of the colliding vehicles, landing clear of the wreckage. The front of the truck had caved in, crumpling under the force of the collision. If the driver had somehow survived the machine gun fire, then he would certainly be dead now. The cabin of the truck had been completely destroyed.

Two of the soldiers did not move out of the way quickly enough and were crushed between the vehicles. The remaining man rolled on the ground as bits of metal rained down around him. The Wolf jumped for him and the man screamed. It tore the gun from his grasp, and with a shake of its head threw the gun thirty feet away.

The Wolf looked at the man and howled.

Three people staggered out of the remains of the truck and stood on shaky legs behind the Wolf. It turned its head slightly, recognising them as kin, and then turned back to the soldier. Its fur started to run back into its body, revealing a blood-spattered face.

"Run," Jack said. The soldier scrambled away from him, moaning, then sprinted after his colleague.

Running the other way, towards them, Jack could see the remaining soldiers of the base. At their head was Knowles.

He was bellowing Jack's name. Jack jumped as a hand patted his shoulder. He spun around to see a man of similar build to himself standing there. Behind him was another man and a really fat woman.

"You must be Stadler," the man said.

Jack nodded. "And you are?"

"Like you, I'm like you. My name is Michael, but I think introductions can wait, don't you?"

Jack glanced back at the rapidly approaching soldiers.

"Come on, Jack. Let's go."

They picked their way through the wreckage of the truck and APC and ran out onto the road by the base. A car came around the corner and slowed when the driver saw the smoke and wreckage by the gatehouse. The driver wound his window down.

"Jesus, is everyone ok?" he asked. "What happened to your clo-"

Michael wrenched the door open and pulled the man out of the car with a speed that was terrifying.

"Borrowing your car," he said. His fingers became topped with razor-sharp talons and he went to slit the man's throat.

"No," Jack cried and grabbed his arm. "Leave him. Take his car and let's go."

Michael looked at Jack with contempt for a moment, then his features softened. "Yes, master."

He pushed the man away and got into the car. The others clambered in, leaving Jack naked on the side of the road.

"You coming?" Michael asked.

Jack looked again at the soldiers who were now only 100 metres away. Knowles was screaming his name, and next to him was the base commander. *Raymond. That's his name. He wanted to cut me open.* Jack looked at the devastation that had once more been left in his wake. He slid into the car, feeling further away from his family than ever before.

14

Knowles watched as the car sped away. The smoke and wreckage of the vehicles by the gate meant that they had no way of giving chase.

146

Raymond was spitting orders into his radio. Knowles jogged past the wreckage, tried not to look at the crushed soldiers but failed. *More dead on British soil. Jesus.* The driver of the car was sitting on the side of the road, holding his arm.

"You OK?" Knowles called.

"My arm, I think it's broken," the man said. *You should be thankful for that.*

"We've got medics that can look at that. Can you walk?" Knowles looked at him, leaving the sentence hanging, a blank to be filled.

"Marcus," the man said, wincing as he stood. "Did terrorists just steal my car?"

"Something like that."

"Why were they naked? You lot been waterboarding them?"

"No, we leave that to the Americans," Knowles said. "Come on, let's get you some help. What's the registration of your car? We'll soon track them."

Marcus rattled off the registration as Knowles helped him back across the road and through the wreckage.

"Don't look," Knowles said. Marcus did and was promptly sick. The smell of vomit did nothing to help make the scene more palatable. Knowles called for one of the doctors to come over and then he went to Raymond.

"I have the license plate sir. We can track them."

"We can't give it to the police, Knowles - are you mad? Look what they did to us. Just think what they'd do to the police."

"Sir, the police can track them. They don't have to corner them."

"Yes Knowles, but just how long do you think they will have that car for?"

"Sir-"

"Shut up Knowles. Your friend has just escaped. We have over twenty people dead back here. There is footage of the wolves on the internet. We are fucked, Knowles, completely fucked."

"Yes, sir," Knowles said.

Raymond put his head in his hands, then ran his hands through his hair. He straightened up, visibly pulling himself together. "Knowles, please pass that registration number to the police. Warn them that, under no circumstances are they to engage the occupants. I want to know where they end up, nothing more."

Knowles nodded. "Yes, sir."

Raymond then turned to the soldiers around them and started barking orders again. First priority was to clean the mess around the gatehouse. Once work had started, Raymond marched back to his office. He had lots of phone calls to make.

Chapter 17

1

The day before, Katie drummed her fingers on the laptop, scanning the search results. She wasn't entirely certain what she was looking for, so had started with searching for Simon Foster. In amongst all the Linked In and Facebook profiles had been a small article about the man's death. That had led her to his blog, but it seemed badly written and smug to her. It was also extremely light on details and had an awful lot of supposition within it.

The comments section had been hilarious in its vitriol though, which made her wonder if someone had done a hatchet job on him. Someone called him a 'deluded faggot' and then that person got attacked for being homophobic and so it went. *Fairly standard internet chat stuff.*

She then tried Doctor Baxter, the man killed in Barnstaple Hospital the night that Jack had been declared dead. This led to lots of plastic surgeons and, bizarrely, the picture of a spider with a human head. It was from some comic, but she clicked off that search quickly anyway. At the bottom of the first page of search results was a link to the North Devon Journal featuring a story about the death of Doctor Baxter and the mayhem that had ensued soon after.

She clicked onto that story and found the name of the detective she had met. Detective Sergeant James Wilson according to the news article, which also included details of the man's death. She had a momentary pang of guilt that she had forgotten his name. *Someone's son.* She typed 'James

Wilson' into Google. A footballer apparently. She read on, clicking onto page two of the results and there she found a police report. It was an obituary. She read it anyway, but it told her nothing relevant. Katie made a cup of tea, checking that Josh was still asleep, then sat down at the computer again. Sunlight streamed in through the windows, making her tilt the screen to avoid the glare.

Katie went back to the North Devon Journal and clicked back through the articles at around the time of the supposed wolf attack in Barnstaple. The Journal's archive was surprisingly thorough and it took a while to sift through them all. Eventually, she found an interview with Detective Wilson. In it he told of the desperate search for the animal before it could attack any more people. He mentioned that the animal was probably wounded because it had been shot by a soldier on leave.

Her heart started hammering, but she forced herself to read on.

Wilson had praised the soldier, saying that without his actions, more people could have been hurt. Peter Knowles. His name was Peter Knowles. Katie gave a shout of excitement, then tapped his name into the search engine.

There were approximately eleven million results for Peter Knowles.

2

She hit the laptop in frustration, then composed herself. She knew she didn't want to read about footballers, whether they were Jehovah's Witnesses or not, so she refined the search and typed in 'Peter Knowles UK army'.

The first hit was now Forces' War Records. That was protected by a pay wall so she returned to her search. She found other sites that promised to give the information, but again, only if she paid. Others said that no current serving records would be made public. Obvious, really, but frustrating all the same.

Next she tried Facebook, but again there were millions of Peter Knowles on record and most of them hadn't done anything more interesting than eat toast for breakfast or share a positive message about the world. *Typical Facebook crap.* Were soldiers even allowed to be on Facebook?

She didn't know. There was so much about finding people she didn't know. Maybe she should hire a professional – there must be a private detective somewhere in Exeter or maybe Plymouth. She was saved from googling that by Josh waking with his usual insistent crying.

The phone rang as she picked him up and she ignored it, letting the answering machine kick in instead. It was Karen, calling to insist that she go for another run. She would be there in half an hour.

3

Despite her intentions and vow to herself, the woods were too close to her house to ignore as a place to run. Katie set off and knew she was running too fast. The path went downhill, going deeper into the woods. Her breathing became ragged and she could feel her legs burning already. She forced herself to slow down. Thick trees combined to make the day seem darker, grimmer somehow, despite the sunlight. She fell into a rhythm, already feeling the frustration of the morning dissipate. The ground passed swiftly and comfortably underfoot and, before she realised, she was running up the hill in the middle of the woods. The hill worked against her, slowing her further, so she gritted her teeth and accelerated until she reached the summit.

Katie waited there, not breathing hard anymore but sweating slightly. She looked back down the hill, which looked even steeper from her vantage point. *Making progress.* The view was pleasant here, not stunning or spectacular like lots of places in Devon, but it still beat looking at a skyline of a city. To her left, in the periphery of her vision, something yellow fluttered on the breeze. She glanced over at it and realised it was the hole in the ground, still taped off with warning signs. *What happened Jack? What really happened?*

There were no easy answers waiting there for her, so she ran on, getting back to the entrance in her best time since starting running again. Without thinking, she carried on past the entrance, running back down the path and starting another loop.

By the time Katie had finished the extra loop, the sweat was pouring from her and she was panting. Her legs had felt the effort going up the hill the second time and she was grateful when the gate came back into view.

She climbed into her car, opened all the windows and drove home. By the time she reached the house, her breathing was back to normal.

4

Karen was cuddling Josh, pulling faces at him and making silly noises. She shook her head, making her cheeks wobble and Josh laugh. Katie smiled at them whilst she took her trainers off.

"He is so gorgeous, Katie."

"Thank you."

"He was bound to be, with you as his mum. You're looking hot, girl."

"I am. Hard run."

"Ho ho, funny girl. That's not what I meant."

Katie smiled at her friend. She had never been very good at accepting compliments, a hang up from her awkward teenage years with short, spiky, blue hair. *It had been a good look. Maybe.*

"You mind if I shower?"

"No, carry on. I've got nothing planned today. Me and the little man were just having some fun." She shook her head again, drawing another laugh from Josh. "I'll get the kettle on."

5

Sipping tea, with a pint glass of water next to her, Katie sank into the sofa. It would need replacing soon, but for now it moulded perfectly to her body. Karen had the TV on, so they watched mindless daytime shows for a while, chatting happily. The news came on, full of the usual human misery and then the local news. The third item made Katie sit up straight.

"Oh my God, it's Jack," she cried.

Karen looked up from Josh. The picture on the screen was of the prisoner who had escaped from Dartmoor a couple of days ago. The report said that the man had been found running away from a lorry at a checkpoint. The driver gave a short interview where he said that the prisoner had jumped him and forced him to drive to London. The driver, a bald man carrying too much weight, was sweating and looked like he was about to have a heart attack. The brief interview finished, and the news anchor talked over a sketch of the escaped prisoner.

Karen looked at the drawing on screen. "It can't be honey, he's-"

"Don't say it," Katie warned.

"You need to face up to this, Katie, sweetheart. It's destroying you."

Katie didn't say anything. She pressed rewind on the television and then paused it at the picture of the prisoner. "Look at him. It's Jack."

Karen took in all the details of the prisoner: long hair, mountain man beard, dark circles under his eyes and tried to marry that with the smiling picture of Jack on the wall. In that photograph, he was holding Katie, both of them grinning from ear to ear: their wedding day.

"Katie, please, honey," she started, but then realised that Katie was crying.

"It looks nothing like him does it?"

Karen shook her head slowly.

"Oh God, I'm seeing him everywhere."

Karen moved closer and patted her friend's shoulder, a manoeuvre made more difficult by Josh. He reached his arms out, and Katie took him. She kissed his forehead lots of times, tears rolling down her cheeks.

"You will get through this," Karen said.

"It hurts. Every day, it hurts."

"It will get better."

"When? How do you know?"

"You can't put a timescale on these things. You know that."

"It's been months, Karen, and it still feels like he should walk in, complaining about work," Katie said. "Sometime, I miss hearing just how shit year ten have been today."

"We're here for you, Katie, me and John. Anything we can do, we're here."

Katie tried to smile but failed. "I'm lucky to have you. I'm sorry."

"No need for apologies, you'd do the same for me."

Now Katie did succeed in smiling.

"I'll make us some lunch," Karen said, "and then we'll take the little man for a walk, get some air."

"I've had lots of air already."

"I know. I was going to steer us to the pub."

6

Later, when Josh was in his cot and fast asleep, Katie poured a large glass of wine and opened the laptop again. She didn't need the drink, having had several glasses earlier, but it made her feel better. *Best be careful with that.* She searched the news websites, scanning them for details of the escaped prisoner on Dartmoor. Most of them had nothing, or if they did, the story was already buried under the weight of news delivered that day. Eventually, she found a piece hidden between a story about hundreds of people taking part in a river swim and some photographs of an otter on the BBC Devon website.

Katie clicked on the image of the prisoner to enlarge it. Using her hands, she covered the long hair and beard, focussing on the eyes. The dark circles made it hard to clearly see them, but they were Jack's eyes – of that she was certain. She read the story. The man had tried to run and he'd been shot. He was now at an undisclosed location under armed guard whilst he recovered. The police had issued a statement thanking the public for their diligence and announcing that they were now safe.

Several things about the article bugged Katie and it took her a moment to realise what it was. First, no-one was named. The prisoner was nameless as was the truck driver who had picked up the dangerous man. *Wouldn't he be hailed as a hero now?* The reason was obvious, now she thought about it: the driver now couldn't be traced. Second, this was supposedly a dangerous man on Dartmoor. Wouldn't that be on the national news? There should be reporters everywhere on Dartmoor, but she could only find this one tiny article.

"He is alive," she said.

Chapter 18

1

They stopped for clothes, stealing them from a washing line. None of them fitted Sally, so they stopped at a shop advertising itself as clothes for the larger frame. They left a poor girl quivering in the stock room before they took clothes for the big woman. Jack insisted they only took one outfit. He also made a mental note of the shop.

Two cars were stolen: one in Tunbridge Wells and the next in East Grinstead. Jack had never been to East Grinstead before and intended to never go again.

Sally sat in the passenger seat, Michael and Jack in the back. The other man, Scott, drove. They were crawling around the M25.

"We should get off here as soon as possible," Michael said. "They will be looking for us."

"They don't know we're in this car," Jack said.

"It's only a matter of time before it is reported stolen," Michael said.

"Where're we going?" Scott asked. "Are we meeting the others in London?"

Michael shook his head, then said, "No. The packs of London are not what they were. Something to do with our new friend here."

"I had nothing to do with that," Jack said and was immediately disappointed with how petulant he sounded.

"Callum used to run London," Michael said. "It was his town. Now he's gone." He didn't finish the sentence, just shrugged.

"Everyone has scattered, gone into hiding," Sally said. "Maybe we could unite them all."

Michael shook his head. "No, leave them. If they survived then they are cowards who ran away or cowards who did not go with Callum to rescue Jack. Either way, they are no use to us."

"It was a bloodbath," Jack said. He remembered the scene, the aftermath of the helicopter attacks on the pack of wolves. The army was probably still cleaning up and trying to identify people from the body parts. *Far too many people died that day.*

"So where are we going?" Scott asked again.

"I think we should go abroad," Michael said. "It's far easier to disappear on the continent. I lived there for years without any problems and without going hungry."

"West," Jack said.

Michael looked at him with eyebrows raised. "The army will find us if we stay here Jack."

"I want to see my family."

"Don't they think you're dead?" Michael said. "That's what Bryant said."

"They do. I want to see *them*; they don't need to see *me*."

"What about Bryant?" Sally asked.

Michael scowled. "Bryant has made his choice."

"Wait, you know Bryant?" Jack said. He was feeling uncomfortable, and it wasn't just the casual stealing that had happened that morning. Something about Michael seemed off. A few years of teaching had given Jack an inbuilt sense of people: who was trustworthy and who was not.

"No, we met him," Michael smiled. "Briefly."

"When did you meet him?"

"You taking the piss?"

Jack looked more confused. The sudden aggression increased his discomfort.

"Michael." It was all Sally needed to say and the cloud in Michael's expression disappeared.

"I've been unconscious for I don't know how long. They were going to cut me open."

"I apologise, Jack. I had no idea." Michael had a large grin back in place.

"We met Bryant in a service station," Sally said. "He turned his back on us."

"He has no idea of his power, of what he can do," Michael said.

"He wants my help," Jack said. "If Bryant turned his back on you, then maybe it's because he can't control it yet." *The man is a killer. If he rejected them, why haven't I?*

"With just you at our head, we could rule the country. With both of you-" Michael said, not finishing his sentence, but there was a gleam in his eyes.

Jack swallowed hard. "I heard that before," he said.

"Callum?"

Jack nodded. Michael waved his hand dismissively.

"He was an idiot."

Sally snorted. "He banished you, and now he's an idiot."

"Sally, I do not remember speaking to you."

The fat woman blanched and looked out of the window.

"Why did he banish you?" Jack's heart was beating faster now. *Even Callum wanted nothing to do with him either. Shit.* Jack had met Callum for no more than ten minutes, but it had been enough.

"He didn't banish me," Michael said, "I had to leave the country for a while."

"That doesn't really answer my question."

"I killed some people. Callum didn't like it." Michael shrugged: no big deal.

"Who did you kill?"

"Couple I found dogging in a car park. Three blokes wanking off whilst they were sat in the car." He smiled at the memory. "I changed their definition of dogging that night."

He killed five people in one night. Christ.

"How was I supposed to know that one of the wankers was a peer with a seat in the House of Lords?" Michael chuckled. "He did taste good though, more tender than the normal folk."

158

Jack fell silent as they swallowed up the miles. *What the hell am I doing?*

2

"Stop here," Jack said. Scott pulled over outside a garage. They were at a crossroads. The garage dominated the left-hand side of the road, with a large forecourt and big workshop behind it. Two cars on the forecourt had 'for sale' signs hanging on them. The main road ran uphill away from the garage, and the street in front of it led into the village.

"So, this is your village? You lived here?"

"Yeah."

"Christ, no wonder you left."

"It's a nice place."

"Sure. What do you do for entertainment when you're not shagging your sister?"

"Really, Michael?"

"Relax. Just kidding. How is wanking with six fingers?"

Jack ignored him. "There's a couple of pubs and a shop up there." He gestured to the road on the left."

"Well that's just awesome, Jack," Michael smirked.

"My house is just down there," he said, pointing down the street opposite the car and garage.

"What now?" Michael asked.

"I just want to see them."

"So you said, but this is a bad idea." He looked at Sally. "Maybe we should do a pub crawl?"

Jack got out of the car, pulling a hood over his head and walking to the top of his road with head bowed. People were moving around in the garage, but he didn't think they'd pay any attention to him and he was moving away from it. He hurried over the main road and stood at the top of his street. An unexpected lump came to his throat. *It's just a street Jack. It's the people in it who are important.*

He could now see his house. The porch looked in need of dire repair, and the front bedroom window had polythene strapped across it. He winced at the memory.

159

A car emerged from the driveway next to his house. Katie looked both ways, eased out and then turned away from him, accelerating down the street. The lump intensified.

Jack turned and jogged back to the car and jumped in. "I have to go to the woods."

"How far is that?" Scott asked, looking at the petrol gauge.

"I can run."

"Jack," Michael started.

"No, just leave it, Michael. I am doing this. Stay here." He slammed the door shut and ran back across the road. A small path, almost invisible from the road, led through to the fields that ran behind Jack's street. He jogged down the path, jumping the fence easily. The fields stretched as far as the eye could see, and disused paths ran to the woods. Katie had been wearing running kit, and he was fairly sure that was where she was headed.

As soon as he crossed the first field, the tree line swallowed him up. He quickly undressed and stashed his clothes behind a large tree. Then he changed and set off for the woods at a furious pace.

3

Katie ran, despite the lingering hangover. She was already getting stronger, could feel it in her legs and lungs, but was still wary of overdoing it. *Get to the stage where this run is easy, then up the miles.*

It was four o'clock and the woods were deserted. She didn't mind: no people meant no-one looking at her in sympathy or muttering about her.

The problem with living in a small village was everyone knew her and what she had been through, regardless of whether she actually knew them. Just going to the shop had turned into a gauntlet of curtain twitching. *At least the streets are usually quiet.*

She reached the bottom of the hill – the one Karen had already dubbed Cardio Hill - then gritted her teeth and pushed herself to run up it as fast as she could. The police tape blurred by and she studiously ignored it. With a roar, she crested the hill and stopped running, hands on knees panting. It felt good.

A twig snapped behind her and she turned to look. The tree line was dark, even though the sun was beating down. All was quiet. *No birds. There are no birds singing here.*

Her heart was beating fast now, faster than just because of the run.

More sounds of sticks breaking came from the tree line, but she didn't move. *It'll be a deer.*

Even as the thought formed in her mind, she knew it wasn't true and she knew she had to run.

Now.

But it was too late. Coming out of the tree line, slowly emerging into the sunlight, was an enormous wolf.

4

Josh was asleep upstairs and Karen sang to herself as she made a cup of tea. The kitchen was as familiar as her own and she was soon sitting down watching some awful daytime TV programme. It seemed to consist of people shouting at each other, whilst the caption read 'twins bed the same girl, but who's the father?'

Sometimes Karen thought that daytime TV was deliberately awful to try and force people back to work.

She heard a knock at the door, the noise so loud, she jumped and spilt some tea over herself.

"Dammit," she said and brushed the liquid off herself as she opened the door.

A good looking man and an obese woman stood smiling on the doorstep. Looking at the woman, Karen felt better about giving up the running. She had some way to go before she should be that worried.

"Hello, is Mrs Stadler in?" the man said.

"No, she's not," Karen said. Later she would wonder how the man knew she wasn't Mrs Stadler, but by then it would be far too late.

5

Michael drummed his fingers on the seat in front of him.

"Scott, fill the car up with petrol, please. We may need to leave in a hurry," he said, tapping the younger man on the shoulder.

"Aren't we waiting for Jack?" Scott asked.

"Yes," Michael said, "but please do it."

"We don't have any money," Scott said.

"I'm sure you'll think of something," Michael said. "Come on Sally."

He got out of the car and crossed the road. Once there, he waited for Sally and then they walked down the street together. He stopped outside the fourth house.

"Are you sure?" Sally asked.

"Can't you smell it? Besides, look at the window." Jack had told them of how he had run away from his family after killing the wolf that was there to eat them. The man had even cried for a bit. *Pathetic.*

A short flight of steps led to the dilapidated porch. Michael knocked on the door, three loud, sharp raps. After a moment, the door was opened by a large black woman. *Well, larger than me, but way smaller than Sally.*

"Hello, is Mrs Stadler in?" Michael asked, smile in place on his lips.

"No, she's not. Sorry," said the woman. "She's just popped out, but will be back soon. Can I help?"

Michael looked at Sally, then said, "We're old friends of Mrs Stadler's. Would you mind if we wait for her?"

A frown crossed the woman's face and Michael knew he'd made a mistake.

"You university friends?"

"Something like that."

"Only she didn't say she was expecting anyone."

"No, we were just passing and thought we'd pop in."

The woman laughed. "No-one just passes through Huntleigh. What are you? Press or ambulance chasers?"

"I beg your pardon?"

"Look, just go away, ok? Katie doesn't need any more grief."

Michael's hand shot out so fast that Karen barely saw him move. She screamed, falling back from the door with blood pouring out of the gash on her face.

Sally saw the claws for a second before they disappeared.

"I didn't know you could do that," she said in awe.

Michael shrugged. "You just have to focus." He stepped inside, pushing the screaming woman back into the small hallway. Sally closed the door behind them. Michael smiled again at the woman.

"I think you'll find the ambulances chase *us*."

6

Scott replaced the pump and looked at the price more through habit than anything else. He didn't have any money, so the fact that this price was bordering on the obscene meant nothing.

The garage had a small shop next to the pumps and he could see an old woman watching him. He smiled at her and waved. *Shit.*

He opened the door to the shop and made a play of scanning the shelves. *What am I going to do? What would Michael do?*

"Nice day," the woman said. Now he was inside, she didn't look that old. Mid-fifties, maybe.

"Yep," he said.

"You on holiday?"

"Yep." He spied something he could use on the bottom shelf and picked it up.

"You need a new battery too, huh? That's bad luck on a holiday, love."

Scott swung the car battery as hard as he could. The woman was so surprised she didn't even scream. The battery connected with a thud, then a crack as the woman's skull shattered. She fell to the floor, blood pouring out of the hollow in her head. He leapt over the counter and hit her again and again until the blood and brains were indistinguishable on the cheap lino floor.

Panting, Scott stood up and then he heard the door open behind him. He turned quickly to see an old man in dirty

163

mechanics overalls standing in the doorway. The man's mouth was open. Behind him were two other mechanics. These two looked much younger and fitter.

"What the-" the old man got as far as saying.

In for a penny. Scott let the wolf burst out of him.

7

The path that Jack was on ran through the wilder section of the local woods. Ferns lined the paths and he could smell badgers and foxes as he ran past. Squawking calls of danger, the birds flew out of the trees as he approached. He ignored them and ran on into the valley. The path was little used and was overgrown in parts. Foxgloves adorned the way as he ran into a tunnel created by trees. Flecks of sunlight highlighted the flowers and the deep green of the leaves.

Soon the trees gave way to a broader track that skirted the woods on his right and fields on his left. This path led further into the valley before rising to Huntleigh Woods proper. He jumped the stream at the bottom. In winter, this could be a raging river, but right now it was just a trickle - not enough even to warrant stopping for a drink.

A short path led up from the stream, this one more maintained than the one he had just run on. There, the smell hit him like a truck. He was not alone. Anger coursed through every fibre of his being and his fur stood out from his body. He stopped and sniffed, focusing his senses.

The *other* one was less than five hundred metres away.

And underneath that scent, a much more familiar one.

Perfume.

8

Katie let out a low moan when she saw the wolf. Its head was down and it glowered at her. Saliva dripped out of its mouth and it was growling.

At me, it's growling at me.

Katie couldn't move. The wolf was less than one hundred metres away and getting closer with every second.

"Leave me alone," she screamed. *Good one, Katie, that'll work.*

The wolf raised its head and howled. Katie flushed with adrenaline and fear as it was answered by more howls, these from behind her and to the sides, within the trees. All around her. She glanced over her shoulder and saw that the pathway was clear. *For now.*

Without warning, the wolf suddenly turned, looking back at the trees. It stood there for a moment, watching the tree line.

Now, run. Now's your chance. Run.

She did.

9

The Wolf heard the howl and the answering chorus and picked up its pace. It was in the woods now, on the main path. It hurtled forward, heading for the main scent. The ground blurred past underneath it as it ignored the *other* scent. The path turned uphill, but the Wolf didn't slow at all. It ran on, hoping that it was fast enough.

10

Katie ran as fast as she could, but she knew it was still too slow. She only had two legs after all. Even in her prime, she'd always been a distance runner. She was very far from her prime now, even with the extra exercise she'd been doing.

Fear, however, proved to be a great motivator. She pushed herself on, even with her lungs burning and her legs aching. She rounded a corner on the path, knowing that the car was less than a couple of hundred metres away.

Too far, it's just too far.

She looked over her shoulder and immediately wished she hadn't. Four wolves were chasing her. The biggest was at the back, and it kept sniffing the air.

"Fuck!" she screamed.

Standing in front of the gates was an even bigger wolf.

She was trapped.

11

The wolves skidded to a stop and growled at Katie, heads low, teeth bared. Katie looked from them to the other one, panic rising. She felt sick and was panting hard. The only way out was deep into the trees, but then what? No-one was here, no-one would find her.

She looked at the big wolf, then back at the other four. The biggest one pushed its way to the front of the pack and walked slowly towards her. She backed away, but then remembered that was just leading to the other wolf and she spun.

The other wolf was less than ten metres away. She could almost see the individual strands of thick black fur covering it. The wolf growled, then howled. She covered her ears: it was incredibly loud. She sank to her knees, still panting hard. Even so, she refused to cry.

Katie looked from wolf to wolf.

"Come on then, get on with it!" she roared.

The lone black wolf planted its feet and roared back, but then she realised it wasn't roaring at her.

Three of the wolves were now lying down. The other large – *not large it's fucking enormous oh fuck oh fuck* - black one was still growling. She looked back at the black wolf and stood slowly.

"I've seen you before," she said.

The black wolf walked towards her, not taking its eyes off the other wolf. It stopped by her side and bared its teeth again. Katie moved her hand but then stopped. *You're not seriously going to stroke a wolf are you?*

She backed away, keeping her movements slow. She didn't want to draw attention to herself. Both wolves were intent on each other only. Her back hit something hard and she only just managed to not shriek. It was the gate to the woods.

Now she ran. She turned and sprinted to her car. Delving into her tracksuit bottoms, she pulled out keys and unlocked the car. It beeped loudly and all five wolves looked at her. The black one furthest from her howled.

Swearing, she yanked open the door and jumped in. She was parked facing away from the woods and had to look in the rearview mirror to see what was happening. The wolf that had howled hadn't moved, but all of its pack were standing now.

Suddenly, the wolf closest to her bolted. It took a vital second for her to realise that it was running straight at her.

She shrieked and started the engine, but then the door was open and a naked man jumped in.

"Drive!" he yelled. She didn't really comprehend what was happening. There was no time.

The four wolves were heading straight for her. They were huge in the mirror, all bared teeth and yellow, malevolent eyes. She floored the accelerator and they sped into the lane. The wolves receded in the mirror and then she looked at the man.

"Hi," Jack said. "I can explain everything."

"I really fucking doubt it."

Chapter 19

1

Knowles watched the film again and swore, again. The mobile phone footage showed a fat lady stripping off and then carnage as the wolves ran amok. Conservative estimates put the death toll at more than three hundred, but they were not releasing that figure to the press.

The internet had exploded with more and more copies of the footage being released to social media. The film company cover story was already failing, even though the BBC had confirmed it was a new film coming out at Christmas. They had given the film a title of 'You Don't Know Jack', which proved that somebody, somewhere had a sense of humour. Even with the BBC onside, the social media hysteria was growing.

Now everyone was seeing wolves. It was hard to cut out the obvious bullshit stories from the ones that might be true. An attendant in a shop for big women had been found crying in her changing rooms. That one was probably true as it was near where they'd found the stolen car.

It was the end of the film that held Knowles' interest now. On the phone, buried on the SD card in it, was a much shorter video. It showed Bryant, clearly, and he said, 'Stadler, I'm coming for you.' To make it easier to analyse, the tech people had put all the footage together into one film.

Every time he saw it, it chilled him. Bryant knew exactly where they were keeping Jack, and yet there was no sign of him. If he was coming for Jack, then where was he? Every time he watched it, Knowles grew more and more certain: Bryant was going after Katie.

Raymond had done nothing bar shout orders into his phone. Knowles had watched him for over an hour now but said nothing. He had started to help clean up the base, but Raymond had ordered him to his side so he sat, impotent, whilst others dealt with the shock of that morning.

So many dead.

"Knowles."

It took him a moment to register that Raymond was no longer barking into a telephone.

"Sir."

"This is a mess. We need a rapid solution. We have lost both Originals. Thoughts?" Raymond paused. "And please be candid."

Knowles grinned.

"Like you wouldn't be anyway," Raymond said, with a rueful smile.

"Sir, I think Bryant means to go after Katie Stadler."

"Why?"

"To get Jack's attention. He thinks Jack is here – he doesn't know he's escaped. Bryant only just got away himself. He wouldn't want to come back here."

"Blindingly obvious analysis so far Knowles." Raymond tapped his desk with a pen. "Do you really think Katie Stadler is in danger?"

"Sir, yes. I think Bryant is going there," Knowles looked at his watch, "shit, will already be there."

"But why? He thinks Stadler is here."

"Their meeting didn't go well sir," Knowles said, trying to keep the sarcasm from his voice.

"It did not. But that doesn't mean he is going for Katie."

"No, but I think we should get some men there as soon as. We can't be too careful."

"And what will the press make of us sending troops to a village in Devon?"

Knowles shrugged. *I don't care what the press thinks.*

"A shrug does not fill me with confidence, sergeant."

"Sir, we have tried to contain this for months. We came close, but today means it's out there now. Our cover story hasn't survived the morning." Raymond nodded at this, conceding the point. "It is likely that the existence of the wolves, and our knowledge of them, will all come out over the next few days and weeks. If Katie dies, and people found out we knew and did nothing-" Knowles left the sentence hanging.

"She is only one person, Knowles. Hundreds of people have been killed by these things today alone."

"Yes, but she is the wife of one of them. The poor abandoned wife of the monster-"

"Enough Knowles. Cut the melodrama. I can have a team out there by nightfall. We can get some of the boys up there pretty quickly if we use the helicopters."

"Thank you, sir."

"Why are you thanking me? I am not doing this for you."

"No, sir."

"Dismissed, sergeant. Get some rest." Raymond nodded at the door. "Close it on the way out."

2

Knowles ignored Raymond's advice and went straight to help the men cleaning up the mess by the gates. By the time he got there, the two vehicles had been moved and people were bagging up body parts. Another man was washing the ground, swirls of red running off the concrete into the grass verge.

"We got this sergeant," said the man washing the ground. Knowles recognised him. Evans. The one who had driven Bryant to Devon. The one who had sat outside Collins' room.

"You've done good work," Knowles said. "Cleared it up quick."

"Thank you, sergeant." Evans paused, visibly mulling over whether to say more or not. "There's talk of the men going after them. We want some payback."

Knowles nodded. "I've wanted payback for a couple of weeks, mate."

170

"One of them is your friend," Evans said looking at his feet.

"Friend is stretching it a bit, but yes, I don't think Jack is like the rest of them."

"Why not?"

"Why isn't he like the rest?"

"Yeah."

"I think he's a good man, underneath it all. The thing inside him is trying to change that, but Jack is not letting it." Knowles paused, realising for the first time that he actually did believe that. "I don't think Jack is a threat at all." *Really? No threat at all?*

"What about Bryant?"

"He didn't do this," Knowles gestured around him, "perhaps he is trying to be like Jack."

"He needs to try harder, sergeant." Evans resumed scrubbing, turning his back on Knowles.

Knowles smiled to himself. On any other day, he would have roared at the man for rudeness, but today he just couldn't be bothered. Today, things were unravelling more than at any other point in his life. He felt worse than when he'd been in an ambush in Afghanistan with Carruthers; worse than when his wife had left him for another man; worse than when Claire's face had been ripped apart by Callum a couple of weeks ago. They were at a tipping point here: the wolves were free, the public had knowledge of them and there were two Originals.

He thought of Katie: the look of confusion she had given him the only time they had met. She had shot a wolf, then the Wolf had saved her from another. Knowles had been far too slow getting there and he'd walked into a bloodbath. He'd made things worse by calling the Wolf 'Jack' and then it had run away into the night, jumping through a window and taking half the wall of the bedroom with it when it did so.

Katie had thrown all sorts of questions at him then, but he'd managed to duck most of them. He had taken her into the other bedroom of the house and stationed two soldiers with her. More and more troops arrived in the next few hours, and they cleaned up the house. They put sheets of polythene over the window, then left. He still had moments of regret in leaving her.

He'd been lucky to keep his job, and he still wasn't really sure why he hadn't been court-martialled. But now, here he was again faced with difficult choices. He had to warn Katie; felt sure the wolves - Bryant - were heading to her, but how could he do that? Raymond had told him to rest, not go to Katie, but Raymond didn't know the danger she was in.

"Fuck it," Knowles said out loud, then he went to look for the team that were about to head to Devon.

3

After speaking to his boss, Raymond picked up the phone and dialled a number from memory.

"Major," came the thick northern accent of Doctor Peacock. She was a slim, harsh woman with jet black hair and even darker eyes. Raymond closed her file before answering.

"Doctor, could you give me a sit-rep on the bones?"

"We are no further along than when you called yesterday, sir."

"Have you seen the news, Doctor?"

"Yes, sir. Was it our guy?"

"No, someone new. We need a solution here and we have run out of time."

"Sir, the bones are normal. Big, yes, but clearly canine as outlined in the initial report. We concur that it is probably a direwolf, but as they died out millennia ago, we can't be certain."

"DNA?"

"We're running the sequencers. However, due to the age of the bones we're not getting much that we don't already have from creatures that died around the same period."

"Meaning?"

"The bones are normal. Whatever is happening to these men cannot be scientifically linked to these bones."

"Shit."

"My thoughts exactly, sir."

"We need them destroyed."

172

"Sir?"

He could hear the shock in her voice, but it didn't surprise him. She was a scientist after all.

"Burn the bones, crush them into a pulp, hell I don't care what you do," Raymond said. "I never want to live through a day like this again. Those things have killed hundreds of people in one day. Destroy it, destroy it all."

"Sir, I really think we need to sleep on this and not rush-"

"Dammit, doctor, I gave you an order. Follow it." He hung up, angrily pressing the red button on the phone which was nowhere near as satisfying as slamming a phone down.

Now all we have to do is wipe them all out.

4

Raymond held the file for Stadler in his hands, rereading it again and again. Katie Stadler kept staring at him from her photo, her eyes judging him although they had never met. The next picture was of the baby, Josh. Six months old now with no idea his father was alive. *Probably no idea of what a father actually was.*

What if Knowles was right? What if wolves were on their way to kill her? Raymond glanced at the news, still leading with the massacre at the service station. The reporter was listing all the different rumours as to what had happened and why. It was quite a list at the moment. The bulletin ended with a clear rebuke of the film rumour.

He was expecting the phone to ring at any moment. He'd been put in charge to keep the problem in check, but it had exploded exponentially out of control. Raymond had no-one to blame but himself: Bryant had been brought in by Raymond. Knowles had been kept on, despite the recommendation of court martial from above. Raymond had gone to bat for him and now this.

He remembered the excitement he'd felt at being promoted to Major. The pride. The look on his mother's face: the relief that he had returned from active duty alive and in one piece coupled with the sheer joy at his promotion. His father watched, as ever, silently from a picture on the mantelpiece.

173

Something me and Josh Stadler have in common.

With a roar, Raymond swept all the files off his desk. *Two months. I've been a major for two months.* He had never felt so impotent in his life. *Time to take charge.*

He looked at his watch. The Devon team would not have left yet. Raymond looked around his office, at the mess he had just created and the constant news stream on the television. *There is nothing but trouble for me here. Paperwork and a demotion at best.*

"Fuck it," Raymond said and left his office.

5

Knowles found four men in the armoury. They were signing forms and collecting their kit.

"Mind if I tag along?" Knowles said. The man in charge looked him up and down, disdain clear in his expression.

"Yeah, I do actually. We don't want no wolf lover along for the ride."

"It's Taylor isn't it?"

The man nodded.

"I know I'm only a sergeant, but you speak to me like that again and not only will you be written up, but I will get you on gate duty for the next month. Am I clear?"

"Crystal." The scowl on his face wasn't going away soon. *Maybe it's his natural look.*

"Good. Now, I saw you take on the Wolf."

Taylor nodded again.

"You lost."

"Nothing but a few bruises," Taylor said.

"Sure, but now you've got a better idea of what we're up against." Knowles grinned at each man in turn. "Now, do you mind if I tag along?"

"No, sergeant, it would be an honour to have a man of your *experience* along."

Knowles ignored the emphasis. "It will be my pleasure. Who are your team?"

Taylor introduced the others: Williams, who looked as sullen as Taylor; Hibbard, whose smile was not genuine and Cockbain whose was. They were all dressed in body armour

174

and carried the standard L85 A2, and Hibbard had a grenade attachment under the barrel of his. Williams had a sniper rifle strapped to his back.

"I need one of those," Knowles said to Taylor, indicating the assault rifle.

Taylor sighed and took another L85 A2 out, pushing the forms to Knowles. "Sign your life away, sergeant." The group moved outside, where a shooting range was set up with targets 200 yards away. Each of them took turns to zero their weapons before returning to the armoury so Knowles could collect his body armour.

Knowles strapped his chest armour on and picked up his weapon.

"Don't you want legs and arms as well sergeant?" Williams had a much higher pitched voice than his build suggested. *Poor sod.*

"The wolves will be licking him, not chasing him," Taylor sneered. Knowles grabbed the man by the chest piece and pushed him against the wall, hard.

"I warned you," Knowles said, "now cut the shit."

"Let Taylor go, sergeant."

They all turned at the new voice, and Knowles swore again.

"We are going to see Katie Stadler and make sure she does not come to any mischief."

Mischief? Seriously? What century does he think it is? Wait- "We?" Knowles asked.

Raymond smiled, and it was as genuine as Hibbard's. "I'm coming with you."

Chapter 20

1

The entrance to a farm approached rapidly and Katie slammed on the brakes, swinging the car into the gateway with a squeal of tyres. Her heart was still hammering in her chest and her dead husband was sitting next to her, as naked as their wedding night.

"You're alive," she said. It sounded lame, even to her.

Jack looked over his shoulder, back up the hill that they'd driven down at a speed that would have impressed Lewis Hamilton. He couldn't see the wolves. The other Original was not following - he would have known.

"Yes."

"How?"

"It's a long story."

"Fucking try me, Jack."

He told her. Everything.

"I knew it."

That response he had not expected.

"That night, when the wolves came. The soldier called you Jack. Who is that man, Jack?"

"His name is Knowles, Peter Knowles. He was kind to me, pretty much the only soldier who was." *Him and his dead girlfriend, who would still be alive if it wasn't for me.* He left that bit out.

"Why did you run?"

"I was scared. I don't know enough about this," he waved his hand at his body.

176

"Are you dangerous?"

He nodded. "Very. I couldn't risk hurting you or Josh."

"You remember his name then."

Jack looked so hurt that she immediately regretted the words.

"The whole time I was with the army, I only worked with them because I wanted to come home to you. It was the only reason, Katie. You have to believe me."

"But you're not home, Jack. You're not with us."

"No, when I saw you," he choked back sudden tears, "I knew I couldn't stay. I knew I'd put you in danger."

"So what was that just now?"

"Proof that I was right to run away." He paused, looking out of the window and blinking away more tears. "There is another guy who wants to be like me. He seems to have found some friends."

"Were they going to kill me?"

Jack shook his head. "I don't think so. I think they wanted you to get to me."

"They wanted me? What about Josh?"

All the colour drained from her face so quickly it was almost comical.

Almost.

"Oh, shit. Josh. Karen." Katie gunned the engine and pulled into the lane. Their house was less than a mile and yet forever away.

2

Between Katie's house and the neighbours, sat a driveway. Katie pulled onto it, nose first and was out of the car before Jack could say anything. He leapt out after her, not caring that he was naked. She threw open the back door and ran into the house.

"Karen?" she shouted.

Jack stepped into the kitchen and was assaulted by smells. Katie had eaten toast for breakfast. Last night she had made chilli. Her perfume was everywhere. He could smell baby lotion and the chamomile cream used for nappy rash. *Where's the dog?* Jack looked around the kitchen, searching for signs of her before he remembered. *Poor Ginny.* The man who had killed her was also dead – one of the wolves that either Jack or Katie had killed the last time he had been in the house.

But underneath, beneath the familiar scents, there were more smells, unfamiliar and yet-

"Katie - wait!"

Too late. Katie had run into the living room and screamed.

Jack followed her, every muscle tense. The room was as he remembered: sofas in the same place; television on its black glass stand that looked great unless it was dusty - which was all the time; books on the bookcase, including his science fiction books and the grandfather clock against the back wall.

Blood covered everything. It smeared the walls, filled the carpet with a wetness that squelched as he walked and he knew his feet would now be red. A dismembered body lay in the middle of the room, completely missing its head and left arm. Chunks were missing from the legs and remaining arm. The legs had been severed and a foot lay by itself on the largest sofa. A trail of intestines led to the door to the hallway where it abruptly stopped.

Katie was still screaming but was now also crying.

"Katie, come here," Jack said softly. He put his arm around his wife and steered her toward the hallway. He sat her on the bottom stair and touched her lightly on the shoulder. "Stay here," he said. "You have to be quiet."

She stared at him, eyes wide and already red from crying. He could see she was about to explode in anger at him. Jack leant forward, and touched his forehead to hers and started whispering.

"You have to be quiet, babe, please," he said. Jack broke contact and looked around the kitchen. He stood, picked up the largest knife they had from its stand on the counter and pressed it into her hand. "They might still be here."

She sat on the step, still sobbing but much more quietly, clutching the knife tightly in both hands. Jack started to walk upstairs.

3

Memories assaulted Jack as he moved. Carrying Katie across the threshold, both of them giggling as he struggled. *Wouldn't be a problem now.* Opening wedding presents, excited about the future. The first time Karen and John had come to dinner. John had drunk too much whiskey and they had ended the night trying to catch a frog that had somehow got into the house. Carrying Josh up to his Moses basket on his return from the maternity unit. The last time he was here, as the Wolf, racing to save his wife and child. That night, blood had spattered the walls, but he had not stopped to question *how* then.

There was blood on the same walls again now, although this time it was the blood of a friend. Jack felt sick but pushed himself on. *How many more people are going to die?* The carnage in his house was incredible. *I am going to kill you, Bryant.*

And how are you going to do that, Jackie boy? He is Special Forces. He kills people like you just for fun.

Jack shook away the other voice in his head. Bryant would pay, that was the only thing he was sure of.

Four doors led off the landing: one to his right, one in the wall in front of him and a further two to his left. He opened the right hand one first, but it was their spare room and had only a double bed in it. Their parents stayed in there when they visited, and he had a moment where he wondered if his parents had ever visited in the time that he was supposed to be dead. He was surprised to see the bed unmade, and Katie's toiletries on the chest of drawers that hadn't been in there when he'd last left the house.

The middle room was the one they had set aside for Josh's nursery, so many months ago. With a deep breath, he pushed open the door to the room.

Josh's cot was empty, with a small amount of blood on the blankets. Jack stifled a shout and looked more closely.

The blood was two small smears, and Jack realised that it was from someone picking Josh up. Karen's blood, covering the hands of whoever had Josh now. He looked around the room, but there was nothing there, no clues as to where they might have gone.

He peered into his and Katie's room, which was colder than the rest of the house. The window was covered with a sheet of polythene, and he winced.

Of course. At least he now knew why Katie was sleeping in the other room.

On the wall opposite the door, written in blood, were the words:

We have your child.
Bring us your husband.
The pub.

4

Jack sank to the floor with a thump. All the air rushed out of his lungs at once and he couldn't breathe for a moment. His heart was hammering hard in his chest and he felt the tell-tale tingle in his arms as thick black fur sprouted along them.

"No," he bellowed, but with a voice that wasn't his own. Deeper, more guttural. Jack shook his head, feeling his face elongate. Claws were emerging on the tips of his fingers and he roared again.

He forced deep breaths into his lungs, keeping the air down, focusing on his breathing and counting. Triangle numbers this time. He felt his face return to normal and saw the fur receding faster than the claws. *Not today, not in this house, not in this room.*

He heard a gasp behind him and turned to see Katie in the doorway. She was shaking, tears streaming down her face. He couldn't tell if they were fresh or not.

"Katie, I will sort this out."

She shook her head. "They have my son. Who are they, Jack?"

"People," he said, trying to keep his voice even. *My son, not our son.* That hurt.

"Wolves?"

He nodded. "Bad ones. It's my fault, Katie. I'm the reason they came here. I told you I was dangerous now."

"Find them, Jack. Find them and get my son back."

This last was said at barely above a whisper, not that it mattered with Jack's hearing. She turned and left the room, walking away from him almost on tiptoe.

After a moment, he heard the bedroom door open, and the tell-tale creak of the wardrobe door. *I should call Knowles.* Jack forced himself to stand and follow his wife. He found her sitting on the floor in the bedroom, a shotgun in her arms. She was loading cartridges into it carefully.

"Shit, Katie," he started. She gave him a look and he shut up. She rarely got angry, but when she did it was best to be quiet. He had learned that years before.

"I am going to kill them if they have hurt him," she said, a quiet firmness to her voice.

"I need some clothes, babe." The words were out before he realised what he had said.

"Don't you fucking 'babe' me!" she snarled. "We were fine whilst you were dead. Karen was alive and," her face creased up and she started to cry again. "We need to ring the police." She pushed past him, still holding the shotgun. "Your clothes are where you left them."

"Katie, wait, don't ring the police."

"Why the fuck not?"

"I'm supposed to be dead."

"So? Karen is dead. Dead, Jack. They have Josh. Nothing else matters," she said. "I don't even know who 'they' are."

"If you ring the police, they will either think you're mad or they will come."

"Good. I want them to."

"No, Katie. If the police meet these wolves it will be a bloodbath." He touched her arm. "Please, no more death, not because of me."

"If they have hurt Josh," she began.

"I don't mean them. No-one innocent."

She nodded at him, seeing the sense in what he was saying. Her lips were thin and she wore a frown like she was used to it. "Get dressed," she said, then ran down the stairs, leaving him.

He went to their old bedroom and looked in the chest of drawers. She hadn't thrown any of his stuff away and he was soon dressed in jeans and a t-shirt.

The pub. Bryant had taken Josh to the pub. Attract Katie to a public place, capture her too. Bryant didn't know that Jack was in Huntleigh too, or at least he hadn't when he'd taken Josh, so would he now change his plan? Would he still be in the pub? Safety in a public place?

What if we both lose control, like in Raymond's office?

Jack didn't think that was likely: they had met once and both now knew what the other was. There would be no surprises.

Something else was niggling away at the back of Jack's mind the whole time he was fixated on the pub and it lurched into the foreground now.

Where's Michael?

Jack slumped to the floor again, once more struggling for breath. *Oh no.*

Bryant was in the woods. He had three wolves with him. No baby. He could not have run back here before Jack and Katie arrived: it was too far, even for an Original and allowing for the time spent in the car. They would have seen him leave: Jack would have smelt him. An Original's scent would have over-powered the reek of blood and death in the room.

Michael.

Josh had been taken by Michael.

5

Katie had the phone in her hand when he got downstairs. She looked at him vacantly then resumed staring at the phone. The shotgun was on the sofa next to her.

"I have to ring John," she said.

Jack shook his head. "And tell him what?"

"She's dead, Jack."

"I know," Jack said, "but I think we leave that to the police."

"Jack-"

"No, for God's sake, would you listen for once," Jack said, far more sharply than he intended.

"Don't shout at me."

"Sorry, I just-" He stopped. No words were going to help. "Look, I think a man called Michael has Josh."

"Who is he Jack?"

"He's a psycho," Jack said. "He's very dangerous."

"Is he," she paused, "like you?"

"No. Not quite."

"What does that mean?"

"It means I can handle him."

"I'm coming with you."

"No," Jack shook his head. "It's too dangerous."

"Fuck you, Jack. I'm coming."

She dropped the phone and picked up the shotgun.

"Once Josh is safe, I am ringing the police, no arguments."

"Katie, please-"

"No arguments," she repeated. "Now, let's go. I'm not staying in this house alone. I want Josh."

Jack sighed. "Ok, ok, but please do what I say. And try not to shoot anyone."

6

Michael looked around the workshop and gave a satisfied nod. "Good work Scott."

The other man beamed, a strange sight given he was naked and covered in blood.

"What do you think, young Josh?" Michael held the baby out, spinning slowly to survey the carnage in the garage.

Five bodies lay at various points in the workshop. All had been ripped apart and their blood covered the walls and cars. Two cars were up on ramps, their wheels at eye level, but even these were smeared with blood.

"Most impressive," Michael said. The baby started crying, and Sally laughed at the sound.

"You're so funny Michael."

183

"Now, Scott, how do you propose we cover this up?" Michael said. His voice was calm, and his smile was still in place, but something had changed.

"We could lock the garage up. We'll be long gone before anyone finds out," Sally said.

"I wasn't talking to you," Michael said. He did not raise his voice and his smile did not waver. Josh cried even harder, arms and legs out straight from his body.

"We could lock the garage up," Scott said, his voice cracking. "We'll be long gone before anybody finds out."

Michael's smile was now beatific. "Excellent plan, Scott. Make it happen." Michael changed his grip on Josh, cuddling him close to his chest. "Shush little one, unkey Mike is going to look after you till Daddy gets here." He strolled towards the entrance of the garage.

"Where are you going?" Sally asked.

"I have a few phone calls to make."

7

"Why do we have a baby anyway?" Scott asked. He was rummaging through the pockets of the dead, looking for keys.

"Leverage," Sally said. She was leaning on one of the cars, examining her fingernails. A small piece of gristle was stuck there, much to her chagrin.

"But he was with us," Scott said, then: "Yes!" He stood with keys in his hands. A white-haired man lay at his feet, considerably older than the others in the workshop. The owner.

"And how long do you think he was going to stay with us once he saw his wife again?"

Scott didn't answer. In front of him was a large opening that cars were brought through. He pushed a button on the wall and the shutter started to roll down slowly. "Come on," he muttered. A cool breeze came through the opening, reminding him that he was still naked. He stood to the side, hoping that the shadows would hide him from passers-by. It was, of course, highly unlikely that anyone would come by: Huntleigh was the dictionary definition of a sleepy Devon village. Scott was already itching to leave.

The shutter rolled into place with a click. *First entrance to this place secure.* At the back of the garage was a similar roller door and he closed this one too. At the rear of the garage were some lockers, and Scott looked through them. He found a very old pair of oil covered shorts and a t-shirt. *It'll do.* He dressed quickly and then went back out to the shop. Michael was talking on the phone, and Scott checked the keys in the door. They were the right ones and the door locked easily.

"We should go," Scott said as Michael hung up.

"Yes, the others will be here soon," Michael said. "We should get to the pub before Jack discovers my handiwork."

"Others?" Scott said.

"I have a plan, Scott. We have our friends joining us."

"Friends?" Scott looked bewildered. "I thought everyone was dead."

Michael laughed and tickled Josh under the chin. The baby giggled. "My name is legion, for we are many."

"What?"

"Forget it," Michael said, waving his hand.

"Didn't Jack say there were two pubs? How will he know which one to go to?"

"Don't worry about that. He'll find us." Michael smiled again. "Come on, let's go. They will be here within the hour."

8

Jack stepped onto the drive and looked over at their neighbours' house. It was dark, but that meant nothing at this time of day. Katie came out behind him, shotgun hidden under a long coat. It was warm outside, despite the cool breeze. In the distance, the church bells chimed, reminding Jack of the last time he had set foot in the churchyard. It was not a happy memory. *Somebody died that day.* He put his arm around Katie and for a moment she didn't resist. It didn't last long. They walked along the street, up the short hill that led to the garage and then into the village beyond. Jack glanced at the garage, a familiar scent hitting him.

"Oh no," he said quietly. Katie followed his gaze. The garage was shut and all lights off. She looked at her watch.

"That's early," she said, then looked at Jack. "What is it?"

Jack watched a man get out of his car and press his face against the glass of the office.

"Something bad," he said. "Let's go before this gets worse."

The colour drained from Katie's face, and Jack got a sense that she was realising, possibly for the first time, just how bad this could be: that Karen's would not be the only death today.

"What if they're not in the pub?"

"Then we look elsewhere," he shrugged. "I'll find them."

"And you're now an expert in baby snatching and where to hide?"

He ignored her. *No point in fighting amongst ourselves.*

As they walked up the hill, he found himself wishing more and more that Knowles was there.

9

Bryant walked with the others through the woods. Jack's scent was clear. He could follow it easily to wherever Jack had gone. Jenny came next, close to him but her lips were thin and she hadn't said a word since the meeting with Jack. The twins walked behind, Joe talking quietly to Henry the whole time.

They had recovered their clothes and were making their way along the path that Jack had run down a short while earlier. Bryant was marching ahead, forcing the others to keep up.

"What are we doing Bryant?" Jenny asked.

He stopped so suddenly she nearly walked into him. "We are going to find Stadler."

"Why?" She looked at him closely. "We don't need another fight, we're done." She made it clear she was talking about Henry by a small inclination of her head.

"He can help me," Bryant said.

"How? Why? Because you make his wife your prisoner?" She laughed. "You really don't know much about families do you?"

186

"No," he said, "I don't. I get close to people, then I go on ops."

"That's not all of it is it?"

"No. I'm a killer, Jenny. Pure and simple." He sighed. "I'm really fucking good at my job."

"So is Stadler going to teach you how to calm down? Control the wolf?" she laughed again.

"I need to try."

"Bryant, you raped me," she said and he saw tears in her eyes. "You killed everyone in that hospital without a thought."

"Trust me, I've thought about it," Bryant said. "It's not like I had a choice."

"No, you did what you wanted. You're a psycho."

He grabbed her by the neck, hand closing tight before either of them really knew what he was doing. Henry made a noise, and Joe put his arm around him.

"If I am really a psycho, then you might need to think about how you speak to me." He let her go and stepped back, a look of horror on his face. Then he turned away from her. "I need to find Stadler," he muttered and started walking at a furious pace again.

10

Jack looked at the pub and felt that pang of guilt again. There were two pubs in Huntleigh, and they were only a couple of hundred yards apart from each other. The Kings Arms was in front of them and was Jack's bet for where Michael was. He didn't tell Katie that he was certain: he could smell it. The scent had led them through the churchyard and out into the square.

"Ready?" he asked.

Katie was very pale, but she nodded and clutched her coat closer.

"Remember, he wants me, not you. We get Josh back."

"And then what?" Katie looked at him. "What happens to you?"

"I don't care. Josh is the only thing that matters."

"But what about us? Will they kill you?"

"No Katie, they can't."

"What do you mean?"

"I heal. Like really quickly." He swallowed a sudden lump in his throat. *Are you sure? Really sure?* "They can't kill me."

"I just got you back Jack. I don't want to lose you again."

He moved to hug her, but she pushed him away. "I said I got you back, that's not the same as I forgive you."

"Sorry," he muttered.

"I want you *and* Josh," she said.

"Me too," he said. "Let's get on with it."

Two men stood in the doorway. One of them was smoking and earned a filthy look from Katie. Jack held the door open for her and was immediately assaulted by familiar smells. The pine of the bar. The ash in the fire, even though it hadn't been lit in weeks. The stale odour of spilled beer. The spirits that ripped the back of his throat out even though he hadn't drunk them. The BO of a man slumped on the bar, a half-finished pint in front of him.

And then: the smell of Josh, so familiar, even though it had been months since he'd seen his son. He had spent one week with Josh, but the scent was deeply ingrained in him. Outside the odour had been masked by the smell of the village. In here, in close quarters, the scent of his son was nearly enough to make him weep.

"What's wrong?"

"Josh. He's here," Jack said.

11

Katie walked into the familiar bar. Two large tables were on her immediate left, more to her right and the bar itself was in front of her. Several bar stools were scattered around the bar, some occupied. One man sat at the bar, head resting on his arms, apparently asleep. Another man and a woman sat close together on the left-hand side of the bar. They looked at Katie when she walked in and smiled at her. She recognised them but didn't know their names. Everybody in Huntleigh knew who she was, even if they didn't recognise Jack. Behind the bar was a barman she didn't know and she was grateful

188

for that. One less person to explain Jack's miraculous return to.

"Katie," Jack said, touching her arm. He gestured to a table on the right.

Sally and Michael sat there, with Josh in the fat woman's arms. She was smiling at him and it made Katie feel sick.

"Give my son back," Katie snarled, stepping towards the table. Jack grabbed her arm this time, but she pushed him away.

Michael smiled at her.

"I see you got my message," he said.

"Shut the fuck up. Give me my son."

The couple sat at the bar were watching now, smirking at each other as they realised they were watching some gossip unfold. The sleeping man sat up, rubbed his eyes, looked around the room then put his head back on the bar with a grunt.

"Such a mouth on her, Jack. Do you like that?"

"I'd do what she says if I were you."

"Why don't you sit?"

"I'm not sitting anywhere with you," Katie said.

"Why Michael? Why did you kill Karen?"

"Who?" He looked confused and mouthed 'Karen?' to Sally, who shrugged. Then he dropped his mouth open and covered it with his hand. It was like watching a comic actor from Jack's childhood. "Oh, the black woman? I needed to make sure I had your cooperation, Jack. I had to incentivise you."

"You already had me."

"No, no, no, Jack," Michael said. "I was about to lose you to this beautiful woman."

A shadow passed across Sally's face for a second. Only for a second, but Katie saw it.

"You killed my friend," she whispered. "You."

"Me," Michael said. He spread his arms wide, then nodded at Sally. "I had some help. She was ever such a large lady."

Josh craned his head at his mother's voice and started crying, arms held towards her. Sally shushed him, holding him closer to her chest.

"Give my son back Michael."

"Or what Jack? What are you going to do in this lovely little pub?"

Jack looked around, counting the people. If Michael changed, four people would die He sniffed as subtly as he could. There were no other people in the pub. *Still four people too many.* The couple in the corner were whispering excitedly to each other. Despite the whispers, he heard the whole conversation anyway and his name was mentioned many times. *Shit.*

"What about the guys in the garage, Michael? Why kill them?"

Katie shot him a look and he winced, but didn't take his eyes off Michael.

"Collateral damage," Michael said. "But that wasn't my fault. That was Scott."

"Where is Scott?" Jack looked around the pub, but couldn't see him. *Something is not right here.*

"That's a great question isn't it?" Michael laughed.

Sally looked up at the window and said, "They're here."

Who are here? What is she talking about? Jack could feel cold sweat trickling down his back. He could sense the situation slipping away from them, but he didn't know how. Katie had the gun and it was too public for Michael to do anything stupid. The man wasn't *that* crazy.

Katie followed Sally's gaze but couldn't see anything moving in the square.

"Excellent," Michael said. "Give the woman," he waved his hand at Josh, "that."

Sally stood and gave Josh to Katie, who almost sobbed with relief. Josh stopped crying immediately.

"What's going on Michael?" Jack asked.

"Let's get out of here, Jack," Katie said, clutching Josh to her chest with one arm. Her other hand was inside the folds of her coat.

"Yes, why don't you go?" Michael said. He was smirking now.

Jack reached across the table with sudden, shocking speed. He grabbed Michael's shirt and half dragged him across the table. "What's going on?"

"Hey!"

Jack looked around. The barman was coming round the bar, a baseball bat in his hands. "Get out of my bar," he said.

Jack let Michael go. Michael sank back to his seat, smirk still in place. *What is he doing? He killed Karen to get us up here. Why?*

"Shall we?" Michael said, starting to rise.

"Jack we've got what we came for, let's go," Katie said. Jack could hear the panic in her voice. *She knows something's up too.* "Leave them for the police"

Michael laughed. "No, no, my dear. The police have been trying to get me for years."

He sauntered to the door, nodding at the people at the bar. "Have a lovely day, well, what's left of it." He stopped by the drunk man and prodded him. "Dude, it's like seven o'clock. Go home."

Jack pushed past him, pulling Katie along behind him. "Get the fuck out of the way, Michael."

Jack opened the door to the pub and stepped into the street. More smells hit him straight away, but by then it was too late. Katie came out after him and stopped with a moan.

There were at least thirty people in a semicircle around the pub entrance. They were all staring intently at the door, and specifically at Jack.

Michael stepped into the sunlight. "You asked me for proof," he roared. "I give you the Original!"

As one the people knelt and bowed their heads. Katie moaned again as she realised what was happening.

Jack couldn't move, couldn't speak. *This is crazy.* All the people in the square kept their heads bowed. Recovering quickly, Jack looked at Michael. The other man was grinning from ear to ear, looking at the kneeling crowd. Jack felt cold inside, a hollow feeling that threatened to consume him. *I don't want this.*

As soon as he thought that, another more pressing concern came to the fore.

How the hell are we going to get out of this?

Chapter 21

1

The sun was on its downward path, giving the world a soft glow. The pilot landed the helicopter in the same field that he had been in a few weeks ago and Raymond led the six of them out from under the downforce of the blades. Seconds later, the helicopter was back in the air.

Raymond surveyed the area in front of him, mentally tallying the actual images with the tactical maps they had studied en-route. They were in a large field, which stretched for several acres behind him. To his left were trees and a path that led to Huntleigh woods. In front of him, hedges marked the borders of the private houses. He could see ten houses and knew that the Stadlers' was the fourth one. The house to the left of the Stadlers had small hedges bordering the field. Raymond pointed at Cockbain and then at this smaller hedge. Next he moved Williams and Taylor to each flank. The three men scanned the row of houses, moving their weapons in arcs to cover the windows. Nothing moved.

Hibbard ran forward and leapt over the small hedge, landing with a roll before sprinting to the larger hedge that bordered the Stadlers property. There was a hole at the bottom of the hedge, clearly created by a dog or a fox, but it was big enough for Hibbard to wriggle through.

He was now in the Stadlers' garden, looking down at the house. It looked dark.

He touched his throat mic. "No sign of anyone."

"Can you get closer without being seen?"

"Yes, sir."

Hibbard ran across the open garden, covering thirty feet in seconds. He pressed himself flat against the wall by the back door. The top and bottom of the door had patterned glass, designed to give the occupants some privacy. Hibbard peered in, looking for moving shapes behind the glass. Nothing. He slowly opened the door and stepped into the kitchen. It was cool inside, but the air was still. The house *felt* empty, but smelt odd. *Not a new baby odd, something else.* Leading off from the right of the kitchen was a door to another room. Hibbard looked through the doorway and could see the corner of a sofa. The living room. He could recall that there were two sofas, a coffee table and TV inside. Was there a bookcase too? He couldn't remember that detail on the tactical map that Knowles had put together for them. There was definitely an old inglenook fireplace as he could see it. Hibbard gently pushed open the door and gasped.

Red stained everything. Blood covered the walls, carpet and both sofas. The coffee table had small lumps of flesh on it, morsels that looked as though they'd been spat out. Bloody footprints led through the carnage and out of the opposite doorway. The trail clearly didn't belong to the foot that sat on the sofa like a discarded toy.

Just a foot. No leg.

"Sir, I have a body."

"Hibbard. Wait one. Hold your position. We're on our way."

2

Knowles ran with Taylor and Williams just behind him. They sprinted out of the field and onto a road. Knowles knew that they had to move fast and make sure all exits were blocked. If the wolves were here, then they had to make sure that no-one else died. Hibbard was currently alone in the house, or at least, he thought he was.

Knowles could hear the engine of an approaching car and increased his pace. The top of the Stadlers' street was only yards away now, but if possible he didn't want them to be seen. The car was coming from behind them, so with luck it would pass once they were off the main road.

They turned into the street. Williams and Taylor had their weapons out in front of them immediately and slowed down. Knowles glanced back over his shoulder, watching the road they had just left.

The car whizzed by at the top of the street and Knowles let out a breath he hadn't realised he was holding. They had not been seen. Knowles had been amazed at how quiet Huntleigh was when he had last been here. You could walk around in the middle of the day and be lucky if you saw another person. He was grateful for that now. *I have no idea how I'd explain this if someone saw us.*

Taylor nodded at Knowles. The street was empty. In the distance, Knowles could see two cars parked but other than that the street looked deserted. *Wolves or people working?* Knowles buried the thought. The wolves could easily have decimated this street, but it was unlikely. What would they gain from it?

Now they moved quickly again,

"Kick the door in," Knowles told Taylor. The other man nodded, their earlier animosity forgotten whilst on mission. Knowles touched his throat mic. "In position sir. Entering in three... two... one."

3

Knowles felt sick, whilst Taylor actually was. His hard man act disappeared as soon as he saw the remains in the living room and he bolted back outside to vomit noisily.

"Is that Katie Stadler?" Williams asked. Knowles didn't bother to reply. The black foot should have been clue enough. Williams left to search the rest of the house, Cockbain close behind.

"Call it in," Raymond said. "Let's get the local force on this."

"This isn't Jack," Knowles said.

"Why do you stick up for him?" Hibbard snarled.

"I'm not. Just stating a fact."

"How do you fucking know?"

"Easy, private," Raymond said.

"Jack can control it, remember? I've seen him in action, first hand. This isn't him."

"Why not?" Raymond asked.

"This is his home, sir. This is all he ever wanted. No way he came in and ate someone, tearing them apart like this. He has never done that to anyone." *Not true Knowles, you know that. Remember that thug, the one they found in the churchyard?* He said nothing.

They heard a shout from upstairs, and Knowles and Hibbard ran up, taking the stairs two at a time. Williams was in a small bedroom with a cot in it, Cockbain next to him with face pale and lips thin. Teddy bear wallpaper lined the walls, and a pile of toys sat undisturbed in the corner. There was blood in the cot.

"What?" Knowles said.

Williams didn't say anything, but pointed at the bedroom next to this one. Knowles pushed the door open and they saw the blood on the walls.

"Shit," Hibbard said.

"Yep," Knowles said with a nod. "Told you it wasn't him." He photographed it with his mobile and then the three of them returned to the living room. Knowles showed Raymond the picture.

Taylor was back in the room, looking sheepish. "Sorry, sir. Won't happen again."

Raymond shrugged. "It happens, Mark. You don't want to get used to it."

Raymond handed Knowles' phone back. "So, the million-pound question is where are the Stadlers now?"

"Sir, this message has basically told Katie that her husband is alive," Knowles said.

"If she believes it," Raymond said.

"If she's even seen it," Taylor said. When the other two men looked at him, he cleared his throat and said, "If she'd walked into this, she'd be in bits, sir."

"Fair point," Knowles said.

196

"Still doesn't tell us where she is." Raymond looked around the room again, searching in vain for a clue as to where Katie Stadler had gone.

Knowles walked back into the kitchen and started opening cupboards. In a tall larder style cupboard, he found a folded up pushchair. "Sir, look."

"Congratulations, Knowles, you'll make a family man yet."

"Sir, the baby is not even six months old. She can't have gone far if she hasn't taken the pushchair."

Raymond nodded, his lips pressed thinly together. "She must be close, then."

"Maybe she's gone to the village. Maybe she doesn't even know about this," Knowles gestured around the room.

"Are you suggesting we walk around a village in full combat gear, sergeant?"

"This village is small, sir. Everyone knows everyone, just about. I reckon we could get up to the square without being seen if we're careful."

"The square?" Raymond said. "That's where the pubs are, correct?"

"Yes sir," Knowles said. "The pubs are basically next door to each other sir, about fifty metres apart, no more than one hundred. I reckon we can scope both easily even dressed like this."

Taylor was already moving back to the breakfast bar. He unfolded a map of the village and pointed to two roads. One ran parallel to the main road through the village, running east to west. It linked to a second road that led to the main square. The other road ran north to south, ending in a path that led through the churchyard.

"Sir, one team goes this way," he ran his hand along the east-west route, "and the other this way. We keep in mic contact."

"Make it happen," Raymond said. "Cockbain, Hibbard, with me to West Street. You three through the churchyard. West Street is Red One, the churchyard Blue One. Square Blue Two." He pointed at the map, indicating various positions on it. "King's Arms will be King, Seven Stars, Star.

Clear? The church can be Green One and it might give us eyes on Blue Two. Knowles, judge that when you get there. Stay in comms at all times. Watch your fives and twenties. Inform me of contact. Any contact. Make no mistake, what we are dealing with is extremely dangerous." The grim faces looking back at him confirmed that his men already knew that. "I want no-one bitten. I do not want to be calling your families tomorrow. No-one else dies today, but especially not Katie Stadler and her little boy. Remember, you must not be seen - clear?"

"Yes, sir!"

Chapter 22

1

"Do you even know where she lives?" Jenny asked. Bryant scowled at her, and she rubbed her neck without realising. She could still feel the press of his fingers there. *What am I doing here?*

"I need a drink," he said and pointed at a sign that said 'Kings Arms 200 yards'. Underneath was the usual stuff about good food and beer, although that was unnecessary. No pub ever advertised itself as bad beer and worse food, regardless of the truth. Joe and Henry exchanged a look and Jenny shrugged. *We've come this far.*

Bryant walked down the road that led to the village square of Huntleigh. He was trembling and kept clenching and unclenching his fists. *What the hell was wrong with him now?*

Jenny jogged to catch up. "Bryant, we don't need to do this you know."

"I know."

"So let's go. We could be somewhere hot by tomorrow night, forget about all this."

He shook his head. "Stadler will help me. I know he will."

"Help you how, Jamie?"

"He controls it, Jenny. Controls the-" Bryant stopped talking. He didn't need to finish the sentence.

"He's very different to you." *He's not an animal.*

"That's what scares me."

They rounded a corner and saw the village square in front of them. It was rectangular in shape, but small: a quintessential small village centre. Two rows of houses ran the length of the rectangle, with a shop and Post Office at the furthest end from them. In both rows, the houses were identical, with doorways that looked small and windows to match. Cars were parked on the left-hand side of the street, with the pub opposite. White washed cottages stopped in line with the end of the pub and a wide lane narrowed as it ran from the square to the church. Jenny could see the church tower, the stained glass glinting in the evening sun. She looked back towards the pub and gasped. The square was full of people and they were all kneeling.

"What the-" Bryant whispered, just as a familiar face stepped into the square.

"You asked me for proof," Michael roared. "I give you the Original!"

"No," Bryant moaned.

"Jamie-" Jenny started.

Bryant's voice was changing, as his face contorted. "No," he said, his voice not quite his own. "*I'm* the Original."

2

"Get up," Jack said. "Please, get up."

No-one moved. Michael beamed at him. "This is it, Jack. Your pack. Your people."

"I don't want this," Jack said, sweat breaking out on his brow. He frowned suddenly then he turned his head to the left and stood stock still. "Oh no," he said.

Michael turned to follow his gaze and the smile disappeared instantly. Bryant was running towards them, changing as he ran. He bulldozed into the kneeling wolves, throwing two into the air with the speed of his impact. He changed back to a man and punched a further two who were rising, then changed his arm and sliced a third open with no more effort than gutting a fish. Five people lay dead in as many seconds.

The other wolves scattered, but Bryant lashed out, cutting down those who were way too slow. The remaining wolves stood at a distance, but still surrounding him. Bryant stopped and looked at Jack. Blood covered his face and torso and he was breathing hard.

"This ends, Stadler."

No, I want you to help me.

Too late, much, much too late. Only one of us leaves here today.

No-

Jack felt the change coming, both his own and Bryant's. "Katie, run!"

The words were barely out of his mouth before the Wolf burst out of him and he launched at Bryant.

3

"I can't put him through this again," Joe said, pushing his brother back, towards the alley that led to the church.

"Go, get out of here," Jenny said, with a nod.

"What about you?"

"I want to see who wins."

Joe shook his head but then started jogging down the alley, half dragging his brother behind him. They reached the gates to the churchyard and then Henry stopped dead. He raised an arm and Joe looked to where he was pointing.

"Back, let's go back," he yelled and turned away from his brother. "They might know who we are." Joe had no idea what the soldiers were doing there, but he had to assume they had descriptions of all of Bryant's pack.

"No," Henry said, the first time he had spoken for days. He turned back to face the men walking through the church yard. They were moving from gravestone to gravestone or keeping flush with the building. One of them noticed Henry and made a strange gesture to the others.

"Run, Joe, run," Henry said. He was smiling and suddenly Joe couldn't remember the last time he had seen his brother smile. With the sudden words and the smile, Joe felt that his twin was coming back to him – returning from the almost fugue state he had been in for weeks. But then Henry turned away from Joe, turning back to the armed men.

"No!" Joe shouted, but he knew it was too late.

Henry threw back his head and bellowed at the sky, then he started to run towards the soldiers, changing as he went.

Joe ran away as the bullets rained into his brother, tears falling down his cheeks.

4

Knowles stopped, holding his hand up. He touched his throat mic. "We just bagged a wolf, sir. Blue 1, proceeding to blue 2. They're here."

"Copy that, Knowles," Raymond said. "How's Green 1? We need eyes on Blue 2."

Knowles scanned his immediate environment. The church rose behind him, ancient and carrying a history all of its own. He looked at Taylor and nodded at the tower. Taylor nodded back and tried the door to the church. It swung open.

Country folk.

"Sir, Taylor and Williams are heading for Green 1. It's pretty high. Should give us a view of Blue 2 and possibly King."

"Excellent, Knowles. We are at Red 1 moving to Blue 2, approx. one minute out. Stay in comms." Raymond was travelling down West Street, heading for the square.

"Sir, the wolf wasn't alone. There was another one who ran when it saw us. He will have warned the others."

"You are assuming there are others, sergeant."

Knowles bit his tongue. *Of course there are others, you utter moron, they are pack animals.*

"Gone firm at Green 1, sir," Taylor said. *He's at the top of the tower already.*

"What can you see?"

"I can see part of the High Street, sir," Taylor said, "eyes on Blue 2."

Knowles shook his head. *High Street. Jesus. Taylor needs to get out more. At least we can now see the square.*

"It's full of people."

5

"You're not going anywhere," Sally said and stood in front of Katie. Michael reached to take Josh, and Katie turned away from him.

"Don't touch me!"

"Katie, I can kill you and take him, or I can just take him. Your choice."

Katie looked into his eyes, saw the intent there and handed Josh to him with a sob. She saw Jack land on Bryant, both as wolves, both snarling and snapping at each other.

Michael followed her gaze. "He's doing well," he said, although it was not clear which Wolf he was referring to. The other people in the square, those still alive, were watching the fight intently.

"What happens if Bryant wins?" Sally said.

"Then we follow him instead. Don't worry, whatever happens here will be good for us."

The Wolves continued to fight. Both were cut in several places, blood splattering the concrete around them. Suddenly one of the wolves stopped and looked around. Katie followed its gaze, towards the church. She saw a man running towards a pretty woman.

For a second, Jack's face appeared through the fur and blood. "Knowles," he said. The other Wolf twisted then, pinning Jack under it. Jack had fully returned to Wolf form now, just in time for the other to tear a large chunk out of its chest. Jack whined and howled and the Wolf bit down again. Jack stopped moving and the Wolf stood, turning back to human. Blood covered the large man.

Bryant stared at Michael, eyes full of hatred. He spat a chunk of meat into the road.

6

"People?" Raymond said.

"Sir, eyes on Bryant." Taylor's voice had gone up an octave: he was excited.

Knowles pictured Taylor in the church tower, binoculars sweeping the square.

"Do you have a shot?"

"No sir," Williams said.

"Sir, I also have eyes on Katie Stadler."

"What about Jack?" Knowles asked.

"There is a large wolf on the ground next to Bryant. I think its Stadler sir, just, God, well, it's huge sir."

"What's he doing?"

"Nothing. He's just lying there. Blood everywhere sir. I think he's dead."

7

As soon as Bryant charged, Jenny slid into the shadows of the alley to the church. She watched the one sided fight, chewing her lip and running through her options. They were limited. Stay and re-join Bryant, run after Joe and Henry or just leave.

Leaving seemed the best choice, but she didn't know how she would survive. The police almost certainly had a description of her, as would the army. Joe and Henry needed time together, to heal their wounds and she had brought nothing but bad luck to them since they'd met. Bryant. She watched as he bit a large chunk of flesh from somewhere on Stadler, and then heard rapidly approaching footsteps.

At some point during the fight, without even realising, she had left the alley and was now standing in plain sight in the square. She turned towards the noise, and heard the gunfire from the churchyard. Joe was hurtling towards her, face pale and streaked with tears.

"Soldiers," he managed to get out. "Henry."

She took his hand and they ran away from the square, towards the rear of the pub.

8

Katie felt bile rise and forced it down. She had to act, and *now*. She raised the shotgun and pressed it to the back of Sally's head. Without pausing to think, she pulled the trigger. Warm blood splashed her face as the fat woman crumpled to the floor. Michael started to turn, still clutching Josh. Katie swung the barrel of the gun and hit him on the chin. Michael swore and Katie dropped the gun, grabbing Josh from the momentarily stunned man. Then without looking at Jack, she sprinted back into the pub.

"Lock the door!" she screamed as she ran in.

She had seen scenes like the inside of the pub when a fight had suddenly broken out. Everyone stood still, not really sure what was going on, and hoping that it would go away before anything else bad happened. The barman reacted first. He ran past her, slammed the door shut and threw the bolt across. It looked gloriously inadequate for the job.

"What the hell is going on?" he said.

Josh was crying, and Katie held him tightly. "What it looks like. It's not safe here."

The early evening drinkers looked at each other, disbelief clear on their features.

"If they get in here, they'll kill us all," Katie said.

"But who *are* they?" said the man at the bar.

"*What* are they is a much better question," she said, "but not now. We need to go. Out the back, now."

The other side of the bar was another entrance to the pub. Katie led the way, opening the door to the street. She looked down the road, the one that led to the square, but she couldn't see anyone. She stepped into the street, shushing Josh, and a pretty woman stepped into her path. The same pretty woman she had seen moments before. A man stood behind her watching Katie with hollow eyes.

"I don't think so," she said. "Back inside."

"Please," Katie said, "my son."

"This is bullshit," the man from the bar said, pushing past Katie. He had been unconscious a few minutes ago and his speech was slurred now. Something changed in the woman's gaze, and suddenly she was a wolf. The man screamed as she howled, and then she was back as the pretty woman.

"Now, I said, back inside."

9

Bryant glared at Michael, who was wiping Sally's blood off his face. "You worship *him*?" He kicked the body of the wolf at his feet.

"No, I want to follow an Original. I made that offer to you, remember?"

"I was weak then," Bryant smiled. "I am no longer."

The other wolves in the square, all in human form, bowed their heads as Bryant glared at them all.

"You are my pack now!" he roared.

"You're bleeding," Michael said.

"I will heal." Bryant brushed at the blood pouring from his arm and then pressed the wound. A frown creased his brow. "Who was the woman? The one with the weapon?"

"Jack's wife. His son too."

"Then she dies next."

10

"I have a shot, sir."

"Take it," Raymond said. "Everyone else, weapons free, go, go, go."

11

Bryant pushed Michael to one side and took a step towards the pub door. The bullet entered him just below the top of his neck, travelling downwards and so blowing out a sizeable chunk of his throat. Bryant staggered forward, involuntarily grabbing his throat. A second shot slammed into the middle of his back, throwing him into the pub door. He bounced off it and fell to the floor near Jack's body.

Suddenly the air was filled with the sound of automatic gunfire. Michael turned from Bryant in time to see the wolves furthest away from him get torn apart by bullets.

Now there were bullets coming from the other direction too. A man was leaning against a car, using its bonnet as a stabiliser and firing indiscriminately into the crowd. Other shots rang out, even louder than the machine gun. *A sniper.* Michael grinned to himself. *Time for phase two.*

He kicked the pub door as hard as he could. Already weakened from the force of Bryant hitting it, the door flew open. He dove into the sanctity of the pub.

A woman screamed as he landed. Michael stood up, his usual smile in place. Katie Stadler stood clutching her baby next to a couple in the corner of the bar. Another man stood watching them, and next to him a naked woman. Finally a barman, easily identified with his Kings Arms t-shirt, was behind the bar.

"Jenny," he said.

"Hello, Michael. This hasn't exactly gone to plan has it?"

12

Knowles stopped shooting. The square was covered in dead bodies. *Christ, I hope no civilians.*

The people of Huntleigh were still in their houses - he could see some curtains twitching now that the noise had died down. There would be a lot of explaining to do, but that was later. Right now, they were showing sense by staying indoors. *At least now the police will be on their way.* All that remained was the clean-up. Although, one man had definitely gone into the pub.

"Sir, multiple targets down," he said into his mic. The others echoed what he said.

"Approach with caution," Raymond said. "Anything so much as twitches, I want another bullet in it."

"Sir, what about Jack and Bryant?" Knowles said. He could see both men lying on the ground, surrounded by blood.

"Use extreme caution."

Knowles walked in a low crouch towards the carnage in front of the pub. He swept the weapon barrel backwards and forwards, covering the pile of dead in front of him. Neither Jack nor Bryant was moving.

"Sir, something's not right here. Bryant and Jack should be healing by now."

"Agreed Knowles, but we need them off the streets. This can only be a good thing."

At the other end of the square, Hibbard was walking forward in the same crouch as Knowles. Cockbain was kneeling behind a car, covering his approach. Raymond was kneeling against a different car on the opposite side of the road, also covering them.

207

Tension and adrenaline were beginning to cause a headache for Knowles and he rubbed his head under his helmet. His forehead was slick with sweat. *No casualties for us. We're getting better at dealing with them.* He reached Jack and pushed him with his boot.

Jack rolled over, and Knowles saw the extent of the wounds for the first time. A large chunk was missing from his shoulder, and Knowles could see the bone through the mess of red and torn tissue. His pectoral muscle was also hanging loose, a long line of ripped flesh running from his other shoulder to just above his sternum.

"Shit, Jack," Knowles muttered, just as Jack opened his eyes.

13

Pain was coursing through him like he had never felt before. Once, on a skiing trip, he had been taken out by a snowboarder and had twisted his knee. That had been his worse accident until he fell into the cave several months ago. Even being shot - several times, at once - had not hurt like this.

This made those laughable.

"Shit, Jack," he heard a familiar voice say and he opened his eyes. Knowles was looking at him, and the soldier was sweating. He was in full battle gear and carrying a gun that looked like something from a video game.

Why is Knowles here? Why is he in Huntleigh dressed like that?

Other memories started coming back to him. Katie and Josh. Where were they? He had to get to them, make sure they were safe. Jack tried to sit up, but his body just wouldn't obey. Nothing seemed to be working.

The wolves. Where did they come from? Where's Michael?

"Knowles, what's happening?"

"I don't know Jack, you're hurt pretty bad."

"But I shouldn't be."

Knowles shrugged. "Bryant bit you, Jack. Probably best not to take on a special forces trained guy, huh?"

"I couldn't help it," Jack said. It was true: something had taken over, something primal.

"Jack, the people I'm with, they won't help you. They will want you to stay hurt until we can get you locked up. I'm sorry."

Jack couldn't even nod. "Find my wife, Knowles, make sure my son is safe."

He closed his eyes.

14

"The arrival of the army has upset my plans somewhat," Michael said.

"What are you?" a woman screamed.

"Shut up," Michael said. "You know what we are."

"Nobody else needs to die today," Joe said. "We can just leave." He was talking to Jenny, but she was ignoring him. "Both of the Originals are down. Maybe the legends are not true," he persisted.

"The Originals will heal," Michael said. "They just need time."

"We haven't got time," Joe said. "How many soldiers are coming?"

"There aren't that many here," Michael said. There was something in his voice – a smugness – that chilled Joe.

Jenny also picked up on Michael's choice of words. "How do you know?"

"You don't really think I put all my people in that square do you?"

15

"Sir, you want us to join you?" Taylor said into his mic. Both he and Williams were lying on the floor at the top of the Church tower. Williams had his sniper rifle resting on its bipod stand, helping keep it steady.

"Negative, keep eyes up there," Raymond's voice was quiet but clear over the radio.

Taylor looked again through the binoculars. He had a view of about three-quarters of the square and it was a bloodbath.

"I hope none of those are real people," he said.

"Bit late to worry about that mate," Williams said. He was still looking through the scope of the rifle, barrel aimed squarely on Bryant's unmoving back.

"What's that?" Taylor said, moving the binoculars up slightly. "Sir, we have movement in the pub. I just saw something at the window."

"We're on it," Hibbard said over the radio. Taylor couldn't see him, but he knew Hibbard – with Cockbain and Raymond - was approaching the square from West Street.

"Careful-" Taylor got as far as saying, then he heard a growl behind him. He rolled over as a wolf jumped at him. "Shit!" he screamed with his last breath as the wolf ripped his throat out.

The wolf snapped at Williams next, grabbing his arm as he tried to roll away. The tower was too cramped for any sort of manoeuvre, and the wolf released his arm. Williams reached for his knife, but his arm was useless. The ruined limb refused to obey any instruction he tried to give it. Too late, he switched to his other arm and his fingers brushed the hilt of the knife. The wolf bit his face. Unlike Taylor, Williams didn't have time to scream. The wolf bit again, this time ripping Williams' throat out.

Scott returned to human form and looked at the sniper rifle. "Fun, fun, fun," he said, licking his lips clean of blood.

16

"Taylor, sit rep," Raymond said. The radio remained quiet. "Hibbard, Knowles I want eyes in that pub."

"Sir." Hibbard said. He walked ahead of Knowles, nodding to indicate he was on point. His weapon covered the door to the pub, whilst Knowles stood five metres behind, covering him. A shot rang out and a sniper bullet smashed through Hibbard's helmet and his head exploded in a shower of blood and bone.

Knowles dived for cover, rolling quickly to one side, but there was nowhere to hide. He sprinted away from the pub, just as another bullet pinged into the wall behind him. He slid over a car bonnet and then took cover behind it. The shots were coming from the church, which meant-

"Taylor and Williams have gone sir," he said. "Get the QRF rolling!" Raymond had been in contact with the base at Lympstone in South Devon and they had a Quick Reaction Force waiting to support in an emergency. A couple of helicopters were ready for the first phase, with two further trucks on standby if more men were needed.

No answer from Raymond. Knowles looked down the street, towards the major. Two wolves were dragging Raymond's body out from behind a car. He was punching one in the head as it dragged him, but the wolf was ignoring the blows. As Knowles watched, the blows became visibly weaker until Raymond was still. Two more wolves came from the other side of the street, both covered in blood. One was carrying an arm. *I'm on my own. Where did they come from?*

"Shit," Knowles said.

17

Where did they come from? Jenny watched Michael with a cross between growing admiration and concern. He was grinning as he looked out of the windows of the pub. He kept moving from side to side, watching events unfold further down the street and immediately outside the pub, in the village square.

"Did you know I split my pack when we arrived back here?" Michael spoke without taking his eyes from the scenes outside the window. "I only took half my people to that service station. Germany made me a bit more careful, I think."

Jenny had no idea what he was talking about, but she stayed quiet.

Four wolves were eating the two soldiers that had opened fire from the end of the street. Outside the front door, the bodies of Bryant, Stadler and the soldier whose head had exploded lay dormant. At least one of them was never getting up again.

The hostages were huddled around a table, Joe watching them with no real vigilance. He looked like he might be sick. The corpse of his brother was out of sight, but there were plenty of others in full view.

"Scott used to be in the army. Did you know that?"

Jenny shook her head.

"He was a sniper in the first Gulf war. His unit got attacked, but he escaped. He was seriously wounded, but then he ran into a pack." Michael shrugged as if to say *you can do the rest of the story.* "I thought he'd be a bit rusty, but that first shot was a peach. The way that soldier went down. I've never seen a head disintegrate like that. It's awesome, isn't it?"

"What's your plan here, Michael? What do you want? All these dead - you won't get away with this."

"I don't need to get away with anything. I will have one of the Originals to do my talking for me."

"But they're both-"

"No Jenny. They are both hurt, yes, but they will heal. It's just a matter of which one first." Michael smiled again. "Shall we go see the soldiers?"

He turned to Joe. "Watch them," he pointed at the hostages. "They go nowhere."

Joe nodded and then Michael repeated, "Shall we?"

He opened the door to the pub and pushed Jenny into the street ahead of him. To her right, the wolves were done with their meal and were walking slowly up the street, heads bowed, teeth bared.

In front of her, the soldier without a head lay in his own blood, arms spread wide. Her foot kicked a shotgun, and she picked it up. It felt good to be armed. Bryant was next in the line, a neat hole in the back of his head and blood in a V shape pattern in front of him. His arms were covered in scratches and bites and blood oozed from these. *So Stadler did get a few bites in.* The thought made her happy. *Finally choosing a side Jenny?*

Stadler lay in front of her of his back. His chest was a mess, blood coming from a long jagged gash. He was breathing, but it was very shallow. It was clear that Stadler was in a massive amount of pain.

"To the soldier hiding behind the car," Michael called.

"Knowles," the man shouted. "My name is Knowles and I have buried hundreds like you. I have watched your carcasses burn and laughed as you've all died."

"Well, aren't you a badass scary motherfucker." Michael looked at her and rolled his eyes. "You are surrounded Knowles, give it up and we'll make it quick."

"Why don't you come a bit closer? You're going first."

A shot rang out then, and one of the wolves stalking up the street whined and rolled over, blood pouring from its chest.

"Sorry, I lied."

Michael stopped walking, and for the first time looked uncertain.

"You will not kill us all, Knowles."

"You wanna bet?"

18

Joe saw Michael stop and knew it was now or never.

"Move, quickly, out the back door."

The three people at the table looked at him in disbelief. The drunk guy was still at the bar. He had poured himself a pint and had downed it. The barman said nothing – his expression did all the talking necessary.

"You're helping us?" the pretty woman said. Bryant had said she was Stadler's wife. She was holding a baby, trying unsuccessfully to keep it quiet.

"I want no part of this," Joe said. "That guy is nuts. My brother died today. I'm guessing you don't want to. Come on."

He opened the back door to the pub and they stepped into the street. It was quiet there. If they went left, they would be back in the village centre as the pub was an island in the middle of the square, so they turned right. Joe jogged up the street, keeping close to the pub wall. The others followed. He stopped at the end of the pub and peered around the corner.

He could see the path leading to the church, and the tower. The sniper would have a clear view of them. About a hundred yards away, the street closed in and there were houses on both sides. They would be in the clear - if they got there.

"We have to run," he said to the others. "When I say, we run for those houses."

Just then, they heard laughter. Joe watched four men come round the corner at the top of the road. They were all wearing shorts and carrying tennis racquets.

"Oh no," said Stadler's wife.

And then, behind her, she heard a wolf howl.

19

"You wanna bet?" Knowles shouted. He was huddled behind the car, shaking. *After all this, I really am going to die in fucking Devon.* He could hear the man laughing. Knowles looked under the car and scanned the street.

Jack was lying closest to him, about halfway between Knowles and the pub. Bryant was next, then Hibbard, whose weapon was on the ground next to him. The grenade launcher attachment glinted in the sun.

I need that weapon.

To his left, three wolves were still advancing, although far more slowly and cautiously. He could shoot them, maybe, but then the leader would be on him. Was he fast enough to get all four?

Maybe. He didn't want to risk his life on a maybe.

There was also the sniper to think about, but for that he needed Hibbard's weapon.

Next he risked a glance through the glass of the car. The leader was standing about five metres away and he was holding a shotgun. Knowles ducked back down as the glass exploded, showering him.

"Not so tough now, eh?" the man said. "Come on, Knowles, stand up and take it like a man!"

A scream pierced the air and Knowles risked another look. Bryant was standing behind the man, holding the other's head firmly in his hands. With a roar, he lifted, his fingers changing into razor sharp claws and digging into the man's neck. Blood flowed slowly at first and then a sudden jet of blood spurted out, covering Bryant. The man screamed again until the claws cut through the windpipe and then Bryant was holding the severed head. He started to laugh, a deep guttural sound. He threw the head in a large arc and it thudded to the ground behind Knowles.

He tried – tried *really* hard - not to look at it.

Knowles stood up, weapon ready.

Bryant stared at him, glowering through the blood that stained his face making him look like a cartoon devil. He howled again, and staggered, before fixing Knowles with a stare he would never forget.

"Run, Knowles, I've lost."

With that, Bryant turned into a wolf and sprinted towards the wolves that had taken out Raymond.

Knowles ran round the car, heart pounding. He wasn't sure what was happening, but he knew an opportunity when he saw one. He slung his weapon over his shoulder and picked up Hibbard's from the floor.

Jack groaned.

Knowles glanced down the street and immediately wished he hadn't. Bryant was tearing apart the wolves, literally limb from limb. Knowles slung Hibbard's weapon over his shoulder too, then scooped to pick Jack up in a fireman's lift. He grunted under the weight of the guns and Jack and staggered to the pub, barging past the ruined door. As soon as he was inside, he threw Jack to the floor and grabbed one of the weapons, swinging it around the inside of the pub, ready to fire.

He had seen people run into the pub. They had hostages in here, surely? He was, therefore, really surprised to find it empty.

20

"You wanna bet?" The soldier yelled. Jenny stopped still, shocked at the accuracy of his shot. Michael snatched the shotgun from her, simply pulling it from her hands. Jenny offered no resistance but took a step backwards. Michael said nothing, so she turned and walked quickly back into the pub.

"Joe," she started, but the words died on her lips. The pub was empty. She looked around quickly, checking behind the bar and the room on the right-hand side of the pub. All empty.

A bang from outside told her that Michael had fired the shotgun. If the soldier was dead he would come back into the pub. She had to get away. Michael was crazy, but not in the overused sense of the word. He was just not wired right. Whatever happened with Jack and Bryant, she no longer wanted any part of it. Michael had changed things, as he always did, and not for the better. Bryant and Jack would kill one another today and then who would control Michael?

She opened the back door and stepped into the street. There she saw them. They were standing on the street corner, peering around it. The narrow street opened there, giving Scott a clear view from the church tower. Joe was at the front of the group, clearly leading them.

Jenny saw four men in sports clothes strolling down the road without a care in the world. One of them was bouncing car keys in his hand. *Leverage. We need all of them to make sure we get away.*

She turned into a wolf and growled.

21

"Oh no," Katie said. She recognised the tennis players. One of them was Chris, a friend of Jack's. They had wet the baby's head together in what seemed a long time ago now. Two of the others were familiar faces from around the village, and she should have known their names, but it didn't seem relevant now. She had no idea who the one with the keys was.

A wolf growled behind her. She spun around but knew it was hopeless. They were not armed, had no weapons.

"Run!" she screamed.

"Katie?" Chris called. The men were looking confused. *Alfie, one of them was called Alfie. Can't they see the wolves?*

216

"Jenny," Joe said to the wolf, "these people need our help." He glanced at the road behind him, risking a look down the alley to the church.

Jenny changed back to a human and the men started shouting. *Great, now they notice her as she's a beautiful naked woman.*

"Joe-"

"No, Jenny, please help them."

"What are you doing?"

"Buying you some time."

Joe took a step into the street, into the sunlight, and a single shot rang out. His head jerked to the side, part of his skull and brains flying out and hitting the ground before he did.

"Run!" Katie screamed again.

22

Knowles swept through the pub, slow and steady, weapon in front of him. As he passed a window, he saw some people outside and he recognised one of them. Katie Stadler. She was with several other people and they were moving away from the pub. *Oh no, not now. There's a sniper out there.* He ran back to the still prone Jack and heaved him back onto his shoulders. Knowles staggered through the pub, Jack a dead weight on his back. He reached the back door and entered the street. He knew Bryant was to his left, devouring the remains of the other wolves but he had seen Katie so he turned right.

A man lay on the ground in front of Katie, clearly a victim of the sniper. Three other people stood next to her, two with ashen faces and the third clearly drunk. Another man and a naked woman stood apart from them. The woman was crying.

He dropped Jack to the ground again and lifted his weapon.

"Don't move!" he yelled, aiming his weapon at the naked woman. "Katie Stadler, have you been bitten?"

"You," was all she said.

"Yeah, me. I'm Knowles. I have your husband."

"I know who you are. Put the gun down Knowles," Katie pushed past Jenny, holding something tightly. It took him a moment to realised she was holding a baby. *Josh.*

On the other side of the street, he could see four men watching them with mouths open.

"Who are they?"

"One of them is a friend of Jack's. You're about to have some explaining to do."

She brushed past Knowles and knelt next to Jack. His breathing was still ragged and shallow, but he was, for the moment, alive.

Knowles turned to the naked woman. "Who are you?" He did not lower his weapon.

"My name is Jenny. I-"

"Actually, I don't give a fuck," Knowles said. "You're one of them."

"So's he." Jenny pointed at the dead body in the sunlight behind her. "And he just died to save this lot. But you have cocked that up. He bought us time and you've wasted it."

Knowles ignored her and turned back to Katie.

"Katie, is there another way out of here?"

She shook her head. "Jack, can you hear me?"

"Katie, focus. We have another Original in the square. Any second now he is going to come and kill us all. Is there another way out of here that doesn't involve crossing that square?"

She shook her head again, tears welling. "Jack, Josh needs you. He's hurt, look, I dropped him and now he's cut his face." She pulled the blanket down, revealing Josh who was crying softly. He had a graze on his forehead that didn't look like much to Knowles.

Maybe that's why the kids don't want to see me.

"We could go through one of the houses," she said to Knowles, without taking her gaze from Jack.

"Actually, I have a better idea," Knowles said. "When I say, run over there and get those idiots to take you away. Call the police, call the army, call everyone and anyone you can think of. Do you understand?"

She nodded. "What are you going to do?"

"Well, you're not going to like that part."

23

Knowles handed Katie his spare weapon. "Point, squeeze the trigger. Not much more to it."

"Shouldn't I have a gun?" said the man. He was very pale, with sunken eyes. He was wearing black trousers and a green t-shirt emblazoned with a logo for The Kings Arms.

"Why?" Knowles said. "Because you're a bloke?"

The man did a good impression of a goldfish. Knowles unclipped his handgun and passed it to the man.

"Listen," Knowles said, "there are only two wolves left as far as I can tell. One of them is up in the tower and I will take care of him. The other is dangerous. Really dangerous. You need to run and keep running. If he finds you, he will kill you. Is that clear?"

The barman nodded. "What are those things, sergeant?"

"Exactly what they appear to be. Now, you ready? You only get one chance at this." The man had gone up in Knowles' estimation by recognising his rank.

Knowles unclipped his belt, letting the extra ammo packs slide to the floor. Next he lifted Jack, letting him rest against him and then he pushed as hard as he could.

"Knowles!" Katie said.

Jack stumbled back into the square. One of the tennis players darted forward to try and catch him.

"No!" Knowles shouted. The tennis player stopped, as Jack fell to his knees. A shot rang out and Jack spun. Blood and tissue flew out of his shoulder, splashing onto the tarmac like rain.

Katie screamed.

The tennis player froze in place.

Knowles stepped into the square and pulled the secondary trigger on the weapon. The grenade round flew into the air in a long arc. Knowles watched for as long as he dared, saw the round fall on the top left of the church tower. He ducked back behind the pub.

"Move!" Knowles screamed at the tennis player. He popped the UGL open and slid out the casing of the spent grenade. He quickly inserted a new grenade.

"What happened?" the barman asked.

"Jack!" Katie screamed.

"I missed," Knowles said.

The tennis player finally turned and started to run, but it was far too slow and far too late. Another shot rang out. The man collapsed, more blood covering the tarmac.

Knowles stepped back out, and aimed slightly to the right of his last shot and he fired again. This time, the grenade landed squarely in the middle of the tower and Knowles set off, sprinting for the alley.

Katie ran into the street and knelt down next to Jack. His shoulder showed no damage, apart from the fresh blood around where the bullet had torn his flesh apart.

"Jack," she said, now realising that this wasn't such a good idea. She rolled him over, watching his shoulder knit itself back together. Black fur rippled across his muscles and his face changed.

"Run," Jack said, "he's coming."

24

Knowles ran as fast as he could. His lungs were burning and legs protesting by the time he reached the church door. Small lumps of stone scattered the floor around the door. He leant against the door, gasping for breath.

Opening the door, he slipped into the church as quietly as he could. The interior of the church was largely untouched. Row upon row of pews lined the way to a grand altar, above which was the usual stained glass image of Jesus.

Knowles was not a religious man, but he knew many who were. Combat did that to you - either convinced you the world was a steaming pile of shit: it already *was* hell, or else it turned you to God. The quiet in the church was oppressive, a feeling Knowles had always had in any church regardless of circumstance. He had even felt it on his wedding day.

A small wooden door opened to reveal stairs on his right, spiralling up to the top of the tower. Knowles started to climb, staring down the barrel the whole time.

Halfway up, the stairs became covered in rubble. It got worse the closer he got to the top. Wooden splinters and larger pieces of wood now littered the floor and then he was at the top. Three bodies, two in uniform, one naked, lay under the rubble, all clearly dead. Knowles sank to the floor, exhaustion and relief flooding through him.

Then he heard the screams coming from the square.

25

Katie looked up and around the square. A huge dark wolf was sprinting towards them. She saw flashes of red in its fur and its teeth stood bright against the black fur. The barman from the pub raised the gun that Knowles had given him and fired, screaming as he did so. The sound was deafening, but the effect on the wolf was immediate.

The shots made it angry.

It pounced and tore the man's throat out with a single bite.

Katie heard a roar behind her, and spun, shielding Josh with her free hand. Another wolf stood behind her, this one just as massive as the other. She felt her knees go weak, and a whimper escaped her throat.

Jack.

She watched as the wolves circled each other with her in the middle. Josh was crying louder and louder. Every fibre of her body wanted to run, but she couldn't. Even the gun in her hand was forgotten and she dropped it. Both wolves stopped moving at the sound. She no longer knew which was which.

She could hear people screaming and someone shouting her name, but it was all so distant. Suddenly the wolves were human again, but still circling her. The other man was huge, muscles distinct on his arms and legs. His six pack was so defined he looked like Action Man.

"Katie, take Josh and go," Jack said. He stepped in front of her, steering her behind him. "Let her go," he said.

221

"I wanted you to help me," Bryant said. He sounded like a petulant teenager. "Why didn't you help me?"

"I don't understand what this is." Jack gestured all around him. "How can I help you?"

"Too late. It's all too late. You are not leaving here today."

Jack nodded. "Probably not, but my son is."

Katie whimpered at the words and instantly hated herself.

"I wouldn't put money on that if I were you."

"What changed Bryant? You wanted help, but now you don't?"

The big man shrugged. "The Wolf won, Jack."

With that, he changed and leapt at Jack.

26

As soon as Knowles fired the grenade that destroyed the church tower, Jenny started running. She dragged the woman behind her, with the two men close behind. The drunk looked a lot more sober now.

"Run!" she screamed at the tennis players. They turned and fled, a blood-spattered, naked woman enough to rouse them from their shock. They ran down the road, the woman sobbing before Jenny slowed.

"What are you doing?" the drunk said.

"Atoning," Jenny said and she turned back to the square, leaving them behind.

27

Katie screamed as the Wolf leapt. Jack changed, and rolled, catching Bryant by surprise and ending up on top of him. He bit down and earned a yelp from Bryant.

"Yes!" Katie yelled. Josh had stopped crying and was watching the Wolves fight with a strange expression on his face.

Jack bit again, drawing blood again. A chunk of Bryant's flesh came away with the bite. He howled again. The bite seemed to galvanise Bryant and he flexed his muscles. Jack slipped his grip and now Bryant was on top. He bit down again and again, blood spraying out of multiple wounds on Jack's body.

"No!" Katie screamed. This was her moment, her chance. She had a small window of opportunity to get away whilst-- *What? Whilst that wolf eats Jack?*

Suddenly a smaller wolf ran into the square. It launched itself at Bryant, catching him with enough force and surprise to dislodge him. The small wolf turned into Jenny.

"Stop, Bryant, stop."

The Wolf watched her for a moment, but only a moment, then it pounced and severed the woman's neck with one snap of its massive jaws.

"Jack!" Katie screamed. Jack had turned back into a human and was trying to sit up. He kept falling back to the ground, his body refusing to let him up. Jack was covered with blood, chunks of his flesh missing leaving angry red holes in his flesh. She could see white in the mess of torn flesh. Earlier, she had seen him heal, but that wasn't happening now. He was breathing hard and blinking fast, a look of surprise etched onto his face. Then his features disappeared, face elongating until he was back as a Wolf. It, too, blinked slowly as it watched her. The blinking slowed until it finally closed its eyes.

"No," she whispered. *I can't lose you again.*

People were now coming out of their houses, shell-shocked expressions on their faces as they watched the wolves fight. Several of them were shouting to her. She felt a hand on her shoulder. She barely recognised the person talking to her; did not hear the words. The man was taking Josh from her and had a firm hold of her hand. He was pulling her towards a house- no, not a house. The butchers. She shook herself free and ran back to the gun on the floor.

When she turned back to face the Wolves, Bryant was back on top, biting down again on Jack. She stepped forward and pressed the barrel to the Wolf's neck. Before it had time to react, she pulled the trigger again and again until it clicked empty.

28

Knowles ran back up the alley, sweat pouring off him. The screams from the square had stopped now, but he could the sounds of animals fighting. *Jack.* He burst into the square, raising his weapon as he did so.

The ground was littered with the dead. The barman from the pub was dead, Knowles' revolver in his hand. It clearly hadn't done him any good as a large part of his throat was missing. Around the square, people were coming out of their houses, shock clear in their expressions.

"Get inside!" he screamed. Some of them ran back inside immediately. *Good.* A soldier with a gun could still have an effect, even here, even today.

One of the wolves was on top, tearing chunks out of the flesh of the other. Knowles saw Katie shake off a man's grasp and pick up a weapon. She pressed it into the neck of the dominant wolf and fired, emptying the clip into the wolf.

The wolf fell off the other, the bullets ripping its flesh apart much more efficiently than it had been doing to the other wolf. The wolf yelped a couple of times, its limbs twitching as the bullets rained into it until finally it stopped moving. The bullet wounds had nearly combined to sever the Wolf's head.

"Katie!" Knowles yelled. "Get back!"

She looked at him dumbly, then at the man who was holding Josh. She let the weapon fall to the floor and sank to the ground, resting a hand on the prone wolf.

"Get back!" he yelled again. She didn't move.

He stopped a few feet from her, gun aimed at the wolf she had shot.

"Jack," she said, stroking his fur. The big wolf was breathing raggedly. It blinked, its tongue lolling out of its mouth.

"Katie," Knowles said, moving closer. "Bryant is not dead, please move away."

"Jack," she said again.

"He will heal," Knowles said. *I hope.*

Knowles nudged Bryant with his boot. The big wolf didn't move. Knowles felt himself beginning to relax. It was over, but at what cost? He knelt down next to Bryant and put his hand on the wolf. *How do you check for a pulse on a wolf?* Bryant's head was held on by bone and strands of tissue. *No way could he survive that. No way.*

Bryant's chest rose, ever so slightly, but it rose.

He was breathing.

Knowles looked at the man holding Josh. He was wearing blood-stained white overalls and standing in front of the butcher's shop. Knowles thought back to the skeleton in the cave – where all this lunacy had started. He had never set foot in it, but his friends had. The skeleton without a head.

"Hey," he called, "you got a really big knife?"

Epilogue

1

Knowles dropped two severed heads at the mouth to the corridor that led away from the main cave. The spiders were there, in force, but he didn't think they would come out. He had returned what should never have been removed.

A unit stood in a rough semicircle behind him. They were all holding flamethrowers and aiming them into the tunnel. Every single man looked scared, and Knowles laughed to himself. *This is a walk in the park.*

Two other men were busy around the cave, digging shallow holes and putting explosives in them. Knowles backed away from the cave entrance. Spiders came out, swarming over their heads, but coming no further.

"Let's go," Knowles said. He clipped onto a rope and heard the motor kick in from above him. Seconds later he was back on the ground, and the rest of his team got out without incident. Knowles saluted the major that was waiting for him.

"Ready, sergeant?"

Knowles nodded. The major gave the order and the men ran back through the woods, heading for the adjacent field. Months before, one of Knowles' men had been airlifted out of here. The first army casualty of this. *Meyers.* Knowles snorted. Who would remember him? So many dead, so many to mourn.

Two helicopters were waiting for them. Once they were in the air, the major gave the order. The ground erupted as all the charges went off at once. Then it collapsed back on itself, creating a crater in the woods. Given time, trees would grow again there and no-one would ever know what was under it.

The rest of the bodies had been incinerated, along with all the other wolves and their victims. The brass had thought it a good idea to keep the parts of the bodies separate, burning them at various locations around the UK. Burying the heads had been Knowles' idea. *Symbolic. Returning what we took.* Now the inquests would begin. The world knew of the existence of the creatures and it was being discussed at a crisis meeting of the G8 leaders.

What a mess.

Knowles closed his eyes and tried to sleep his way back to Lympstone base.

2

A week later, it seemed that every house in Huntleigh was up for sale. Rumour had it that the MOD was considering buying the lot. *Turn it into a training ground in case this happens again. Bit fucking late.* Knowles sat in his car, outside the Stadler house. Removal men were carrying things out, all laughing and joking. Sighing, he got out and went to the door. Katie opened the door and smiled when she saw him.

"Sergeant."

"Not for long," he said.

She raised her eyebrows.

"I'm getting promoted. Head of a new unit. Somehow I'm a hero."

She nodded. "A lot more people would be dead if it wasn't for you."

"I don't feel like a hero." He shrugged. "Maybe more would be alive if it weren't for me."

A cry came from the next room and Katie left, returning with Josh. "Where are you moving to then?"

Katie laughed. "Probably best you don't know that."

"I can always find out."

She nodded, a wistful smile on her face. "Please don't."

"Most of your village seems to be on the move."

"Yeah, can you blame them?"

"Listen, if you ever need anything-"

"I know. Thank you, Peter."

"Everyone calls me Knowles, Katie, and I think you've earned that right."

She smiled at him, and this smile was a bit more genuine and warm. "I think this is over, though. Now everyone knows, we'll be able to deal with it, right?"

"That's the idea." He paused. "Listen, I don't know if you're interested, but we figured out where Michael's pack came from."

Katie shook her head.

"We have footage of him arriving at Dover. He had about a hundred people with him. We can track them to the train station, where they split. Some of them head to the bus-"

Katie shook her head again. "I don't really care, Knowles. They're all dead, right? His pack."

"We think we've got them all, yes."

"What about the other wolves. That woman, Jenny-"

"What about them?"

"They don't all need to die, Knowles."

"In your opinion."

"That one in the pub. He saved us. He wasn't like the others. The woman too. She came back. She saved-"

Knowles shook his head quickly. "Don't finish that sentence Katie. He's dead remember."

She nodded, but not before glancing upstairs. A shadow crossed there, moving slowly. *So that's where he is.*

"They're not all bad, that's my point."

"That makes two in the hundreds I've met. That's not good odds Katie."

"It's a start," she said. "Besides, you knew three that were alright."

"Yeah." He reached out and stroked Josh's head, then shook her hand. "See you around, Mrs Stadler."

"I seriously hope not," Katie said.

Knowles returned her smile and left.

Acknowledgements

Writing a book is a solitary task that involves many people. If you know any writers, then that sentence will make sense and if you don't, well, trust me: whilst I wrote the words, the effort was not solely mine.

Tinu, Josh and Ethan – I cannot thank you enough for your patience whilst the various drafts of this were written. Tinu has now read this more than any other book, each draft slightly different from the one before. I think you need some kind of medal.

The beta reader team – Dad, Jer Fisher, Cath and Chris Kenny (Ok, first page only, in Andorra, but you found a mistake so you're in!), Richard Evans, Shani White, Tracey Evans, Nadine Marchant, Angela Peters and Katie Samuel. Many thanks are due to all of you: you have helped make this a better book.

The Smith family for the cups of tea during the tricky third draft. Unfortunately, it was too late to turn the hero into a dour Yorkshireman. Maybe in the next one!

Frank at gfivedesign for the cover, and Rowan Kendall-Torry for the image. Good job fellas and more beer coming your way soon.

Pat for technical expertise and advice. As always, any errors are mine. I still think it would have been cool for Jack to have been a human shield, however unrealistic that is. Ah well, maybe in the film..!

Finally, thanks to everyone who enjoyed the first book: I hope this lives up to your expectations. Please leave a review on Amazon and drop by on Twitter to say hi @joshfishkins.

Made in the USA
Coppell, TX
20 April 2022